INCITEMENT, CONSPIRACY, AND DARK DOINGS

"I speak to you and tell you the great words given to us from Makfaril, the leader, directly from the Great Chyyan.

"Look around you in your island! Where are the slaves that once did your bidding? Gone, all gone. And why? Because your new High Kov, this high and mighty Prince Majister of Vallia, this Strom of Valka, decrees that you honest working people shall no longer run slaves. Is this fair? Is this justice?

"Tell me, brethren in the Great Chyyan, if this is a sample of the usage to which this Dray Prescot puts you, then will you lie down beneath it? Will you give the tyrant the full incline? Will you be slave?"

"It is the express command of Makfaril himself that Dray Prescot be delivered up to me for judgment. Hearken! The torments Prescot would then suffer are beyond mortal men's comprehension."

"I rode disguised through this strife-ridden land."

SECRET SCORPIO

by
ALAN BURT AKERS

Illustrated by
Josh Kirby

DAW BOOKS, INC.
DONALD A. WOLLHEIM, PUBLISHER
1301 Avenue of the Americas
New York, N.Y. 10019

Cover art by Josh Kirby.

FIRST PRINTING, DECEMBER 1977

1 2 3 4 5 6 7 8 9

DAW BOOKS

PRINTED IN U.S.A.

Table of Contents

LIST OF ILLUSTRATIONS

A Note On The Vallian Cycle

Secret Scorpio is the first book of Dray Prescot's adventures in the Vallian Cycle on that marvelous and exotic world of Kregen he has made his home.

Dray Prescot himself is an enigmatic figure. Reared in the inhumanly harsh conditions of Nelson's Navy, he has been transported to Kregen many times through the agency of the Star Lords and of the Savanti nal Aphrasöe, those mortal but superhuman men and women of the Swinging City. There is a discernible pattern underlying all his breathtaking adventures—he is sure of that—but the pattern and its meanings remain veiled and unguessable.

His appearance as described by one who has seen him is of a man of above middle height, with brown hair and level brown eyes, with enormously broad shoulders and powerful physique. There is about him an abrasive honesty and an indomitable courage and he moves like a great hunting cat, quiet and deadly. On the savage and beautiful world of Kregen he has at various times and for various reasons risen to become a Vovedeer and Zorcander of his Clansmen of Segesthes, the Lord of Strombor, Strom of Valka, Prince

Majister of Vallia, King of Djanduin and a Krozair of Zy, a plethora of titles to which he confesses with a wryness and an irony I am sure masks much deeper feelings at which we can only guess.

Now a new page of action turns in his life. The volumes chronicling his life are arranged to be read as individual books. Now he is plunged headlong into fresh adventures beneath the hurtling moons of Kregen, in the streaming mingled lights of Antares, under the Suns of Scorpio.

Alan Burt Akers

Chapter One

Black Feathers of the Great Chyyan

A foot scraped in the shadows. Instantly we seven came to a dead halt in the blackness of the alley. Ahead the darkness lowered down as mufflingly as in the alleyway, for massy clouds covered the night sky of Kregen, concealing the glitter of the stars and the radiance of the moons.

My left hand gripped Roybin's shoulder and I could feel the fine tremble as he waited, poised like a wild leem, savage, suspicious, ready to leap out in perfect and deadly silence if that scraping foot heralded a murderous enemy.

In single file we seven stood, half-crouched, stock-still, invisible. The foot scuffed the slimy cobbles again and then the disappearing patter of feet told us that the wayfarer of the night was about his business. Seg's left hand on my shoulder pressed, but in the same instant Roybin moved ahead again. We followed, silently. Behind Seg, Turko the Shield fretted, I knew, that he did not stand at my back, a place he considered his by right. Inch, stooped to bring his great height beneath the evil-smelling brick overhang, prowled after Turko, and our rear was brought up by Young Oby, young and a boy no more, who perforce clasped Inch's belt, and by Balass the Hawk whose dark skin blended perfectly with the shadows.

In single file we stole out from the mouth of the alley, aware of the vanishment of the pressing walls and the feeling of greater space about us. The tiny square lay shrouded about us. Yes, I suppose on reflection, we were a pretty ferocious bunch. I know I would not like to stumble upon such a crew as that on a pitchy night when all manner of deviltries are afoot.

Roybin led. We were experienced enough to know when to follow a man who had knowledge of the terrain. This alley led around the back of the fish market in the town of Autonne, on the island of Veliadrin that had lately been Can-Thirda, and our objective lay across the fish-scaled cobbles of the square.

No one spoke. Here, in the pressing darkness before the first of Kregen's seven moons made an appearance, there was no need for words to know what we were about.

Soundlessly we emerged from the mouth of the alleyway, feeling that cloying pressure of pent-up air give way to the freer sense of the square, small though it might be. Water ran between the cobbles and there would be fish scales and heads and tails aplenty strewn about. A scattered rain could not decide whether to cease altogether or to drench down in the long shafting downpour of a Kregan storm.

We inched ahead and cleared a brick buttress, our right hands trailing along the crumbling mortar. A spark of light jumped into life ahead.

We froze instantly.

The light shone from a small lantern set outside an arched gateway closed by a moldering lenken door. That wooden door blended with the decay and dissolution of this tumbledown section of the fish market. In the crazily leaning brick walls stained with the patina of time, in the powdery and splintered timbering, in the gap-tiled roofs queasily lurching at incongruous angles, the archway and door betrayed nothing unusual.

Yet Roybin had certain information so we were here, prowling like wild leem, and the night ahead of us might soon explode with fury and action.

A long running roll of thunder boomed distantly away to the east in the interior of the island.

On the tail of the rumbling echoes Roybin whispered, "Lookouts."

We had expected a sentry. Peering across the darkened square into the isolated pool of radiance shed by the lantern, we made out the forms of three men. An edged weapon caught the light and glittered. They were quiet over there, probably talking desultorily together, resentful at their watch. But they would keep a lookout. All Roybin had told us convinced me that whoever these people were that we intended to spy on this night, they were ruthless and efficient.

For we knew why we were here, creeping like villains along vile, fish-stinking alleyways in Autonne, a city of the western coast of the island of Veliadrin. Veliadrin, of which I was still High Kov, that large island between Vallia and my own wonderful island of Valka, had once been called Can-Thirda. The name had been changed for certain reasons. The island had at one time, in the long ago, been a kingdom, before the Empire of Vallia had obtained the supreme power over all the islands fringing the coasts of the main island of Vallia. Veliadrin was still split into distinct regions. Over on the west coast the people were mostly fisherfolk, given to wild boasting of the old days, not overly rich or well-endowed, but sturdy and resourceful and also, as we had discovered, too prone to superstition.

Oh, yes, we knew why we were here, stalking the shadows like leems.

Rumors and suspicions, malicious gossip and ugly conjectures had at last come together to make a picture that displeased me greatly. That picture spelled evil days ahead if we did not act at once. There are many and varied religions on Kregen, and some are fine and worthy of the utmost effort in a man or woman. And some there are dark and secretive and baleful in their influence.

From the main island of Vallia a new creed was attempting to make a lodgment in Veliadrin. The west coast, a port, a poor and credulous people—the new creed found fertile ground.

Mind you, I knew who must take the full blame.

We had known for some time there were deep stirrings from Vallia, long ground swells of troubles to come, and the emperor was once more a worried man. Many forces, many ambitious men and women, many fanatics, sought to topple him. I had been told that there were far more potential insurrectionists these days than there had been when I had last spoken to the emperor in any privacy and confidence, before my absence on Earth and my adventurings in the inner sea, the Eye of the World.

Now this new creed threatened close to home.

As I had said to Seg Segutorio back in Valka before we left: "My Freedom Fighters did not clear Valka of the slavers and the aragorn and make of it an island where they might bring up their children in pride and justice and freedom, for some Opaz-forsaken devils to worm their way in and overturn all we have accomplished." And I had slammed a dagger into the sturmwood table beneath a mullioned window overlooking a stupendous view of Valkanium and the bay.

Seg Segutorio, the Kov of Falinur, a Bowman of Loh, and the truest comrade a man could hope to find in two worlds, had replied, "Valka is indeed a paradise, Dray. Falinur, well, I try, and hard it is, by the Veiled Froyvil! The people there do not forget the old times, when their kov went up against the emperor and they followed, exultant, and they cast a deal of blame on me, the new kov, for the old kov's failure."

Delia had told me some of Seg's problems with the recalcitrants in his province, and he seemed to be having a worse time of convincing them that he was their new leader than was Inch in his Black Mountains, a province which had also been involved in that old revolution against the emperor.

Seg had gone on, staring moodily across the sun-lit expanse of the bay: "But as Inch and I are here in Valka, we think prevention in Veliadrin may aid us in our own kovnates."

Thus spake Seg and I warmed to him.

There was no need for fulsome words between us. I understood him—and, by Vox, he understood some of me—for, because he was Seg Segutorio, a black-haired, blue-eyed fey maniac from the wild hills of Erthyrdrin, he had added: "Mind you, my old dom, I can tell you a kovnate goes to rack and ruin if you aren't there to keep an eye on things."

He was right.

At least, he was right if an absentee noble could not find a loyal and trustworthy person to run an estate in the absence of the owner. I, to my shame, own I am probably the greatest absentee landlord of two worlds. But then blame the Star Lords, blame the Savanti—blame also, if you will, my own accursed facility in picking up titles and the possessions that go with them on Kregen. I already had a plan to deal with these problems, plans you shall hear of in due course, and already I had consciously begun the hazy opening moves to unite all of Paz.

"Veliadrin is not Valka," I had said. "Here in Valka, Tharu and Tom and the Elders run things, with Drak. In my kingdom of Djanduin, Kytun and Ortyg handle affairs perfectly. In Strombor Gloag rules the roost. And as for my clansmen, well, Hap has them so well organized we took over another clan without bloodshed, all through obi."

In his dry way, Seg had said, "You're really a Vovedeer as well as a Zorcander, now."

"Aye." He knows when and how to puncture complacency, does Seg Segutorio. "I've been more than lucky in having found good friends to run affairs whilst I'm away. But Veliadrin is split up, occupied by diffs and apims who don't really get on, for the damned Qua'voils still resent their defeat."

"But the Pachaks you have settled in Veliadrin."

"Ah!" I had said, feeling pleased. "I have great hopes for my Pachaks of Veliadrin." This was ture. "And the Pachaks of Zamra have finally freed all the slaves. That is progress."

"But this damned new creed." Seg had run his eye along the true shaft of an arrow, brushed his fingertips lightly over the brilliant blue fletchings. "Chyyanists, is it?"

"Aye. Roybin is a first-class spy and he has received a certain report. A preacher or a priest or some devil of that kind is loose in Autonne. He holds meetings. I think a little firsthand information will prove of value."

"There's nothing like seeing for yourself," said Seg.

So that was why we were here, creeping like a gang of piratical cutthroats through the rain-swept darkness, toward the speck of light over the gateway leading on to what unknown horrors we could only conjecture.

Inch had refused to stay behind, swinging his enormous two-handed ax absently as he told me that if Seg and I were going off for some fun he wasn't going to be left out. Turko the Shield considered the matter closed. Oby was raging for adventure and Balass the Hawk deserved some fun. So they all came.

"As to fun," I had said just before we ventured out into the rain from our secluded inn, a place where the attention we attracted had been mitigated by pretenses and stratagems, "this Chyyanist nonsense is likely to lead to a few smashed skulls. At least, that is what I feel in my bones."

"All reports speak of the creed as evil," said Roybin sagely, nodding his head. "But they are all outside observations. No one really knows."

As I padded forward through a few opening flurries of rain toward the gateway and the moldering lenken door, I wondered just how much we could hope to discover in there. The center of the new religion lay in Vallia, or so we believed. It had been brought here by a priest or preacher who sought to rouse the simple fisherfolk hereabouts. As an absentee landlord I had no right to criticize my tenants if they rose up against me, in a just cause.

However intolerant and objectionable I may be, I do not think I had given any cause to these people to rise up in justice. Maybe that is just another facet of my supposed meglomania. But the fisherfolk of Autonne made a living and did not starve and were housed. I had ordered the freeing of their slaves. This Opaz-forsaken priest of Chyyan sought to stir up trouble out of willful spite, a sullen resentment, a sense of ill-treatment, and if I could not understand and sympathize with feelings like these then no one else in two worlds could do so. And, too, there were far weightier reasons for Chyyanism, as you shall hear. . . .

Not one of my six comrades appeared to think it strange that Roybin no longer led on, that I had pushed on in the front to take the three guards. I mention this to indicate that my thoughts had allowed me to act without thinking about the action I was taking. A bad habit. A nasty habit. A habit that had brought me into dire trouble in the past and was to pitch me headlong into further horrors, a habit that was just one against which I continually strove.

My guard went to leaning sleep with a tap of a dagger-hilt along his skull.

Turko's lolled unconscious from cunning finger pressures.

Roybin's collapsed with a dagger through his throat.

I looked at my spy. Well, Roybin had dealt with these people before, so he should most likely know. The guards were cloaked heavily, but they wore armor and carried weapons and were not of Autonne. I put my mouth to Roybin's ear.

"The roof?"

He nodded.

That cleared up the protocol over the local man leading.

Roybin, who was called Roybin Ararsnet ti Autonne, had served me before, in various dubious capacities. I do not mince matters where brave men are concerned. Roybin was a spy. I gave him credit for that, for credit was due.

Around the side of the building the rain spattered more strongly against the corroded brick, lashed on by a rising wind. The darkness was not as absolute now, for the clouds were piling away invisibly above and every now and again a sliver of the Maiden with the Many Smiles, who shines forth most bravely in the night sky of Kregen, glimmered through the rack. Inch wore a tightly fitting leather helmet and not a scrap of his yellow hair was visible.

I looked back at him as I set my hands to the climb. In the fragmentary light his incredibly tall frame looked angular and sinister with the immense long-handled Saxon ax swinging handily from his wrist-thong. Yes, it was a great comfort to have Inch of Ng'groga at my side.

Seg's Lohvian longbow was unstrung and the string safely in the dry of his belt pouch along with the spares. We all wore decent Vallian buff tunics and breeches, with rapiers and daggers strapped about us and, therefore, looked like perfectly ordinary Vallian koters, although, of necessity, being marked as apim, for we were all *Homo sapiens.*

The crumbling brickwork afforded good handholds and in no time we were all on the roof. I had no intention of leaving any one of these bonny fighters alone, below, as a lookout.

It behooved others to look out when we wandered along.

Megalomania, maniacal, vicious, I know, I know. But I harbored frightful suspicions concerning this new creed of Chyyan. Nothing must hinder us tonight.

Over the roof where the rain blustered and then fell away, only to return with just that little extra edge in its sting, we crept cautiously. Roybin led us to the skylight. The iron was new, replacing worn-down bronze.

Young Oby pushed forward, taking a slender tool from his pocket. Opaz knew what deviltry he had been practicing in my absences, but the lock snicked open and with a single heave Turko hauled the iron bars up and out. He placed their weight down as though replacing one of Delia's priceless cups of Linkiang porcelain on its saucer.

I looked down. Only darkness, until my eyes picked up a faint glimmer, the merest wraith of an orange glow, and I made out three-quarters of the outline of a door. A well-made and tight fitting door sealing off the lower portions.

One after the other we dropped down onto a loft floor where stinking fishnets tangled beneath our feet, and where no doubt the scales clumsily brushed into the corners might once have graced a coelacanth. The door yielded to the forensic ministrations of Oby. I did not shove it open, as a soldier might, the sword mighty in his fist.

Gently, I eased the door inward. The orange glow brightened. I put an eye to the crack. For a moment the world consisted of orange whorls of fire, and then I saw that the door opened onto a narrow gallery surrounding the central area. Here was where the fishermen hung their nets. A low drone of voices lifted. Lights threw orange reflections upon the far wall and struck in slivers of radiance up through the warped planks of the gallery.

Chances were that we could open the door and sneak out onto the gallery before the people gathered on the floor below might look up and see us. It was the kind of chance that always attracts.

I might have listened to Roybin when he made his first report and simply ordered out a detachment of guards. We would have surrounded this odiferous place and swept up all who worshiped here. But then we would catch men and women who had come here out of mere curiosity. We would have taken the priest of Chyyan. But it was my guess that he would say nothing.

So we went about our work nefariously, like criminals.

Like wraiths we seven slid out onto the gallery. Not a board creaked, not a single item of harness chingled. We were old hands, feral as leems, deadly as Manhounds.

We each found a crack in the planking and set an eye to observe what went on below.

My first fears vanished the instant I clapped eye on that scene. Gathered in a mass at the end of the room a crowd of people were in the act of rising from a deep genuflection—we had chosen our time well, the chance swiftly and surely taken—and the priest himself, clad all in black vestments, lifted his arms high, leading the congregation in the opening bars of a chant. The chant proved to be a moaning, miserable, oafish thing, and most of the people did not know it. But the priest raised his voice to lead them. At all this I glanced with the swift calculating eye of the fighting man, seeking to weigh possible odds. The words of the chant came so garbled they were practically impossible to make out. Over it all I glanced up and to the wall behind the priest. And I let out a soundless puff, and felt vastly relieved.

For, set against that back wall draped in its rich cloths and golden tassels, there stood no pagan silver idol of a leem.

A calmness came over me. Whatever of vileness this new creed of Chyyan might bring, I did not think it could be as vile as that of the cult of Lem the Silver Leem.

Against the rich cloths of the back alcove lifted a bold image of a heavy-winged bird, an image as tall as a man, with feathered wings spread to encompass a full twenty feet. All a rusty black, this bird, save for its scarlet eyes and scarlet claws and scarlet beak. Four wings the chyyan possesses, like its distant cousin, the zhyan. The four wings were undersize in this image for the body size, but the whole effect was at once impressive and ominous.

At once surmises sprang into my brain. Native saddle-birds were unknown in Vallia and Loh, being, at the time, generally confined to the hostile territories of Turismond and to Havilfar and islands thereabouts. The mighty continent of Havilfar, south of the equator, was the home of zhyan and chyyan. I frowned. This bore a little more investigation. Havilfar boasted as its most powerful nation the Empire of Hamal, and the mad Empress Thyllis was sworn to destroy the Empire of Vallia. Was this creed of Chyyan a gambit in that game?

Incense rose, stinking and abominable. The chant ceased. The crowd stood to listen as the priest spoke. As I listened I watched their faces as well as I could, and some lapped up the ranting words, but others were more critical. A couple of trident-men near the door came as close as may be to openly jeering. I marked them.

This priest had journeyed to Veliadrin from Vallia, and no doubt Autonne was his marked target town. I tried to size him up, wondering from which city, country or continent, even, he hailed. A full-fleshed man, with the bright staring eyes of the fanatic—or the diseased—he presented an imposing figure. His robes were all of black, relieved by embroidered motifs in golden thread and imitation jewels, motifs mainly of chyyans doing unmentionable things to their victims.

Chyyans have not yet been generally tamed to the saddle. They remain unbroken, wild, flying freely over the wide spaces of Havilfar, a dread and a terror to lesser animals and to man. The white-plumaged zhyan is notorious for the uncertainty of its temper, for all that the bird is valued above ten fluttrells, and yet the zhyan in its power and mastery has been curbed to the rein and the bit and the flying harness.

Not so the chyyan. Its rusty black plumage shares none of the brilliant sheening highlights of the impiter of the hostile territories of Turismond. The chyyan is a bird to steer well clear of when you ride the level wastes of the air, astride a saddle-bird, or piloting a small model voller.

So this priest, who may have come from Hamal to wreak the Empress Thyllis's vengeance upon Vallia, lifted up his voice and harangued the simple fisherfolk of Autonne, which is a town under my care.

"It is not for the distant future when you are dead and gone to the Ice Floes of Sicce! No, my children, I tell you in the sacred name of the Great Chyyan, upon whose black breast is taken every arrow that seeks your heart, I tell you that the Great Chyyan brings hope and comfort, delight and joy, prosperity and wealth to you in this life. Do not wait until you are dead to enjoy yourselves! Listen to my words, for they are words from our leader, he who has been chosen in the divine twinning by the Great Chyyan to lead us into the new darkness of the Black Feathers, in which is there light beyond our meager understanding."

At this guffaws broke from the two trident-men. Not for them the finicky parsing of metaphysics. They heard words that appeared to contradict, and they brayed their derision.

"By the silver flukes of Shalash the Shining!" bellowed one, clapping a bronzed hand onto his thigh. "Your riddles make no sense to a coy, Himet the Mak!"

"Hush!" and "Quiet, impious onker!" broke from those standing near the two trident-men, who I guessed were brothers.

The priest, this Himet the Mak, lifted a hand. I saw his black robes stretch over the hilt of a sword belted to his waist.

"I tell you that the Great Chyyan leads us into the darkness in which there is light. . . ."

"The blasphemers speak their own destruction! The word of the leader twinned with the Great Chyyan is to be obeyed. The leader is the spirit of the One made Two, spirit and flesh, spirit made manifest to men. Our leader and the Great Chyyan are in duo, twins, radiant with the Black Feathers, leading us to light. And the word of our leader tells us we must wait for a sign. He will come among us. He will tell us when to lift the banners of the Black Feathers. Then, my children, then all that you do not have will be yours. When Makfaril our leader gives the divine word you will gain all, not when you are dead and rotting in the ground, but here and now, in this life, soon!"

People were dancing up and down and the two tridentmen had fallen silent. It was mumbo jumbo, but the promise, the passion, the pride of purpose, these drove home keenly into everyone present.

"Listen to me, my children, to Himet the Mak, who comes to tell you of the Great Chyyan and of our leader, Makfaril. You must do all the things necessary and pray for guidance, that in the Black Day you will be spared and live to enjoy the fruits of luxury handed to us by him of the four wings, Chyyan of the Black Feathers. In that glorious day will you find resurrection in the here and now. All will be yours. Only believe! Believe and pray to our leader that he may intercede for you with his divine twin, in spirit and in flesh, pray for your salvation in the day from the Great Chyyan."

One or two shrill yells broke from the embryonic congregation. Again and again the priest harped on the desirability of achieving one's heart's desires in the here and now. He gave only a sketchy metaphysical plan for life after death, for salvation, for the delights of paradise, of being reborn higher in the circle of vaol-paol, or for the joys of Valhalla; he hammered home his message that the Great Chyyan and Makfaril the leader sought to reward their devotees *now*.

When he reverted to supernatural arguments they were all cant phrases, rolling rodomontade mixed with elements culled from many minor creeds of Kregen. I have made a little study of the beliefs of Kregen—vastly edifying!—and could recognize this curious mixture as an artificial construct, alien, almost thrown together. The priest had skill. I wondered who had trained him.

And yet, despite his skill, despite the lure of grabbing it all now, the two trident-men grew restive, so that Himet the Mak was forced to take notice of them.

From the resplendent cloths draped over the alcove at the back of the statue of the rusty black chyyan stepped forth armed men. They appeared, suddenly, between the tall drapes. I eyed them.

First I looked at their faces and the way they stood and held themselves, next at their weapons and then at their uniforms.

They were all apims, like me, and their faces were all of that low-browed, brutal cast that does not in any way invariably mean brutality in the possessor. I rather fancied these men would be hard and merciless and take more than a trifle of joy in sinking their weapons into the guts of any who opposed them. They stood alertly, poised, and I knew that at a signal from Himet they would kill and go on killing until he called a halt.

Their weapons remained scabbarded. They wore rapiers and daggers, but as I looked at the way they were belted up I frowned. It seemed to me the thraxters and the parrying-sticks belted to their waists were their prime weapons.

Their uniforms were black, beneath boiled leather armor, well oiled, and they wore profuse ornamentations of black feathers. Their iron helmets carried tufts of rusty black feathers from chyyans. All in all, they looked a formidable bunch. I judged them to be masichieri mercenaries who had never aspired to the quality of paktuns—for paktuns are in general finicky about questions of honor—and who combined a little thievery and assassination and slaving into their mercenary way of life as the opportunity offered, without reaching the power of the aragorn. There were twenty of them, led by a hikdar.

My instinctive reaction was that I wished I had taken up my Krozair longsword when we'd first ventured on this escapade.

The two trident-men eyed the guards uneasily, and their taunts fell away. They were tough and wiry, but they carried only their fishing tridents and degutting knives in their belts. They wore old buff breeches with frayed and unlaced ends, singlets of a coarse weave, and they were barefoot.

Balass the Hawk at his crack in the boards began to stir himself around, reaching for his sword. I turned my head toward him and he stilled. Of us all, perhaps, Balass was less accustomed to stealth in his fighting, being a hyrkaidur and master of the ritual combats of the arena.

Silently Oby drew his vicious knife. Seg had already strung his bow, all done simply and silently and with enormous professional skill. Inch's ax glittered in a shaft of the orange light. If there were to be handstrokes, we were ready.

Turko, who could rip a fully armed man to pieces with his bare hands, had grumbled and cursed when I'd told him to leave the great shield. Now Turko the Shield flexed his muscles. Oh, yes, if it came to a fight those twenty hard men down there would be in for a surprise.

But I wanted no fighting.

I wanted to observe, to fathom out just what lay behind this new and evil creed of Chyyanism, and then to withdraw and debate, calmly, what best to do.

With a tiny gesture of my left hand I indicated to Roybin that he should retire, and we would follow, one by one.

No one questioned my right to leave last.

Himet the Mak was shouting again, lifting his voice, and I detected a strained hoarseness there, very surprising to me considering the circumstances and the clear power he had been exercising over these credulous people.

"I speak to you and tell you the great words, the great words given to us from Makfaril, the leader, directly from the Great Chyyan. Yet you seek to mock me, to deny the great words. Do you not desire salvation and wealth and luxury in the here and now?"

His voice sharpened, took on an undisguised note of contempt and anger—and a tinge of fear? My comrades withdrew from the little rickety gallery, but I stayed, listening.

"You two, trident-men, brothers, you have been tainted with the falsehoods put about in the island. You know your island is called Can-thirda. Whatever it was called in the ancient days of the kingdom, ever since your island has been part of Vallia it has been called Can-thirda. Yet now you must call it Veliadrin. Why?"

A certain grumbling rumble from his listeners brought a wolfish smile to his lips.

"Aye! I well tell you why! Because the power-mad incubus, the Prince Majister of Vallia, decrees it! That is why.

Some unknown master from no man knows where tells you your fate. He holds your future in his hand. Has he visited you? Have you seen him? No, and you have not see his bitch of a wife, the Princess Majestrix, either!"

My muscles jumped. I took a breath. But I remained lying still, watching and listening. Yes! Well may you who have followed my story marvel. But I remained still and did not leap down and choke this fellow's throat a trifle to induce him to show proper respect for the most perfect woman in two worlds. And, I confess, I not only marveled at my own iron self-control, I actually relished it, as showing how I had matured and grown wise.

"Some forgotten child they had, spawned from their evil union, this Princess Velia, dead and abandoned in some foreign country debarred from honest men's knowledge. Who knows where she died? Who cares? Why should your island be called after the slut?

My fists gripped and my muscles trembled as a leem's flanks tremble in the instant before he charges. But, despite all, I remained still.

Through the confusion roaring away in my head I understood that my own private problems, my own petty pride, must not interfere or injure the interests of my people, their lands or the intangible debt I owe all those who look to me. If this is pride, so be it; if it is duty, so be it. To me, a simple sailor and fighting man, it was and remains a mere matter of common decency.

So I battened down the hatches on my anger and made myself listen to what this fellow was saying. After all, there was more than a grain of truth in his rantings. . . .

If, because this priest of Chyyan insulted my Delia and our dead daughter Velia, I acted as I was wont and hurled myself down to choke him a little and bash the skulls of his ugly-faced guards, then I would forfeit the advantage of listening and learning in secret. Whoever had sent him would know that much of their designs were privy no more. I must force myself to swallow all that intolerant choler which makes of me a laughing stock, a fighting man and, sometimes, makes me do the right thing.

"Look around you in your island of Can-thirda! Where are the slaves that once did your bidding, that worked for you and made the days light? Gone, all gone. And why? Because your new High Kov, this high and mighty Prince Majister of Vallia, this Strom of Valka, this Kov of Zamra, decrees that you honest working people shall no longer run slaves. Is this fair? Is this justice? Why should a man do his own hard labor, why should a woman slave in the kitchen when she might buy and thrash a slave to do the work for her? Tell me, brethren in the Great Chyyan, if this is a sample of the usage to which this so-puissant Dray Prescot puts you, then will you lie down beneath it? Will you give the tyrant the full incline? Will you be slave?"

They yelled it back at him.

"No!" And, "No! We will not bow down to Dray Prescot!"

I fumed up there on the gallery. I didn't want the famblys to bow to me. I'd already cut out all this fawning and inclining nonsense in Valka. But, equally, I did not want them buying and selling and flogging slaves either. This is the old conundrum, with an answer, and I brushed it aside as I peered through the crack between the sagging boards.

The mood of the embryo congregation had turned ugly. They were sucked in. They saw a hope before them that not only might they return to the slave-holding of the past but might aspire to a seizure of the goodness of life, now.

Useless for me to condemn them. Had I spent more time in Can-thirda, had I even consulted some of the people about the change of name, had these folk seen me more clearly, instead of hearing about their High Kov only by hearsay, then, perhaps, I might have prevented all this, have nipped in the bud the horrors to come. For I knew well and made no mistake that far more lay behind this artificial religion of Chyyan than ever Himet the Mak would tell these poor famblys.

"If he were here now! If this infamous Dray Prescot, Prince Majister of Vallia, were standing before you, what would you do?"

The answering yells bounced in ugly echoes in that tall net-room below the gallery.

"Chop the cramph!" "Cut the rast down!" "Feather the tapo!" And, "Make him slave and run him for the good of us all!"

Things had gone to rack and ruin indeed, in Valiadrin, since I had been away. Seg Segutorio spoke the true word. I swiveled an eye back. Seg's face showed in the crack of the doorway. He looked vexed. Clearly, since we had obtained information, he was wondering why I did not join the rest of the party.

I made a face at him, and he smiled, amazingly, in return, as I looked back at the scene below. The people were waving their fists and many brandished degutting knives and tridents. The leather-clad guards in their black feathers stared watchfully on.

Himet the Mak gesticulated for silence.

"Not so! It is the express command of the leader, of Makfaril himself, that only in the last resort shall Prescot be slain. Make him slave at your peril also. Deliver him up to me so that I may take him to Makfaril. Yes, my children, leave the fate of the wild leem to me and my guards here, my bonny masichieri, to take him to the leader."

One of the trident-men shouted, his voice shrill and cutting through Himet's words to the listening people.

"Dray Prescot has a fearsome reputation as a fight—"

No doubt he was going to say as a fighting man: Himet chopped him off with, "A fearsome reputation! Yes. Truly, by the Great Chyyan, a horrendous reputation!"

That is true, by Vox.

Howls spurted up, execrations against the name of Dray Prescot and dire promises of what would befall him should he be foolish enough to fall into their hands. Himet bellowed.

"You would do well to heed my words and deliver him up for the judgment of Makfaril! Hearken! The torments Prescot would then suffer are beyond mortal men's comprehension."

They had not missed the neat turning of what reputation I had in Vallia from that of a warrior prince to that of a villain. Oh, yes, I am a villain. But only in certain matters.

There was little more to be gained here. We would have to think on what best to do about this new creed of Chyyanism. We were now acutely aware of the problem and its methods.

I cast a regretful glance at the two brothers, the trident-men who stood near the far door. Although uneasy, they showed no more signs of being cowed by words. But their glances at the guards, the masichieri, spoke eloquently enough. One brother shouted above the hubbub.

"And if the Prince Majister were here, among us now, who would know him?"

"Aye!" bawled his brother, red of face. "Who would know?"

Himet quieted conflicting answering yells. He smiled, a slow evil smirk that informed his listeners of his own importance.

"I have seen his representation. I would know. I would know the evil-hearted cramph among a thousand!"

The way the priest phrased this interested me. But it was time to go. The two brothers were scarcely likely to come to serious harm. The thought occurred to me that perhaps Himet had planted them, shills to give him arguments from which to strike sparks. If so, they were consummate actors.

"To the Great Chyyan with Dray Prescot!"

The chant from below grew in volume. I took no notice. What they wanted to do with me sounded highly unpleasant. What I intended to do with them might be highly unpleasant, at first; afterward they would see clearer. At the very least, this new creed had brought to my attention disquiet in Valiadrin, a disquiet I would see was dealt with fairly and rectified, so that the people of Valiadrin might be as happy as the people of Valka, as was their right.

So, still more confused than I probably realized, still holding down my anger, still blanking out what had been said about Delia and our dead daughter, I took my eye away from the crack in the floorboards and prepared to wriggle soundlessly back to the doorway. Seg had gone and the gap showed only a dark slit.

The boards beneath me creaked. They groaned. A spurt of ancient dust puffed past my face. I froze.

The gallery moved.

They were bellowing on about what they would like to do to Dray Prescot, making a hell of a noise, shrieking the most bloodcurdling threats. The groan of the ancient timber might be lost in all the uproar.

The rotten timbers under me sagged. Even to this day I do not know if the pure welling of savage satisfaction justified or condemned me.

The whole wooden structure shrieked as rusted nails gave way, as wooden pins snapped, as corroded bronze linchpins bent and parted. Rotten wood powdered to dust.

A miasmic stench of long-dead fish gusted over me. I was falling.

The yells of hatred for the Prince Majister of Vallia belching up from below, the shrieks of venom for Dray Prescot, changed to a shocked chorus of surprised screams as the wooden gallery collapsed in a weltering smother of dust and chips and flailing timbers upon the mob.

Head over heels, I, that same Dray Prescot, of Earth and of Kregen, pitched down onto the heads of the blood-crazed rabble beneath.

Chapter Two

"It is Dray Prescot, the devil himself!"

For an instant I lay flat on my back amid the splintered wreckage of the gallery. A damned infernal chunk of wood jabbed sharply into my back. The people broke away in a circle, yelling, struggling to tear themselves free from the descending debris. The noise and confusion, the spouting dust from the ancient building, the struggles of men and women, I suppose all the furor was rather splendid.

But I had an eye out for the black feathers and leather armor of Himet's masichieri. They'd recover more rapidly from the shock of surprise than the fisherfolk.

I sprang up. I did not draw my weapons.

People were turning to stare back at me. Broken planks slipped beneath our feet and the dust made us cough. Dust and muck festooned my hair and shoulders, and my face, I suppose, knowing my own weaknesses, revealed the struggle between laughter and downright cussing fury possessing me. To be thus chucked down like a loon among a mob yelling for my blood—well, it was funny rather than not.

Himet stood with arms uplifted, his mouth open, glaring as though a demon from Cottmer's caverns had miraculously appeared before him.

Oh, yes, the cramph recognized me.

Whoever his leader was, this Makfaril, that rast would not be pleased with his priest. For, forgetting what he had been enjoining the folk around, Himet pointed a rigid forefinger at me. His wide-eyed stare blanked into stupefaction.

"It is Dray Prescot, the devil himself!"

After the thunder of the gallery smashing into the floor a silent moment expanded. Himet's voice shocked out. The fisherfolk understood the enormity of what the priest of the Great Chyyan had said.

"Dray Prescot!"

They repeated the name. A quick babblement flowed through the crowd. They stared at me. Like a monstrous tidal wave growing and surging landward from the wastes of the sea, like a tsunami running from continent to continent, their hatred burst up and broke. In the next instant they roared upon me in a shrieking mob.

A skip and a jump cleared the wreckage. Somehow, the rapier and dagger leaped into my hands. I beat away a reaching trident. A knife whistled past my ear and thunked into a shattered upright. These people were out for blood. These fisherfolk, wrought upon, forgetting what Himet had warned, were out to lay me flat on the floor, to slay me, to kill me stone cold dead.

"Do not kill him!" screeched Himet the Mak. He might as well have shouted into a Cape Horner.

With a shout of rage Himet turned and violently gesticulated, a savage, unmistakable gesture of command. At once his guards, his bonny masichieri, leaped down into the press, their weapons glittering.

Then began as weird a military dance as you could desire. For I had no wish to be forced to kill these simple duped fisherfolk, yet they sought to slay me. I did not mind if a few of the masichieri were cut down, but the guards were under orders not to slay me. And the fisherfolk would not willingly kill the guards of the priest but, as I quickly saw, the guards would slay the townspeople if necessary. This was a ludicrous three-sided encounter with each of the three sides willing to slay one of the other sides but not the third, and therefore, it must follow, to be slain and not reply. I saw a guard run his thraxter through a burly fisherman who poised to hurl his trident at me. So the preservation of my life for the future evil intentions of Makfaril had already cost the life of one fisherman of Veliadrin, and was like to cost more if I did not act now to stop this blasphemy.

I let out a yell. I bellowed over the hubbub as I had been wont to hail the foretop in a gale.

"Yes! I am Dray Prescot! I am your lawful High Kov. I

wish you no harm. I have listened to your grievances and they will be redressed in justice. On this you have my word as a Prince of Vallia!"

I might as well have saved my breath.

The business about listening to them provoked only the shrieked response: "He has been spying on us! Slay the rast! Kill Dray Prescot!"

"No! No!" bawled Himet. "He must be taken before our leader. Makfaril demanded him for his own justice!"

Enough of the congregation in the hall had not been fully persuaded by Himet's exhortations and promises to obey blindly the dictates of the priest of the new creed. They had been roused to a sense of injustice. They had been cruelly treated by their new High Kov, and here he was, alone, ready to be chopped down in the violent way of Kregen and thus prove the justice of their own ends.

There followed a bout of confused struggle, wherein I found myself backed up against the far wall, beating away the crude implements of the fisherfolk and ever and anon striking with more deadly intent at a black-feathered guard. To defend oneself and not to slay the attacker—yes, there is a skill in that. It was not too easy in the press. A bulky lad staggered back with red blood pouring from his cheek where my main gauche, in whipping back to parry a trident, had gashed his flesh. Weapons flashed before my eyes. The guards were having difficulty in breaking through the fishermen to get at me, and when they did they died. The masichieri tumbled the fishermen away and advanced with scowls to an unwelcome task.

They handled their parrying-sticks with a fine free skill. As for their thraxters, the thraxter is a weapon of Havilfar, the straight cut and thrust sword, and these masichieri preferred it to the rapier in work of this nature.

The wall at my back was not altogether a good idea. No one was going to sneak up behind me and chop my knees off, but I could not skip and jump with the freedom I prefer in this kind of bash and batter fighting. I began to angle around and a trident passed perilously close under my left arm as I leaned away to flick a neat rapier slash that unhitched the belt from a portly fisherman's waist. His breeches started to slide down. He let out a furious yell and tried to degut me with a knife so admirably adapted for the purpose, and the breeches tangled while he staggered, purple-faced, enraged, striking ineffectually at me. I did not laugh. Truth to tell, this whole fracas smacked of the ludicrous and I was in no mood for petty levity.

I leaped away and one masichier tried to be clever and earn his hire. He brought his thraxter around, flat, a blow aimed to stun. I slid the blow and bashed him with the hilt of the rapier. Instantly I had to duck a savage sweep from a parrying-stick from a fellow masichier. I almost ducked into a wickedly unstabbing trident.

"By the Black Cunkrah!" I bellowed at them all. "Must I break all your heads to make you see sense?"

They snarled and roared at this, pressing in as I foined them off.

"You are not wanted in Can-thirda!" "Go home, Dray Prescot!" "Go back to your palace and your bitch wife!"

The fellow who said this, leathern-faced, scarred of jaw, abruptly somersaulted backward. My fist in the rapier guard tingled with the force of the blow.

"Kill him! Kill him!"

It was all a flurry of blade and tine and parrying-stick, and I smashed them back, beginning to feel my frustrated fury working on me. Soon the guards would tire of their fruitless attempts to take me alive. Then the fighting would begin.

"Slay the tapo!" screeched a lean and emaciated fisherman, hurling his trident. My rapier angled up and flicked the thing away. But the weapon was a trident, three-tined, and the sharp tines caught in my blade. Like the jaws of a shark the trident wrapped around the slender blade. I did not let go of the hilt, but my rapier was angled up and deflected, uselessly pointing to the cobwebby ceiling and the smoking lamps.

A fat and sweating man wearing more ornate clothes than the others, with a narrow gold chain about his neck and embroidered sleeves, even though silver fish scales caught in folds of the cloth glittered as marks of his trade, cursed with joy and thrust his trident hard for my guts.

I wriggled away at the last moment, striking a guard with the main gauche, wrenching it free in a gout of blood. I swung back to meet the next attack of the fat and wealthy trident-man. His sweating face showed a grimace of fierce joy, of that awful crazed desire to kill. I do not think he would have had me. But he would have come close.

He was not given the chance.

One of the two brothers who had mocked Himet the Mak stepped in and wrapped a burly forearm around the fellow's neck. With a chopped off squeal the crazed man was hauled bodily backward.

There was no time to gasp out thanks, for with a swish my rapier came down into line and extended into a bar of gleaming red-stained steel and the guard who had decided it was time finally to deal with me shrieked and spun away, clasping his neck where the long blade had kissed him above the edge of his leather armor.

"Take him, you fools!" Himet the Mak danced about frenziedly, well back of his guards, yelling orders and curses. His fanatical obsession with the instructions given him by Makfaril did not induce him to step forward and take an active part in the fray. Steel scraped and men yelled and bodies fell.

The pressure at least gave me some chance, for the fishermen maintained their yelling and their desperate attempts to get at me, and the masichieri continued to belt them away and so preserve my miserable hide. The rapier smeared with blood and the main gauche a similar reeking blade darting and flashing before me, I hacked and cut and kept them off. The rapier glistened before the eyes of a guard, distracting him, cut back viciously. He fell. As he fell so the dagger in my left fist sliced at a precise angle under the chin of his fellow. He staggered away as the rapier went in, slickly, withdrew, and a third guard spun away, shrieking, coughing out his life blood.

Now the masichieri were finished with this tomfoolery. Now these hired guards were out for blood.

A masichier stepped up, bulky in creaking leather armor, bold and confident, his thraxter held in a practiced grip, the parrying-stick slanting and catching runnels of jagged orange light. He thrust. He began his thrust as I whirled away from thunking a fisherman over the head and kicking another off.

The masichier halted his thrust in mid-action.

His shaggy hair beneath the iron helmet fluttered as his head lolled. Blood and spittle began to dribble foolishly from the corner of his mouth. He slid slowly sideways, upsetting a fisherman and his trident. As the guard toppled slowly to the fish-stinking floor I saw the long Lohvian arrow sprouting from his back, driven clean through his boiled leather armor, driven with exquisite force so that it did its business and no more, for it had not burst on through the man's chest.

I did not look up.

Another arrow punched through the neck of the nearest guard.

Oh, yes, you who have read accounts of my life on Kregen, that marvelous and horrible, beautiful and savage world four hundred light-years from the world of my birth, will understand. For Seg Segutorio, the master Bowman of Loh, had shot over me more than once in the past, had preserved my skin with superb displays of archery.

The guards' yelling changed in tone. The viciousness I had known could not be battened down for much longer broke and brought them surging forward with all the old hateful, expected, demoniac desire to slay.

A fisherman sailed up into the air from the back of the ruck. He went spinning up like a catherine wheel and he landed plump on the heads of a group of others trying to get in at me and they all collapsed like ninepins. I saw Turko grasp another unfortunate wight and hurl him like a bag of beans. Turko, the famed Khamster, a high Kham, a man who had reached very high levels of achievement within the syples of the Khamorros, disdained edged and pointed weapons. Now he bore through the throng like a snowplow through six-foot high drifts.

Inch's long Saxon-pattern ax removed the head of a masichier. No one who wishes to retain their anatomy entire is advised to stand within the sweep of Inch's great danheim ax. His leather cap was slightly askew, and a long braid of brilliant yellow hair swung wildly as he fought.

That meant trouble.

Balass the Hawk, matched as a swordsman without his usual shield against a thraxter and parrying-stick man, made nothing of the disadvantage. The guard's parrying stick was a klattar model, of balass and steel, and suddenly it slanted where he had no intention of allowing it to go. His thraxter swirled as Balass's own superb Valkan sword slid in. Himet was short another guard.

As for young Oby, his wicked long-knife did nasty things to a guard who thought that he, at least, stood a chance.

The fisherfolk fell back, gasping, dazed.

Himet the Mak . . . I whirled, for the moment freed from immediate opposition. The priest was nowhere to be seen. He had fled. Well, that was sensible. It was all of a piece with the man, with the artificial religion he sought to introduce to Valiadrin, and with the warped morals of the situation.

"Himet the Mak!" I bellowed up to Seg, who stood braced in the doorway above the vanished gallery. His bow was spanned, ready, and a stray gleam of light from the lamps struck a glittering spark from the steel arrow-point, most comforting to me, but most disconcerting to the poor wights huddled below, I daresay.

Seg spoke clearly, barely lifting his voice. "He vanished beyond the curtains behind the idol after the first shots."

There was no need for me to ask why Seg had not feathered him. Seg had loosed to clear away the guards pressing in on me. He had taken what he regarded as the prime objective. There is no use arguing with Seg Segutorio on these matters. As well argue with me, for I would have done the same had Seg been down there in that riot instead of me.

As Inch said, "Let us go and chase him, for he has made me break a taboo, and I shall have to perform unsightly things hereafter," Oby ran off with a whoop.

Again, there is no profit in laughing at Inch's taboos, which embroil him in ludicrous situations, at least, not too much laughter, for we could always make Inch stand on his head with the mere scent of squish pie. I hauled a guard toward me by his harness. I used my left hand, for my right held the main gauche as well as the rapier in a somewhat awkward grip. Now had I been a Djang, or a Pachak, I could have done that little trick without trouble.

I glared on the guard who rolled his eyes and flinched away.

"Tell me of Himet the Mak, my friend," I said, quite pleasantly, staring on the fellow. He blanched at this and his wild eyes went wilder still. He considered himself a dead man, that was certain, yet he had only been wounded, a long cut down his cheek. He made no attempt to lick at the blood. "Where has the arch-devil gone? Tell me that and you may live, dom."

Whether he believed me or not I do not know. He opened his mouth, slobbering, and I saw the stump of tongue there and felt the disgust in me. Had Himet done this? Did he employ dumb guards? But some had shouted as they fought.

"Can you write?" demanded Roybin.

A rolling, lolling shake of the head.

That was to be expected. Illiterates, even if through no fault of their own, tended to end up in the lower levels of whatever trade they entered. I had no desire to play dwazn questions with him. Vallia, Havilfar, the islands, there were far too many boltholes to go through even if this dumb devil knew. And, if Hamal was the homeland of the masichieri, I might ask all night and not get the right answer.

Balass, cleaning his sword, said, "They use the thraxter and parrying-stick. That is not of Vallia."

"They wear rapiers and daggers," said Roybin, fingering his chin. "Yet they left them in their scabbards and chose thraxters. It adds up. Hamal it must be."

Seg had jumped down to join us and we talked, taking no notice of the fisherfolk. I wanted these people of Veliadrin to see the picture and use their common sense. "Not Hamal, Roybin, surely?" Seg's bow gleamed in the orange light. "Shields there. More likely the Dawn Lands of Havilfar, or over to the west . . ."

"Wherever they come from," I said, "and this Himet the Mak, their target is Veliadrin. Right. Tell me, how far have they infiltrated Vallia to venture out here?"

The question was the obvious one, of course. Why bother over an island off the east coast of Vallia, an island moreover split into different provinces, when the main island remained?

Roybin looked worried. "You mean, my Prince, they have already completed their foul work in Vallia?"

Now that he phrased it like that I realized I didn't mean it . . . quite.

Perhaps I was growing paranoid. The word is of this later time and my thoughts then were more earthy. I had thought that Himet the Mak was after me personally. All this business about capturing me and taking me to the leader and torturing me was pedestrian stuff. I had thought, perhaps, the Star Lords might be taking up again their interest in me or, perhaps, the Savanti. But this kind of rowdy fracas was not their style, never had been so far. If they wanted me they could reach down and by means of a gigantic and ghostly representation of a Scorpion they could snatch me up from wherever I happened to be on Kregen and dump me down anywhere else they desired. Aye, and they could send me packing back to Earth four hundred light-years off through space.

The Star Lords and the Savanti between them had caused me great grief in my life, as you know, but I was no longer the same blind, ignorant, gasping puppet I had once been. Yet I was still painfully aware that at the whim of forces I did not understand and the dictates of superhuman men and women I might be flung willy-nilly into fights and adventures, into danger and unwelcome distractions, at any moment of any day.

I would not again struggle against the Star Lords in the same stupid way I had done the time they had summoned me and, because Delia and my friends were in peril, I had refused them. Then they had flung me back to Earth for twenty-one miserable years. No. This was not the handiwork of the Star Lords, who sought to work out a destiny for Kregen I could not comprehend.

The fisherfolk were growing restless. We were, as I have indicated, a right tearaway bunch of fearsome fighting men. But once we had seen off the black-feathered masichieri, why, there we stood, all talking and arguing away together as though the fisher people of Autonne did not exist. What were those good folk to make of that?

They had heard of Dray Prescot, their new High Kov, and they did not like him or his high-handed ways in renaming their island or of freeing their slaves. Fingering their tridents, shuffling their feet, they began to edge toward us.

Their faces hardened with determination ousting shock. They formed a half circle about us with their women safely in the rear. Their feet shuffled with more purpose as they advanced.

The way the orange lights caught on the sharp tines of their tridents and flashed sparks about the lofty room reminded us that perhaps we had not finished here yet.

Seg was saying, "More news would have come out of Vallia about them if the Chyyanists had grown really strong. In Falinur there have been rumors only, with nothing positive. This is the furthest I've gone yet in discovering—"

"They're a secretive bunch," observed Inch, who had come back in after chasing after Oby. Now the tall man was carefully winding his braid of yellow hair and stuffing it up under the leather cap. He looked more than a trifle put out, adding, "Secretive. And they preach revolution."

Casually, unhurriedly, Seg Segutorio turned around. His superb muscles put out their awful power and the bow string drew back. The arrow cast cleanly. The sharp steel point struck fiercely into the floorboards before that advancing semicircle of men determined to slay us out of ignorance and folly and hatred. The blazing blue feathers with which the arrow was fletched quivered as the shaft thrummed in the floor.

Seg turned back and answered Inch. "We'd have known something, you long streak."

It was magnificently done.

Instantly the forward shuffle of those desperate men stopped as though each man had been stricken with paralysis.

I said, "There is no profit, really, in running after Himet. Oby is on a fruitless errand. He will seek us out, all in due course. He will come to us, of that I feel sure."

As though on cue Oby walked back in looking disgruntled. He shook a few raindrops from him and the wind gusted in through the rotting doorway, half sagging from broken hinges.

"He took a flier and went—whoosh—and I can tell you, my Prince, the voller was a good one. Made in Hamal for a damned Hamalese."

If anybody would know about airboats, Oby would.

As Oby spoke I was fretting away about my response to Roybin and my insistence that Himet would seek me out. Were these the responses of a magalomaniac? Did I see conspiracy everywhere, plots to drag me down to destruction in every unusual occurrence?

I just was not sure.

"I believe this Himet the Mak will seek us out again. This is not just a fresh religious creed, which is open and exultant about its origins. If Hamal is involved, and that certainly seems to be so, we all know that Hamal has not been crushed but only halted in her aggressions. So it makes sense to strike at us in this new way. When this Himet returns we will deal with him. And, Roybin, I did not exactly mean what you suggested about Vallia. . . ."

Seg and Inch and Turko!

Oh, yes, I caught their delighted mocking smiles. Each

one of my true comrades favored me, each in his own way, with that secret, mocking, almost indulgent smile each one reserves for me. I sometimes think they humor me as they would a little child. Clearly they must have been thinking something along the lines that this so-puissant Dray Prescot, who was Prince of this and Kov of that and Strom of somewhere else, needed a little of the old headlong action to bring his addled senses back.

Since when, it seemed to me their sly and good-humored smiles were saying, since when has the high and mighty and great Dray Prescot not been sure of anything? Ah! If they only knew! If they only knew of the torments of indecision I suffered then—and still do suffer, by Zair!—then they would revise their opinions drastically.

I supposed they thought of me as a rough and ready soldier of fortune who had won through to great wealth and power—as indeed, with their help I had—and so therefore a man fit to be gently mocked. So I thought them. This amiable irony, this cheerful mockery of my comrades is returned by me, and it is never hurtful or cruel between us. Rather, it adds a zest to our comradeship, a spice, for each one of us knows that if he does a foolish thing—as who does not, by Vox!—the others will remind him of it, from time to time, gently.

So, being a cunning old leem-hunter after my own fashion, I pointed at the two brothers in the pressing crowd halted by Seg's single arrow standing in the floor as though held back by a solid wall of granite.

"You two. Step forth."

They stepped out, apprehensively, and other men near them hurriedly drew away to give a clear path as though afraid of contamination or the plague. What the two trident-men thought, or what the people thought lay in store, Opaz alone knew.

"You two. Brothers. Twins. Names?"

They swallowed, alike as twins, alike as twins ought to be and so often are not.

"Please, your honor, I am Tarbil the Brown."

"And, if it pleases your worship, I am Tarbil the Gray."

"It pleases me, Tarbils both," I said. "I saw. And I heard. Why did you attend this meeting tonight?"

Both spoke at once, then Tarbil the Gray yielded to Tarbil the Brown. "Our lives are poor, your honor. We thought there might be a little . . . fun."

"I would like to know why you did not shout for Chyyan with the rest."

"These people, your honor, would bring back slavery."

"Ah!" I said, understanding. I looked at the mob. "And that sweaty one whom you dragged back. He was your master?"

"Aye, your honor. We were slaves from childhood until the High Kov said all slaves must go free."

He looked at me under his eyebrows, his head ducked, this stalwart, muscled, hardy fisherman. He would go out in his little dory all night with a light, spearing fish. He was whipcord tough. Now he swallowed and shuffled his feet and wet his lips. "And, your honor, you are really him? You really are, your honor, you really are the new High Kov, Dray Prescot?"

"Yes."

I did not add, as I might unthinkingly have done once upon a time: "For my sins."

That was true enough, Zair knew. But they would have misunderstood, believing the words rather than the oblique thought behind them, an altogether too common failing, and a false word could have spread. I was hated enough in Veliadrin as it was.

Both brothers began the full incline until I stopped them, somewhat roughly, with a word, and then bade them stand up like men.

"There is no slavery in any place where the people look to me," I told them, trying not to give the impression of smugness or of righteousness. That never wears with simple folk. "You who once were slave are now free. It is your right. And I would thank you for your help."

I did not there and then, in view of some of the murderous looks bestowed on the Tarbil brothers, give them a gold piece each, or a ring or any other trifle. That would come later, when I confided the details to Panshi, my Great Chamberlain. He had remained at his post in the palace fortress of Esser Rarioch overlooking the bay and my capital city of Valkanium in Valka. And it would be no trifle. The Tarbil brothers would be useful.

Yes, I own it. Already I was thinking how they would fit into my schemes to free all the slaves of Vallia.

The Tarbils bobbed again and then drew back. They were given plenty of room. I looked questioningly at Roybin.

"They will be safe, my Prince. I believe you have put such a fright into these folk they will be quiet for a space, to the glory of Opaz and the Invisible Twins."

Oby and Balass were busy picking up the scattered weapons dropped by the black-feathered masichieri. They knew my ways. I did not give the Tarbils a rapier or a thraxter. Giving a man a weapon he does not know how to use is no act of friendship, and is a good way of getting him killed. But Roybin, who would stay in his home town of Autonne for a space, would see to the Tarbils before they were brought to Valka for the greater work.

I lifted my voice so all could hear.

"And we have more work to do." I spoke to the fisher-folk of Autonne. "Go to your homes. Ponder on what you have seen. Remember that the spirit of the Invisible Twins made manifest in the heavens above us is a beneficent spirit; but remember also that Opaz will strike down the wrongdoer. Put away from your thoughts this evil creed of Chyyanism. It is a fallacy to dream that each one of us may have exactly what he wants in this life, all at the same time, without effort. You must work, I must work. You will say I am your High Kov, and so I am and may be. The burdens laid on me are different from those laid on you, but they chafe no less harshly. But if any one of you wishes to take that task upon himself he knows the ways, both in law as elsewhere, and I warn you, he will grieve mightily."

Yes, all right. I know that was double-edged. I damned well meant it to be double-edged.

On Kregen land and wealth and titles are for the taking, but only by due process of law after the battle, despite a forest of dead bodies. I was legally the High Kov of Veliadrin. I could give the title to whosoever I wished, obtaining the emperor's agreement. Anyone could fight me for it and, if he won, have the emperor ratify his success if he could. That battle might be harder than the preceding one. A man might marry into lands and wealth and, perhaps, into a title. The system is not the same as those obtaining on this Earth. On Kregen it is far more what a man is and what he does that makes a man, and not what a man is born into.

As for women—the whole gorgeous world of Kregen is their oyster.

The famblys shuffled out, still dazed, and some, as I was

very well aware, still resentful. We desperadoes were left in the deserted hall, with the shattered gallery and the stink of ancient fish and the four-winged black idol of the Chyyan.

Turko bent and picked up a parrying-stick. He turned it over in his hands, weighing it, studying it. "A klattar," he said.

I recalled how in Mungul Sidrath Turko had bent and picked up a shield.

Roybin coughed and began to say, "I will arrange for everything to be cleared up here," when Oby let out a strangled screech that snapped us all about to glare at him.

"Dray! My Prince, *look*!"

We all stared where his rigid finger pointed.

The black idol against the rich cloths glowered down somberly upon us, the four wings black and seeming to span the heavens. And the idol's eyes glowed! Twin pits of emerald fire, they shone down with an eerie, baleful flame of malefic evil.

Chapter Three

Burning eyes of a pagan idol

Glowing with baleful fires, the eyes of the idol poured out a malevolent radiance. Twin pits of flame beside the arrogantly beaked nose, the eyes smoked greenly with a sense of contained horror most unnerving.

Impossible to say which one of us moved first.

As one we rushed toward the idol in its alcove.

What we shouted, what we said, I do not know. I think each one of us wanted to get a grip on the bird-idol and rip away the masked face to discover just what trickery was at work. The emerald fire blossomed into a fierce blaze of green fire. Then it vanished. As we reached the statue only cold lusterless glass eyeballs gazed dispassionately down on us.

"Sink me!" I burst out. "Here's a task for Khe-Hi and old Evold!"

We prowled around the idol, glaring at it, hitting it experimentally with our sword hilts. It sounded hard almost everywhere save for the center of the back, where it gonged with a hollow note. Those tearaways of mine would have pried the back open there and then, but I halted them.

"Let the wizards deal with this. There is bound to be trickery here, protection against opening."

They grumbled, but they saw the sense of what I said. We all knew a little of the powers of the Wizards of Loh, although no man not a wizard could comprehend them fully, I judged, and it seemed likely it might need a wizard to open the idol without disaster. Inch, hefting his ax, was maundering on about an idol of deepest Murn-Chem that had opened to let loose a flood of poisonous insects. Oby, eager to display learning, could cap that with the story of Rosala and the Eye of Imladrion. Seg and Inch stood back and Inch lowered his ax. I fancied a blow in the right place would open the idol of the chyyan easily enough, but we might not welcome what emerged.

Only later, thinking back, do I realize that the horrific appearance of those eyes suddenly glowing with sentient light, gleaming emerald pits of fire glowering down upon us, had not scared us witless as, doubtless, had been intended.

We'd simply yelled and charged straight for the idol.

I fancied that was behavior the manipulator of the idol was unaccustomed to.

Truth to tell, this whole affair of the Great Chyyan was a most serious business, but levity kept intruding. I'd fallen head over heels into a secret meeting. A horrific light had flashed from the glass eyeballs of an idol, and we'd simply gone for the thing baldheaded instead of shrieking and running off. When one gets into low company, one's habits tend to lower also. Like Oby having to be told to take his damned great long-knife out of the idol's eyesockets.

"If there are demons and poisonous insects or what not in there, Young Oby, you'll let the things out if you pry its eyeballs out, will you not?"

He jumped down agilely, saying with some resentment, "I've always wanted to prod out the fabulous gems from the eyesockets of a pagan idol."

So, sharpish, I said, "Then you can help the wizards when they dismember this thing, you imp of Sicce."

Whereat he scowled and fingered his knife and then, when Balass whispered to him, perked up. Balass had hinted that the fabulous gems might accrue to a light-fingered young scamp, when the wizards were otherwise occupied....

As you will readily perceive, after a little exercise and for all their forebodings, my comrades did not take the new creed of the Great Chyyan with overmuch seriousness. I hardly think it necessary to remark that in that they made a grave mistake.

There would be much to do, I considered, to stamp out Chyyanism. I would stamp it out, for it posed a threat to Vallia, my adopted country. Had the creed been genuine I would not have interfered. Religions originate and take root and flourish when there is a need for them. Changes of religion occur when the times cry out for new vessels for old wine. But this Chyyanism was artificial, a hodgepodge, a deliberate throwing together of ideas culled from the deepest recesses of the wish-fulfillment sections of the human mind. Chyyanism had been created as a weapon, for a far deeper purpose than merely to stir up credulous men and women resentful that their slaves had been taken from them.

In all this I tried to remember that my own origins were those of the rebel. I detested authority imposed by brute force without concern for evil results. Despite my friends in whom I joy, I am a loner. I have resisted authority all my life, often enough to my sorrow. Now that I had certain responsibilities I could see the other side, but, even so, I knew that Chyyanism merely used resentment against authority as a weapon, that the glib promises of luxury and paradise now were hollow, false and could only lead to ruination for all.

"Very good, Roybin, then you will see to this. Before I leave for Valka you must have a settlement. We owe you much."

"My thanks, my Prince."

So we left Roybin to summon his own people to clear up the mess and we took ourselves off to our secluded inn. The innkeeper was Roybin's cousin, and he asked no questions of these strangers recommended to him. But we all knew the word that the High Kov of Veliadrin was in Autonne would be all over the town by morning. It was high time to pack our traps and leave.

We had discovered certain things about Chyyanism and our agents would continue to burrow and pry and we would discover more. We had the great black idol. And I still felt convinced that this Makfaril, the leader of the Chyyanists, was aware of my interest and would take steps to counter the threat.

All this would make life interesting, as though life on Kregen can ever be anything other than fascinating!

We had flown here in small, inconspicuous fliers. Even so, airboats are rare enough in the backcountry of any nation of this continental grouping of Paz, with the natural exceptions of those countries where vollers are manufactured. So folk would still look up from their work on their nets or in the long tended rows of their fields when the shadow of an airboat skipped over them.

Seg would be leaving for his province of Falinur and Inch would be leaving for his province of the Black Mountains, both in Vallia. They would be flying west and north; I would be flying east.

We made our partings brief, with a compact to meet up again shortly.

The twin suns were just lifting above the eastern horizon as our fliers took off, the last shouted Remberees ringing in the limpid dawn air. Well, Seg and Inch are the finest company a man can wish for, and at every parting I sorrowed, but all the same, acknowledging that I am a loner, I could look ahead with some fascination to the future.

The journey to Valka proved uneventful, although we spotted a flier which contrarily kept pace with us for a time and then vanished behind clouds. Oby, who was piloting, looked at me enquiringly. But I shook my head.

"The fellow may be something to do with the Chyyanists, and he may not. Our task is to get home and have the wizards inspect the idol."

Oby's face expressed a certain disappointment.

"Don't fret! By Vox! Makfaril and Himet and their crowd will cause us enough strife to keep you well occupied, you bloodthirsty leem."

Only a little mollified, Oby drove us on through the morning as the mingled lights of Antares fell about us, streaming in jade and crimson across the voller and the fleeting countryside below.

By Zair! But it was good to be alive and on Kregen!

Turko kept twitching his new parrying stick about and Balass sat out of the slipstream methodically polishing up his sword blade with an oily rag.

A few seasons ago I would have gone blindly off charging after that elusive flier and thereby dropping myself headlong into fresh adventure or, most likely, failing to find him in the scattered clouds, so my present conduct gave some small indication of maturing. I wanted to chase the fellow. But the mystery of the idol fascinated me more.

So we bore on steadily through the levels, homeward bound for Valkanium, the capital city of Valka, and the high fortress therein of Esser Rarioch.

Since my return from Earth and the adventures in the Eye of the World I had a deal to do in catching up with events on Kregen. Things had changed. The sparkling vista of the Bay and the city opened up as we flew down in a beeline for the high landing platform of the castle. I did not sigh. The sound of a sigh in that bright scene would have been out of place. Just as I felt out of place. My son Drak, Prince of Vallia, appeared to be running Valka very nicely, thank you.

He was called the young strom, and I had heard men refer to me, unaffectedly, as the old strom. This was an eventuality I had not entertained, for despite what might happen on Kregen I had always thought of Valka as my home.

Oh, yes, I had other homes on Kregen, there was Strombor and Djanduin and the wide plains of Segesthes where my clansmen roamed. There was even Paline Valley in hostile Hamal. But Valka . . . Well, as Oby brought the airboat around in a sweeping line for the landing platform and touched down with that perfect sweetness of touch of the master flyer, I choked back that ridiculous sigh and hopped over the voller's coaming with a riotous bellow for the guards and attendants.

For a space it was all yelling and Lahals and rejoicings, and then Delia appeared and everyone fell respectfully back, and we touched hands. I looked into her eyes and, as always, saw there the amused wonder at these carryings on, the deep love between us and also that damned mocking smile which told me, clearly enough, that she had a word or two to say to me when we were alone.

Balass, I noticed as we turned to go into the palace, was engaged in a very close conversation with a superb black girl, a maiden of Xuntal, and so I rejoiced for him.

As for Oby . . .

"Yes, Dray, he has to run very fast to keep ahead of all the girls who have matters to discuss with him!"

Delia smiled as she spoke, so I knew the matter was not serious.

For Oby had ducked down beneath the voller, crept around the other side, and the last I saw of him that day was a fleeting glimpse of his breechclout as he vanished down a back stairs. Hot on his heels ran half a dozen rosy-limbed girls, all yelling after him, waving their arms like a bunch of love-crazed nymphs. Well, they were, in a way.

I found my craggy lips twisting into a smile.

"It seems Oby has made himself at home in Esser Rarioch."

"Very much. Which," added my Delia tartly, "is more than can be said for Esser Rarioch's strom."

But she smiled as she spoke. One day I would have to tell her about Earth and all the rest of that story, which she, dear girl, would find almost impossible to believe. How could any intelligent person believe in a world that had only one sun, only one moon, possessed only *Homo sapiens* as intelligent people to live on this fantastic world, did not have flying saddle-birds or any other of the everyday marvels of Kregen?

It would take a lot of belief to believe a story like that.

The only consolation I had was simply that there is no woman more perfect than Delia on two worlds. She, at least, would listen in her grave, lightly ironic way, half laughing and yet deadly serious, and would give me the benefit of her love. She, at least, would not condemn me out of hand as a madman, makib, fit only for the ice-chains of Hegenor.

So, together, we went into the palace where everyone seemed pleased to see me back, and where we were soon served up a capital meal in a small private room. Melow the Supple, the ferocious Manhound who had dedicated her life to the care of Delia, as her two children cared for my first twins, prowled in, splitting her frightful muzzle in a grin of welcome.

We drank tea and ate miscils and other light pastries, and munched on fruits of all kinds, with the ever-present dish of palines to hand.

"And this new creed is then a serious menace?"

"Most serious, I judge. To tell simple folk that they can have all they want, here and now, for the asking, is ruinous folly. By Zair! Had I all I wanted, here and now—" And then I paused. I had so much. Was I then so greedy?

Delia had told me the news of our children. Each was about his or her business in the greater world of Kregen. I had seen my three sons in action, and in them I could feel content mingled with apprehension. Drak, as the eldest, handled my affairs for me. Zeg was now a famous Krozair in the inner sea, the King of Zandikar. Jaidur had remained in the inner sea to finalize his acceptance into the Krozairs of Zy. I value my membership of that order among the highest of the good things that have happened to me on Kregen. I had ideas to put the mystic disciplines and teachings of the Krozairs to a wider use. So the lads were accounted for. Our daughter Velia was dead, but we had another new daughter, Velia, and she I looked upon with a dread joy, for the stories about lightning are not true.

As for the other two girls, Delia simply told me that Lela, Drak's twin, was busy with the Sisters of the Rose. And Dayra, Jaidur's twin, should—and then Delia corrected herself, and said was—also concerned with the Sisters of the Rose.

"But they are making arrangements to visit Valkanium to see their father. They have to call at Vondium first."

I nodded, thinking. So with Delia and the children I had all I wanted. Why should I then cry out that I did not have all I wanted? Perhaps the thought of the perils and problems besetting Kregen prompted the remark. All I knew then was that I felt a gnawing sense of anticlimax, and a restless desire to be up and doing once again.

"As soon as the idol is here the Sans can probe and pry." I munched palines, tasting the flavor, forcing myself to feel a content foreign to me. "To promise anyone instant success in the here and now rings false."

"But there is more to it than that?"

"Yes, my heart." Trust Delia to see through my mumblings. "The idea of this creed could be a new attack from Hamal." I outlined some of my suspicions. "I shall have to go back there at some point. The devils still sell us inferior fliers, so I believe."

"Oh, they do not fail so much as they used to do. But the silver boxes go black and fail much earlier. And they charge us greatly inflated costs. And—"

"If nothing else turns up, then I'll go back to Hamal and this time rip the secrets from the very throats of the Nine Faceless Ones themselves."

Delia did not say in an arch way: "You mean that too!" For she knew I meant it. But I caught her expression, and at once felt deflated, an idiot, a veritable onker. To talk about going away again so soon after so long an absence was thoughtless cruelty. I reached over and touched her arm.

"Let us open up the idol and see what we find. Then we can talk with more sense."

She took the words as an apology. And then she said, "This time, I think I shall come with you."

So I laughed and we drank more tea, and Panshi, the Great Chamberlain, came in to tell us that the black pagan idol bird had arrived. So up we went through the colonnades and passageways and along the long hall of the images to Evold Scavander's laboratory. The black idol squatted against the wall opposite the windows, and dominated the room with an aura of evil. The thing looked just as impressive and malignant there as it had in the makeshift temple of the fisherman's net-room.

Old Evold sniffed and hitched up his robes and fussed around his princess, bellowing for Ornol to find chairs and refreshments. Delia sat calmly, smoothing her trailing skirts, accepting the services with that delicacy that marks her as a true princess born.

Turko walked in with his loose limber prowl and settled down quietly and watchfully by the door. I noticed the parrying-stick thrust through his belt, the jags turned out, and I fancied he'd have Balass foining away at him with a rudis in short order.

Evold Scavander, given the honorary title *San*—which means sage or master or dominie—was the wisest of the wise men of Valka. His wizardry extended into different spheres from those of the famed Wizards of Loh, who are, I must confess, real sorcerers. If they are not genuine, then they are the most consummate confidence tricksters of two worlds. Much remained to be learned of the Wizards of Loh. I was engaged in a long-drawn-out struggle with the master-wizard, Phu-Si-Yantong, a man who was more evil than could be understood by mortal men, and yet who was not a cardboard villain without features that made him both darker and, contrariwise, human. Yantong had not bothered me in the inner sea. I surmised he knew I was back in Valka and therefore I must expect a visitation from him, a ghostly apparition that would spy on me.

The Wizard of Loh, Khe-Hi-Bjanching, whom I had brought out of danger to a position of importance in Esser Rarioch, had been erecting defenses against Yantong. I knew these defenses must be put to the test. I did not look forward to that time.

Evold, spluttering and blowing, prowled around the idol, peering up at it, tapping, feeling, prodding.

Once he would have started in to prize the back off without a second thought. But for all their arguments and quarrels, Evold and Bjanching had come to a kind of understanding. I felt only a little surprise when Evold burst out: "Now where by Vox is Khe-Hi? He's never here when he's wanted, and always underfoot when he's not." So that salved some of Evold's *armour propre.*

By my orders there were few people in the laboratory. The tables were loaded with the paraphernalia of Evold's studies. Here we had broken some of the secrets of the silver boxes that powered airboats. Here we had sought to uncover the secrets of past ages, and to make experiments for the future well-being of Valka. But my concern now was for what might happen when the idol was opened.

When Khe-Hi-Bjanching came in I saw that look that flashed like two flung stuxes between the two wizards. Like two flying spears their looks clashed and crossed. But much had changed in Valka since I had been away, and I knew I would find much had changed as I took up once again the threads of life on Kregen, so I watched with a small sly inward approval as the two wizards prepared to cooperate. Young Khe-Hi and Old Evold, wasn't that becoming the story of my homecoming?

"You have touched nothing, San?"

"Nothing, San."

Their exquisite politeness one to the other tickled me. I remembered them yelling at each other and hurling scathing remarks about aptitudes and abilities. Now the two wizards walked together all around the black chyyan and cocked their heads back to stare up at the malignant eyes and drew long thoughtful expressions. In short, they behaved as professional men consulted on a case of intricacy behave.

Finally, Khe-Hi said, "The idol is certainly sealed by sorcery. I know that."

We all understood. A wizard of Loh who deals all his life in sorcery knows when sorcery is being used, or, at least, knows most of the time.

"You say the eyeballs flamed emerald, my prince?"

"Aye."

"Yet they are plain glass with a yellowish tinge." Khe-Hi gestured and Ornol, Evold's assistant, brought across a ladder which was propped against the statue. Khe-Hi, hitching up his pure white robe cinctured by the crimson cord, mounted and peered closely at the eyes. I wondered what would happen if they blazed their incredible malignant green into his face.

Many men of the continent of Loh have red hair. Not all. Loh is a land of mystery and terror and remained locked away from exploration after the collapse of its famous empire. Khe-Hi's red hair shone darkly against the black of the statue. He peered this way and that. Then he descended and stood looking thoughtfully upon the back of the idol where a single light tap gonged a hollow note.

"There are preparations I must make," he said at last, coming to a decision. "San, I would value your help." Evold nodded without speaking.

"Will this take time?" I spoke calmly.

"Three burs only, my Prince."

A bur is forty Earthly minutes. There would be time for more tea and a slap-up meal in two hours. I nodded. "Then I leave the idol in your care." Then, because of reasons that remained too obscure to be articulated, I added: "And Oby has settled a lien on the eyeballs with his longknife."

There was a laugh at this. Delia rose. We went out together and Turko followed. Like my return home, this first investigation of the idol had been an anticlimax.

Chapter Four

Eggs of evil

There was so much for me still to learn about what had chanced on Kregen during my absence that every spare moment was occupied in Delia's dredging her memory to retail the choicest bits of information. We had recourse to the records of Valka, of course, kept by the stylors in Esser Rarioch. How all this fresh torrent of facts and conjectures would influence my life had to be weighed and judged. I think it best if I simply fill in what it is needful to know about any given situation as it arises in this narrative.

For instance, I was fascinated by the scraps of knowledge gleaned from distant Hyrklana, where Queen Fahia, poor soul, was having trouble finding fresh fodder for the Jikhorkdun. Likewise, I was mightily impressed by the progress made in raising and equipping three full regiments of Pachaks mounted on flutduins from the Pachaks of Zamra. But these and many and many another affair of state had nothing, as I saw it, to do with my present concern with the Chyyanists. I mention these two to give examples. Also, I handled some pressing affairs of business that my son Drak would have taken care of had he not been in Zamra dealing with the construction of a new seawall, jetty and pharos for the new town of Veliasmot put in hand to provide another secure harbor for the great galleons on which rested our trade.

So, as I ate vosk pie and momolams, I listened to Jiktar Larghos Glendile recently returned from Vondium, the capital of the Empire of Vallia, telling me of the latest decrees of the Presidio. The Presidio ran the country although the emperor as well as holding titular power controlled enough real power to maintain the balances so necessary for government. It was all a matter of balancing one power group against another, of taking advice and of making laws that would maintain.

"But the racters, my Prince! They have shrunk in numbers but have increased their powers through carefully placed men in the right positions."

The racters, the most powerful party in Vallia, who wore the black and white, held their wealth and positions through high commerce, through land, through slaving, through mining. There were other parties, notably the panvals, who stood against the racters. But all, as I well knew, had their own candidates to take the emperor's place.

"They maneuver the emperor so that he will stand alone. Then they can reduce him."

"Do you know who it is whispered will take his place?"

"No, my Prince. That information is held close."

This Jiktar Larghos Glendile presented an imposing picture as he reported. He was a Pachak. Now Pachaks, being blessed by nature or by gene manipulation with two left arms, are among the most renowned of Kregen's fighting men. Also, they have a hand on their long whiplike tail. Loyal were Pachaks, and first-class mercenaries. I had built up centers of Pachak habitation in both Valka and Zamra that were based on a full life. That is, the towns occupied by the Pachaks were proper towns, with all the facilities of towns. They were not mere military barracks for mercenaries.

Larghos Glendile was a jiktar, a rank I suppose most nearly equated with that of colonel. His uniform of the brave old scarlet glowed. He wore two bobs, the medals given by my Elders of Valka. His tough face, with the harsh yet human features of a man who has had wide experience, betrayed his desire to do well not just as a hired fighting man, which he no longer was, but as a full-fledged citizen of Zamra. Zamra, the larger island to the north of Valka, of which I am kov, was to prove of surprising worth in the seasons to come.

The necessity of thus building up a powerful fighting force was one I loathed. Yet the necessity remained. There are many foes in Kregen who will cheerfully sail up over the ocean rim, or drop down out of the skies, and seek to take whatever portable property is lying around not chained down. My duty as a prince was to protect my people. And, equally, when I called on them for help, their duty was to help me protect them. But of course it is not as simple as that.

Jiktar Glendile of Zamra went on to tell me more of what was transpiring in Vondium, and I listened and ate my fruit and quaffed tea and finished with a handful of palines.

The clepsydra indicated half a bur to go.

Delia came in looking radiant. I rose. Glendile straightened to ramrod attention.

Delia looked at me accusingly.

"And have you kept the jiktar standing all the time?"

I gaped.

Neither Glendile nor I had noticed. We were warriors.

So the moment passed and Jiktar Glendile finished up his report sitting down, drinking, his booted feet stuck out, his rapier cocked up and his tail curled decorously around the chair legs. That tailhand could whip a long blade up between his legs and have a foeman's tripes out in a twinkling.

When the Pachak had gone I said to Delia, in more of a groan than I intended, "There is so much to learn! By Zair! Things have moved on Kregen since I have been away!"*

She laughed and tinkled a fingernail against the clepsydra.

I stood up.

"Then let us go and see how the Sans have got on with that damned black idol."

So I stood up and spoke I saw Delia, half turned in the

---

* Although a fresh supply of cassettes from Dray Prescot has come into my possession, for which we should thank all the gods of Kregen, I am convinced there are some cassettes missing. *Krozair of Kregen* finished with Dray Prescott and Delia reunited in the Eye of the World. They must have rescued Didi, the daughter of Gafard and Velia, from the Grodnims. Textual evidence lends support to the idea that the rescue was hairy in the extreme. But the present volume, Secret Scorpio, begins with Prescot and his friends on Veliadrin seeking out the secrets of the Chyyanists. How much is missing we cannot tell.

A.B.A.

doorway, looking back at me, and the breath caught in my throat.

Often and often I have tried to find expression to convey some sense of the beauty of my Delia. How impossible a task! As she stood there, half laughing at me, the sheer ivory-white gown relieved only by a small brooch of brilliant scarlet scarrons, her brown hair with those shimmering tints of chestnut striking through and making a wonder and a halo around her head—yes, I felt my flinty old heart thump and the blood pulse through my veins. By Zair! Was there ever a girl like Delia, my Delia of Delphond, my Delia of the Blue Mountains?

Sweetly she looked at me, mocking, knowing very well what thoughts were prancing through my mind.

I scowled. What chance of that! The scowl died and I realized I was smiling, grinning away like a loon.

"There will be plenty of time, my love," said Delia, the Princess Majestrix of Vallia, "for you to catch up."

If I do not give my reply to that I fancy each of you, in his or her own way, will furbish up the retort suitable. The effect of all this was that we were smiling foolishly away as we walked through the hall of the images toward the laboratory. These images, of ivory and bronze and precious stones, commemorate the Stroms of Valka. I still had not made up my mind if I relished their presence forever lowering down on me, the latest Strom, or if I resented them as reminding me of past glories and past shames.

We had just passed the bust of Strom Natival, I recall, around whom legends clustered, when we heard the explosion. For a single shocked instant I thought gunpowder had been touched by a spark. But gunpowder was not used here. All my old training in a wooden ship of the line, with felt slippers and flash curtains and water buckets and hoses forever at the ready, reared up in me. With a curse I leaped forward and the billowing mass of black smoke choked around the far corner and boiled swiftly forward. The black smoke engulfed me. I swung about, reaching for Delia, waiting for the blast to take us. It was all a screaming nightmare with the concussion still ringing in my ears.

The smoke roiled and eddied. I blundered into Strom Fagan's bust—I knew it was his by the size of the vinous nose—and it went over with a smash. Delia clung to me, saying nothing. Our eyes and noses ran with the stink. This was not ordinary smoke. There was about it a charnel tang, a foul-tasting vileness on our tongues, rasping our throats.

No further blast came.

The smoke thinned. I gasped for air. We waved our hands about, wafting the smoke away.

Delia's ivory dress was spattered with black dots, like mold on cheese. My eyelids felt redly granular, itching. I spat.

"By the foul intestines of Makki-Grodno!" I bellowed. "The infernal idol!"

I pushed Delia away.

"Go back, Delia!"

I started to run for the laboratory.

My Delia ran at my side.

"Go back! Who knows what has happened?"

"I intend to find out. Why don't you go back?"

I saved my breath.

As I ran on I was cursing away at myself for being such a fool as to bring the damned idol into the palace. What a blind idiot! Had I never heard of Troy, and the White Horse? What sorcerous mischief had I unloosed in Esser Rarioch?

A figure blundered into me and I grasped old Evold by the arms and shook him.

"Tell me, Evold!"

"My Prince—" He babbled on, shaking. "The eyes lit up again, just as you said!" He coughed and choked and spluttered and I let him go as he swiped at his streaming eyes. "San Khe-Hi, he was almost prepared as he had promised, and then it was as though the lightning struck. The idol shrieked! There was smoke and flame and a blue-green fire and—"

He had no need to say more.

From the wrecked door of the laboratory Khe-Hi-Bjanching stumbled, beating wildly at the darting black forms surrounding him. They dived from the air, swirling their ebony wings, and their shrill chittering filled the hall with the rustling whispers of the tomb.

Chyyans! Scores of tiny chyyans, with a wing spread of no more than two feet, swooped and darted and struck and clawed. I saw their baleful red eyes, the raking dart of their scarlet talons. Their beaks gaped wide. Khe-Hi stumbled and fell. I leaped forward, ripping the rapier and main gauche free. I stood over him, straddle-legged, and at once my blades swirled and swished to cut down the fluttering horrors.

They appeared almost like bats, vampire bats, lunging in to sink their fangs into my neck and suck me dry.

But each black chyyan had four wings, four wings clad in rusty black feathers. They swooped and darted and struck, and I felt the sting on forehead and arms as they clustered thickly about me and sank their talons into my flesh.

"Wizard!" I bellowed, slashing about me wildly. "Cast a spell or something! Drive them off!"

"I have spelled them already," came the gasping wheeze from the wizard. He tried to crawl out from between my knees and a tiny chyyan slashed at him, so that he cried out and scuttled back.

"Well, for the sweet sake of Mother Diocaster! Spell them again!"

I heard a furious yell from along the hall and between slashing and ducking turned. Turko was there, laying about him with his parrying-stick. And my Delia, slim and glorious in her slashed ivory gown, my Delia sliced and cut with the long slender jeweled dagger in whose use she is so superbly skilled.

"San!" I bellowed. "You must run for it!"

I shoved the dagger into my mouth, ricking my lips back in the old way so my teeth could grip the blade. I reached down with my left hand and hauled Khe-Hi out by the scruff of the neck. My right hand seemed of its own volition to be flickering the rapier about, chunking great swatches of black feathers away, slicing and cutting, never thrusting, for in a game like this that was the sure way to die.

I gave Khe-Hi a good rousing kick up the backside and sent him scuttling and staggering down the long hall.

Then I reached my Delia and with three blades we wove that old deadly net of steel. She flashed me a single smile. We went to work, then, in real earnest.

Jiktar Larghos Glendile appeared, raging, roaring into the fight with a rapier and two daggers, and with a blade gripped in his tailhand. He was worth two men in that kind of fight. Others of my people showed up, and soon we could actually count the numbers of chyyans remaining.

I bellowed.

"Save some! Do not slay them all!"

Then ensued a riotous chasing rout as the fluttering birds sought to escape from the palace, and my people, whooping as though on a rampage, chased them through the corridors and up and down the stairs, seeking to cast nets and sacks and whatever came to hand over them. In the end we caught three of them, penned in sacks, and the stout material bulged and strained. Turko hit a bulge with the parrying-stick and the bird in the sack quieted down.

Once again what had begun as a drama, as tragedy, ended in farce.

"Khe-Hi!" I said, and at my tone he stiffened up, looking woebegone in his ruined finery, but nonetheless still retaining his dignity as a Wizard of Loh. "*Well*?"

We went back to the laboratory and Khe-Hi pointed out what was left of the idol.

Bits and pieces of black stone were scattered about the chamber. The windows were blown out. The tables were overturned. The place was a shambles.

"Khe-Hi!" squeaked San Evold. "You've ruined my chamber!"

"Not me, old man. Rather this Makfaril of whom the prince speaks."

"I'll do more than speak about him," I said, very nastily. "You said you had spelled them."

"So I did, my Prince." Here Khe-Hi pulled himself together and became again a famous Wizard of Loh. "Had I not done so we would have been beset by full-size chyyans."

Turko whistled. Jiktar Larghos Glendile flicked his tail-hand about.

I said, "So you did well, wizard. Did you seek to open the idol before I arrived?"

"No. No, my Prince! The eyes lit up again as you described when my preparations were almost complete. I understand what happened. A wizard was controlling the idol and saw what I intended. He released the hidden sealing spells and there was a sound as of thunder and a blue-green light as of leprous lightning."

That was as good a way as any to describe an explosion to those who did not know of gunpowder.

"The spell I had set reduced whatever was in the idol in stature and power. So the eggs—"

"Eggs?"

"The idol was packed with chyyan eggs that would hatch into full-sized chyyans instantly, bypassing normal growth. It is a trick some wizards employ. My counter-art reduced the size of the chyyans."

"Lucky for us," said Glendile. He had four weapons to clean, and was hard at work even as we stood talking.

"And the light was blue-green?"

"Yes."

That did not square with a gunpowder explosion.

"Damned sorcery," I said. "I don't hold with it. Another wizard?"

"A most potent practitioner of the arts."

I looked at Khe-Hi-Bjanching. We all knew of whom we thought.

It was left to Delia to say, in a calm, even voice, "Do you think, San, it was this infamous Phu-Si-Yantong?"

Khe-Hi scowled. "I do not know. By Hlo-Hli, my Princess, I do not know!"

This was a poser. I was prepared to credit Yantong with any evil you care to imagine. Once a fellow has run into evil of that nature he tends to see his opponent as more black than a night of Notor Zan, until, with wisdom, comes the understanding that character shades into gray and purple and bilious green. All the same, Phu-Si-Yantong!

"I have told you of the Wizard of Loh, Que-Si-Rening, kept by the Empress Thyllis in Hamal. Do you think it could have been him? After all," I added, trying to appear casual and making a dismal mess of it, "after all, everything about the Chyyanists points to another ploy from Hamal."

"I swear by the Seven Arcades, my Prince! I cannot tell. The sorcery was sealed by great power. It is possible among high adepts to conceal ego-traces, to hide the personality patterns. I can do this to an extent. There are few wizards, I venture to think, who would discover what I did if I did not wish them to, but of course there could be a few who would have the power."

This was mighty humble pie for Khe-Hi, I saw.

I nodded, not satisfied, but unable to do anything about that dissatisfaction for the moment.

A clatter of dislodged stones and debris from one of Evold's smashed tables turned our attention to Balass, who straightened up lifting a dusty round object from the jumble. He blew on it and dust flew.

"Now what is this?" he said, turning, walking across with the round plate balanced on his upturned palms.

I was aware of Khe-Hi at my side, of the way a tremor shook through him. I shot a swift searching glance at him. The wizard's face looked strained, a deep furrow dinting down between his eyebrows. He sucked in his breath.

"Whatever it is, Balass," I sang out cheerily, "our potent wizard knows!"

"Aye, my Prince! By Hlo-Hli. I know!"

"Well, then, tell us."

He took the plate from Balass, by which I judged the thing exerted no immediately dangerous evil influence. He turned it over. We all craned to look. The plate was fashioned from bronze, as thick as two fingers, as wide around as an Och's shield. Inset around the edge were cabalistic signs; these Khe-Hi ignored and I judged them decoration. Nine sigils surrounded a blank center. That center either had once had or had space left for five further signs. Each of the nine signs was different and I recognized none.

"Well?"

"This was secreted in the compartment in the back of the idol."

"Well," exclaimed Balass. "Anyone knows that!"

"Go on, Khe-Hi," I said. Balass shut his jaws with a snap.

"The wizard controlling the idol is able to observe at a distance without the necessity of forcing a representation of himself to the needful point and looking through his own immaterial eyes. This saves psychic energy."

Delia was looking carefully at the disk and its nine emblazoned signs, and Turko lifted it from Khe-Hi's hands so the princess might view it more easily.

I said, "You mean when the eyes light up with that baleful green fire this damned wizard is spying out of them?"

"Yes, my Prince. I also think this is a sign for the priest in this case Himet the Mak, to open the back in safety."

"But the confounded thing blew up when the eyes lit up!"

"Yes. Because the wizard observed what was happening

and knew that in the next few murs I would have reduced his sorceries and rendered the chyyan eggs harmless."

"Hmm," I said. "And these signs? Nine of them?"

Nine is perhaps the most magical number on Kregen. There was a fanciful touch about this round plate and the nine symbols that reminded me, vaguely, of the Krozairs of Zy and their sign, the hubless spoked wheel within the circle.

"Each sign, I think, is a location. Probably where a temple of the Great Chyyan is situated. When the sign lights up, it must be a signal to meet there."

Every symbol lay flat and dull and lifeless.

"The first thing," I said with enough acerbity in my voice to make them understand the seriousness of all this and my inflexible determination to rise above the farcical element that had been dogging us lately, "the very first thing is to read the symbols. We must find out where these damned temples are."

Evold peered at the plate. "They mean nothing to me at the moment. But mayhap I have books. San Drozhimo the Lame may have somewhat to say on these signs. And there is the *Hyr-Derengil-Notash*. Also I have hopes of the hyr-lif of Monumentor ti Unismot."

There were one or two small smiles in the group. We all knew old Evold and the lore he culled from his musty books. All the same, he did come up with answers to problems. No one could deny that.

Khe-Hi sniffed. "This is wizard's work, San. The *Hyr-Derengil-Notash* was compiled by a great wizard two thousand five hundred seasons ago. I know it well. If whoever is controlling the idol used it, you may find what we seek. I doubt it."

San Evold did not look disgruntled. He was used to this kind of deprecation from Khe-Hi.

The *Hyr-Derengil-Notash*—the title means, very roughly, the high palace of pleasure and wisdom—is used by philosophers and in its pages they can find whatever they seek. It is read as the heart commands. If, and I did not savor the thought, if Phu-Si-Yantong was the wizard controlling the idol I did not think he would have recourse to that hyr-lif. Only very important books on Kregen are called lifs, and only the most highly important of all receive the appellation of hyr-lif.

The signs meant nothing to me. One looked like a mess

of worms. Another like a ship of no recognizable type, with a fork of lightning joined to the mainmast. Another seemed merely a formal angular maze. Delia looked up at me, and at the look in her eyes I jumped.

"I think," said Delia slowly, her face more flushed than usual, "I think I know where is the place one of these signs refers to."

Chapter Five

The Stromni of Valka explains

The plate, with its outer ring of nine symbols and its inner ring of five empty places surrounding the blank center, was very heavy, being fashioned of bronze. The idea, undoubtedly, was to make it difficult to steal. Khe-Hi-Bjanching told us that this kind of plate with symbols used by the wizards as a means of conveying information was called a signomant, employing signomancy to give instructions that could not be misunderstood by those who had the key.

I refused to allow Delia to speak until we had all left the laboratory, Turko and Balass taking turns to carry the signomant, and until we had all settled down in an airy upper chamber after we had washed the muck of the explosion from ourselves. A light white wine was served, for the suns were almost gone, and the birds flitted about the grim stone face of the castle. Wearing a delicious cool laypom-yellow gown, Delia sat in her comfortable chair, gazing upon us in some delight, her cheeks still rosy and her eyes bright with the secret revelations she was about to tell us.

No one was fool enough to mumble some sycophantic nonsense about not being at all surprised that the Princess Majestrix should understand the signs. We all sensed that only some local knowledge had given the clue to Delia. This proved true as she spoke.

"I am called Delia of Delphond," she began. "My estate of Delphond is very dear to me and I have studied all that I can find about it."

Now I am aware that I have said very little about Vallia. One reason is that its puissant empire tended to stifle coherent thought in me. Also, much of my adventuring on Kregen has taken place in countries outside Vallia. But, all the same, as I go on I must tell you of important facts. In the long ago the main island of Vallia and the surrounding islands were all separate, petty kingdoms and kovnates—and some not so petty—and it was only after long-drawn-out and bloody wars that finally the empire drew together with its capital at Vondium.

Delphond is situated on the southern coast of Vallia, not too far to the west of Vondium, and it had been a kingdom in its own right, small and tight and sweet. When the empire-builders advanced from Vondium the kingdom of Delphond retained an individual identity for much longer than anyone might have expected. There was much trouble with the far southwest, and Rahartdrin resisted stubbornly. Also the northeast maintained a hostility to Vondium that persisted for centuries. So it was that when at last Delphond was incorporated into the empire the final capitulation was swift, with little damage done to the ancient monuments of the past. The old history twined with passion and intrigue—just as these times of which I tell you now hummed with plot and counterplot—and Delphond when at last she entered the empire was given over to the empress and her descendants, alternating the generations with other estates of Vallia.

Now Delia pointed to one of the nine symbols ringing the bronze plate.

"The Temple of Delia," she said, and looked up at me like a small girl embarrassed at picking the largest fruit in the bowl.

I laughed.

Now I understood the meaning of the flush in her cheeks, the brightness of her eyes. She may be a princess, a Princess Majestrix, but my Delia is a woman with a mature and yet girlish heart that derides pomp and circumstance, that makes mock of titles, that understands that if Opaz has seen fit to burden her then she must brace up and shoulder those burdens.

Old Evold nodded with quick understanding.

"You are right, my Princess!" That, of course, was a silly thing for anyone to say to some common princess, for whenever can a common princess be accused of being wrong? But Delia is no ordinary princess and we were all friends here, eager to seek out the devil's work threatening our people.

"See," said Delia, her slender fingers busy tracing the lines of the sign. "Here are the pillars, and this is unmistakable." Two dots surrounded by twin circles and with a V-shape joining them had been linked with the architrave. "This has always been taken to be the sign of Delia in her manifestation as Mother Goddess. It is scarcely known outside Delphond. When Delphond lost her kings and became a province of Vallia the religion of the time sought to stamp out all knowledge and memory of the Mother Goddess."

"That was before we were blessed with the knowledge of Opaz," said Evold. He pulled his nose, blinking. "That would have been in the time of Father Tolki the Almighty."

"Yes." Delia knew all about this. "The fearsome warriors in their bronzen mail trampled down all Vallia, bringing with them their own belief in Father Tolki. They were hard days. The old records show that Delphond escaped lightly, for we are cut off there, a backwater, out of the stream of events."

"But a mighty pleasant backwater!" I said, incensed. "I am particularly fond of Delphond, and I have read of how the mailed hosts of Father Tolki ravaged the land. But they did institute the first Empire of Vallia."

"Which broke up, as empires do. There were many religions and many new peoples and kingdoms and empires before the Light of Opaz guided . . ." And then Delia hesitated, and stopped. How could she go on to say that her family had taken the ragbag of Vallia and shaken it into an empire, that her family had taken the power thrust upon them by Opaz—or by greed and cupidity and sheer downright cunning and skill and ruthlessness?

"It is a story not unknown in Havilfar," said Turko. "The ancient mysteries of the Mother Goddess, and then the newer, harsher, military religions of men. We Khamorros have fought against oppression for all our history."

"We rejoice in the Invisible Twins," said Delia seriously. "For in them made manifest through Opaz we see the fusion of male and female, of mother goddess and warrior god, and all the other aspects of godhood." She looked around and added not so much tartly as with finality, "As it should be."

How this brought home to me the ancientness of Kregen! Civilizations had risen and fallen, cities built and vanished, kingdoms waxed and waned. And, far back into the past, the Sunset Peoples had lorded it over a young Kregen with the freshness of dawn. Now all that was left of them were the Savanti, locked away somewhere in their Swinging City of Aphrasöe. One day I would return to Aphrasöe, and with a purpose. But that day could not be now, for there were too many other pressing problems in Vallia to occupy me.

Old, is Kregen, and yet the world is populated now by new vigorous peoples thrusting out to conquer fresh territory, waves of migrations passing across the continents and casting up new kingdoms and republics, new confederations, hurling down the old into ruination. The famed Empire of Walfarg, generally called the Empire of Loh, had fallen into a pile of dusty refuse, and now Loh slumbered, her Bowmen mercenaries in the other continents, her wizards scattered and serving other monarchs.

One day the dark continent of Loh would be opened up again and hosts would march. Perhaps a host of Vallia would penetrate that land of secret walled gardens and veiled women, hear the silver trumpets screaming, bring the Light of Opaz to the deepest darknesses.

But first we had our own stables to clean.

"But which," I asked Delia, "which temple is it?"

"Oh," she said with quick confidence. "It must be the chief temple. Much of it still stands, garlanded with vines and ivy, overgrown, moldy. But the sacrificial pools are still there, with water still in them. The last time I was there—you were gone off, Dray—the golden roofs still stood. Although, of course, the gold was gone long since and only the tiles remained."

"Just the place for a secret rendezvous for a congregation of the Great Chyyan."

"Oh, Dray! I hope not! My poor people!"

"Yes." I was grim about it. "There is no guessing when meetings have been held, or even if any have been held so far. But one thing is sure. This devil Makfaril intends to use Delphond as a base for his Chyyanists. For all we know they are already strongly entrenched there."

"I am not so sure." Delia looked troubled. "My Delphondi are a lazy lot, as you know, slow to anger. They prefer the easy life, sitting in the sun, yarning, eating, singing. It would take a very clever and cunning man to rouse them against their wills."

"Makfaril is clever and cunning. Make no mistake about that."

"Then we must go there at once."

"Agreed. But we go carefully."

Delia's troubled look persisted. She shook her head.

"What a business this is! I love Delphond. I am the princess—it is an imperial province—and I am sure the people love me. Yet I must go creeping back like a spy!"

"Exactly!"

Then I paused, trying to think. "On the other hand, if you went as the princess, in all pomp, acting as you usually act—and I know the people love you—that would show them your care for their welfare persists. I feel convinced only a few may have gone over to this damned creed. You will have to work from the outside, bedazzle them, show them that Opaz is still the religion of their fathers and mothers. Yes," I said, brisking up, seeing a cheerful glow on my mental horizons. "Yes, that's it. You are the Princess of Delphond. The people will welcome you as they always do. But, as for me . . ."

"Yes?"

"I am not as well known there. Oh, a few of the nobles would know me. But I shall go in my own way, and creep about and ask questions, and prod and pry. I'm looking forward to it. Between us, my love, we'll have these damned Chyyanists in the open where we can get a shot at them!"

She stuck her bottom lip out at me."

"I can put on a disguise!"

I shook my head. "As soon seek to disguise a shonage in a bowl of squishes."

"Inch!" we both said then, and laughed, for the thing might be serious. But life was for living and Inch was, well, Inch of Ng'groga was Inch, Kov of the Black Mountains.

"We'll have messages sent to Inch and to Seg, apprising them of what is afoot. I know Seg was more perturbed than he said. I think Falinur smolders. Her people are still resentful over the lost coup of that dratted kov of theirs. Seg has a handful with Falinur."

Khe-Hi indicated the other eight signs. "Where are these places? The answers must be sought, my Prince, but I will hazard a guess. We may not know what the five blank spaces are for, but is it not possible that the single central blank space is reserved for the sign for Vondium?"

Old Evold cackled. "A puffed-up Wizard of Loh you may be, San Khe-Hi. But in this you speak sense."

It did make sense. If Makfaril intended to destroy Valia he would have to strike at the capital. The central space meant Vondium, I was convinced. Also, I fancied that the existence of a sign indicated that a center of Chyyanism had been set up there. A blank indicated the Black Feathers had not yet opened up shop at whatever place they next intended. So we have a breathing space.

"We leave first thing in the morning," I said. "Panshi can organize everything tonight."

There would be a lot to do before we could leave. Didi would have to be left in good care. A message would have to go to Drak warning him. The Elders of Valka, with Tharu still in control and with Tom as his right-hand man, would carry on as they always did when their strom vanished. But this time their stromni, the Princess Majestrix, would be absent also. . . . More and more I could see that Drak was taking over here, and much though I resented it, the circumstances of my life made it inevitable and cruelly precluded me from taking and steps to halt the process of takeover. Drak was my eldest son, and he was fully entitled to look out for his inheritance.

With preparations made for an early start on the morrow we turned in. Just before she went to sleep, Delia turned over, smiling at me, her hair a torrent of bronze-gold upon the pillows. "When we get to Delphond they'll expect me to behave like a princess. But, my grizzly graint of a husband, be very sure I shall make a journey to the Temple of Delia to find out just what deviltry you've been up to."

Chapter Six

At the Temple of Delia in Delphond

I, Dray Prescot, Lord of Strombor and Korzair of Zy, hitched up the ragged brown cloak over my left shoulder and took a firmer grip on the tatty cloth bundle that held my worldly possessions.

Leaning over the bulwark of the flier, Delia handed me the bamboo stick.

"You look a mighty savage ruffian, my love. Try not to scowl so, and cast your eyes down. To act a poor wayfarer is not going to be easy for you."

"Maybe not, my heart. But I've done it before and, by Vox, I'll do it again."

Parting with Delia is always so cruel an experience that I wondered, every time I parted from her voluntarily, why I was such a fool. To hell with Vallia! What did it matter if an evil creed overturned everything? What mattered beside life and love that meant everything with my Delia? But then I would return always to the harsh understanding that I was driven, a man doomed—perhaps by the Star Lords, perhaps by the Savanti, perhaps by Zena Iztar. For all of them I could feel anger, and yet, for Zena Iztar, who had materially helped me in ways beyond belief, I had to feel an affection that transcended my feelings for either Savanti or Star Lords. I might resist them; in fact I had worked cautiously on ways of circumventing their commands, and had succeeded and failed, yet would continue to struggle against them as I could.

But Kregen itself, the world of people, the beauty and grandeur and horror, this drove me. This made me both less and more of a man. So I could stand in the dust of a

"Parting with Delia is always a cruel experience."

Delphondian lane with the green of orchards about and say goodbye to Delia and put a brave enough face on it.

"And do not be late for our rendezvous," she said. So we called up the last Remberees and the flier lifted off. I waved as the voller rose and swung and swooped away into the bright morning air beneath the streaming mingled light of the Suns of Scorpio.

I was alone.

Well, that was what I wanted.

This was a decision I had made.

I tucked the bamboo stick into my belt over the old scarlet breechclout, draped a fold of the tattered brown cloak about it and with a final look around started the trudge to the Temple of Delia, about a dwabur off along the coast.

Very soon I found I could take an interest in all I saw, for the world of Kregen is always marvelous. My hand touched the bamboo stick. It was not real bamboo, of course, but it held the same deep orange glow and was ridged at intervals. Just such sticks are carried by the poor folk when they venture out from their own villages at least, just such a stick to outward appearances.

My hair was uncombed and tousled up, and my face bore the marks of grime, although this was fresh dirt newly rubbed on. I was barefoot. Well, I am still more accustomed to going barefoot than to wearing shoes or boots. So I strode on out of the orchards and over the brow of a hill and across springy turf with seabirds wheeling and calling overhead, on along the edge of the cliffs with the wind in my face.

Far out to sea a galleon of Vallia bore on, the spume breaking from her bows, her canvas all stiff and curved, a stately and gorgeous sight in the light of the suns.

And, as always, the smell of the sea wafted in to brace me up and bring the memories flooding in. By Zair! But all this wonderful display of nature—a naive but a feeling thought—deserved to be savored.

Soon I passed a small group of cottages, set in the lee of a low hill. Gray smoke wafted. I did not stop and skirted around past the fences where the bosks nosed up, squealing. The people here would be like all Delphondi, easygoing and lazy, or so I then considered, but I felt disinclined for any company since I had voluntarily debarred myself from the only company for which I care.

The Temple of Delia was set in a wide dell, a kind of lush ravine, through the center of which a narrow and rapid river helter-skeltered to the sea. No one lived hereabouts any longer. The grass and moss-covered outlines of ancient buildings, reduced to mere low mounds, told of the busy activity here when the Goddess Delia was worshiped in the land.

Now I proceeded cautiously. If this Makfaril called his freshly garnered congregations to worship here they must travel a fair way. There were towns within riding distance. Many of the richer sort might own an old airboat or two. The poor people would walk, or ride their draft animals. I kept into the side of a grassy bank and moved steadily forward until the first of the standing columns came into view. The green and emerald suns struck conflicting shadows from the flutings and ornamentation. Beyond the row of pillars a gray slate roof lifted, much worn and, as I judged, repaired within the memory of man.

The quietness seemed very peaceful, with the droning of insects to deepen the hush, but I fancied that quietness to be deceptive. Slowly I inched forward, trying to peer into the blue shadows that lay in cool swathes beyond the pillars.

Nothing moved. The suns beat down and the mellow heat lifted from the warm earth and the insects droned and the air and sky breathed a sweet stillness.

I scouted the ancient temple thoroughly. Nothing human lived within those moldering walls. The place had been surprisingly large, the shattered walls and columns and fallen roofs lushly overgrown, giving clear indication of a rich and thriving community centered around the temple. When this place had hummed with life and worship and the continual processions, on Earth the men of Sumer were considering how best to fashion bricks into the form of ziggurats to reproduce the mountains they had deserted. Well, the ziggurats of Kregen are notorious, as you shall hear, and I was doing no good mooching about here. It occurred to me that the nine sigils of the signomant might not mean nine temples for the worship of the Great Chyyan.

The thought did not depress me. That had been a guess. There would be many wrong guesses before this business was over. Far more likely was our first assumption that the signs indicated places of rendezvous. This temple stood near the coast so it could be the place where ships landed, gliding into the pebbly cove where the small river tumbled headlong into the sea, disgorging money, weapons, priests, to further the cause of the Black Feathers in Vallia. That made sense.

There had been no sign among the nine that we could make tally with the town of Autonne in Veliadrin.

Ignoring the cluster of cottages I had passed, the nearest village lay two dwaburs off. I fancied I would walk there and quaffing good Delphondian ale and eating cheese and bread and pickles, I would ask cunning questions. The villagers would most likely know if torches had been seen in the ruins, if the weird sounds of chanting had been borne on the night air.

No thought that Delia had been wrong in her identification could be entertained. Of course, she could have been deceived by some fancied resemblance of the sign to the ancient symbol for the Mother Goddess aspect of Delia, but I did not think this. What I had been half-consciously looking for I found in the same instant that I heard voices drawing near, voices engaged in the age-old complaint of the soldier performing guard duties when he would rather be off in an ale-house.

Even as I bent and from the broken angle of moldering masonry retrieved the scrap of black feather, I heard the voices.

I held the feather in my fingers, a tip of the rusty black plumage of a chyyan, the feather proved everything. If the mission on which I was engaged resembled some eerie detective story, then this was a clue of the first water.

The voices complained on and I shrank back into the shadows and listened. I put the feather down onto the moist green ferns struggling from the cracked masonry and blew it gently so that it drifted down out of sight. I marked the spot in my mind.

"That Shorten is a right bastard." The voice rolled, rich and fruity, lubricated through the years by many a flagon of medium red. "As a hikdar he'd be a great zorcadrome attendant."

The second voice, sharper, more intense, carried on the bitter complaints.

"We've been nobbled for picket duty three times in a row. By the Black feathers! I've a mind to appeal to Himet the Mak himself."

"Do that, old son, and he'll just refer you back to Shorten. That's how they run things."

I waited silently until the group came into sight. Four lumbering quoffa carts, bundled high and with canvas lashings protecting and concealing all, followed eight masichieri marching two abreast. Right in front and about to enter the ruins, the complaining two marched well ahead.

They were unmistakable. Fruity-voice, glowing of nose, broken-veined of cheeks, with bright protuberant eyes, marched with a rolling swagger that churned his swag belly inside his leather armor. They wore plain black tunics, with the well-oiled leather and the parrying-sticks and the thraxters. The second masichier, smaller, weasel-like, kept in step with his bulkier comrade; and both of them grumped and groused to amuse Vikatu, the Old Sweat, Vikatu the Dodger, that archetypal old soldier, that paragon of all the military vices, that legendary figure of myth and romance loved and sworn by with great vehemence by all the swods in the ranks.

"Get down behind that busted wall, Naghan," squeaked the smaller. "As soon as we're outta sight of Deldar Righat I'm gonna take a good long swig."

"Me too, and it won't be from my water bottle, either."

The moment the two scouts were out of sight of the main body and the deldar in charge they ducked behind a broken wall, driving up a green lizard who sprang away, a flash of green light under the suns. They hauled out squat bottles. Dopa. Well, dopa is a drink wise men steer clear of. But a man generates a thirst marching in armor and girt with weapons.

"By Vikatu the Thristy!" said Naghan, wiping his mouth. "That feels better, Little Orlon."

"Aye!"

I studied them from my concealment.

They were masichieri, among the lowest form of mercenary, yet they spoke like soldiers, like swods in the ranks. Perhaps the Great Chyyan could enroll people into his new religion and change them, turn an honest soldier into a thieving masichier?

I could believe that, which meant the new creed, through the leader Makfaril, could change other men and women, turn honest men into rogues. How far into the society of Vallia had the disease spread?

No arrogance in these thoughts of mine touched me

then—or now. There were many religions on Kregen and some of the smaller were remarkable, seeking to do good, perhaps remaining small purely because their high ideals were too difficult for mortal sinful souls. But the simple basics of Chyyanism were plain. They were revealed as Naghan, sweating, stowing away his dopa bottle, spoke:

"When the Great Chyyan gives the word and it's the Black Day—ah!—then I'm gonna take what is my due from those high and mighty lord muckamucks in Vondium!"

"Too right!" Little Orlon spat vindictively. "I've my eye on a shop run by a fat Relt. I'll wring his scrawny neck and twist his beak until he stares over his shoulder blades! I'll have his shop, and the Great Chyyan will bless me."

If there was a more basic approach than that—excluding a purely sexual lure—then much of history would be falsified.

The quoffa carts lumbered on and the creak of their wooden axles and the grinding groan of their wheels drove the lizards away. The deldar—deldar Righat—bellowed his orders and the column broke up and helped guide the carts into the shade of a half-standing wall. There were the two scouts, the eight men of the main body, and the four drivers.

I fancied I'd test them.

So, hitching up the ragged blanket, I stepped out into the suns-shine and walked, a little slowly, a little unsurely, across to the group.

Hunching my shoulders I put on that old imbecilic look and prepared to act out my part as a wandering laborer.

"And what have we here?" said the deldar in that knowing, gloating kind of voice that immediately spells trouble.

"If it please your honor," I said, getting a splendid wheeze into my voice, "I'm Nath the Gnat and I'm just passing through."

"And why should you be passing through here?" The deldar drew his sword to show me how important he was. He gestured. "Grab him! Hold him fast and let me look at the rast."

I allowed them to seize my arms. They held me and the deldar eyed me up and down, slapping his sword flat-handed, the steel smacking against his palm.

"A foul-looking specimen! Speak up! What are you doing here?"

"I'm just going through," I squeaked, shaking my shoulders. If these men were ordinary soldiers they'd laugh and offer to share a cup of wine and a handful of palines with me. But I thought I recognized these masichieri. They were of the cruel persuasion. If they could not have a little fun with a broken-down old fellow, well, by Krun! what was the world coming to?

"Through? Through where to?"

"To Dinel," I said, naming the next village where I'd thought to eat bread and cheese and quaff ale and ask questions. "There may be work for me there."

"There's work for you here, my lad!" said the deldar and the soldiers laughed dutifully. I called them soldiers, for they aped military ways, but I had to remember they were mercenaries of the lowest sort, masichieri.

They did not beat me up there and then. But I was kept very busy unloading the carts along with the four drivers, who were slaves. They were all apims. We carried bales and bundles into the main roofed section of the still-standing temple. I managed to get a glimpse of the contents of one box when it was dropped awkwardly from a cart and the lid sprang open. A mass of rusty black feathers within told me what I wanted to know.

We worked for a few burs until everything had been carried in and arranged to the deldar's satisfaction.

More than once I staggered under the weight of a bale that I could have thrown one-handed. These men were convinced I was a simpleton, and they were pleased that they had found a pair of extra hands to help. They offered me no dopa as they drank; to have refused would have looked odd, so I was spared the expected fight breaking out before I was ready.

"All out!" shouted the deldar.

We went out into the declining rays of the suns and I expected that, if there was to be a fight, it would begin fairly soon. I said, "I left my sack in there, your honor," and turned to go back.

The slaves were drinking water and fighting over a crust of bread and a scrap of cheese. The masichieri were lighting a fire and preparing to cook a meal. I went back inside and no one offered to stop me.

The knife over my right hip slid into my hand like an eel. I slashed open the bales, pulling the contents out. Yes. Black robes and cloaks fashioned from feathers, with fierce beaked headdresses in which the priests could dress to look like chyyans. The chests contained food and drink of a refined kind, reserved, not for the use of the guards. There was a little money, gold pieces of Pandahem among the golden talens of Vallia, and these I left strictly alone. There were weapons also. I left them.

Everything pointed to this collection being the paraphernalia for a gathering of Chyyanists.

An iron-bound chest was heavily locked. I did not attempt to open it, guessing it to contain the alter vessels and the more valuable impedimenta to be used in the rites of the Great Chyyan.

While a certain amount of spying is great fun and serves to thump the blood along the veins, I felt I had accomplished enough. I have no truck with those imbeciles who consider all spies as rogues—many are, of course—and during my wartime experiences on Earth I had seen some incredible disasters through the disdain in which spies were held. But enough was enough.

A quick glance outside showed me the masichieri around their fire, the shadows lying long in their twinned bars from the columns, the quoffas munching quietly, the slaves tied to the tailgates and trying to rest. Now was the time for me to walk briskly over to Dinel, find a mount and try to reach the nearest sizable town, Arkadon, where I might find a garrison in time to make it worthwhile to return here. Arkadon is a pleasant place, one of Delia's nicest towns, but the garrison troops would be like most Delphondi, as I then thought, a lazy and inefficient lot. But we ought to be back here before dawn and in time to sweep up this little lot and the worshipers and the priests. I wanted to get my hands on Himet the Mak and find out what he was really up to. He most probably would not talk, but I had grown suddenly weary of spying. Enough was enough. We would at least lop off this branch of the Chyyanists.

A flicker of movement in the tail of my eye caused me to spring abruptly and silently to one side.

I glared into the shadows. An indistinct figure stood impassively staring at me. I could not make out the features, merely a vague blur with deep pits for eyesockets. Clad all in a long robe, dark in the shadows, the figure remained motionless.

I knew.

Phu-Si-Yantong!

Yes, this had happened before and I knew it would happen again. As I spied on the Chyyanists so the wizard of Loh spied on me.

Somewhere in the forbidding world of Kregen Phu-Si-Yantong had placed himself in lupu, in a trancelike state, and his incorporeal body had visited me, spying on me. I felt the chill in the air, the shiver as of millions of tiny needles pricking into my skin. As I started forward the appearance vanished. There could be no mistake. The blurred figure did not move. It simply winked out of existence.

This ghostly apparition filled me with a fury that was purely ridiculous, for there was nothing I could do about it.

Cursing the damned wizard and all his misdeeds, I took up my sack and my bamboo stick and prowled to the far opening, peered out, saw the coast was clear and so stalked out into the dying light of evening as the twin Suns of Scorpio sank toward the horizon.

There was no direct proof that Yantong was mixed up with the Chyyanists, although circumstantial evidence pointed to that eventuality. If he was, then I knew I was in for the fiercest struggle I had faced so far on Kregen.

In my ugly mood I positively relished the confrontation.

Poor fool, I, Dray Prescot, Prince of Onkers!

Chapter Seven

Koter Rafik Avandil, lion-man

The suns sank finally as I rode from the little hamlet of Dinel.

In the last of the light drenching the western horizon with shards of blood and washes of viridian I rode, cursing that the farmers of Dinel had no better mount to offer than this stubby four-legged hirvel, kicking him in the ribs to make him go faster. As I cantered on through the rich farmlands under the night sky, I reflected that even if the farmerfolk of Dinel had no fine zorcas or fancy sleeths to offer me, their work demanding the use of krahniks and calsanys and the occasional quoffa and unggar, at least this hirvel, whose name was Whitefoot, made some claim to be a quality saddle animal. He belonged to the chief man of the hamlet and was superior to a preysany. I could have done worse. So I kicked my heels in and away we went.

She of the Veils, Kregen's fourth moon, rose to shed a fuzzy pink light, golden and glorious. I was in no mood to enjoy the wonder of the night sky of Kregen, even when two of the smaller moons went hurtling past close above. I had to reach the garrison at Arkadon, the marketplace for the surrounding area, rouse them out, select the best-mounted—for I doubted if they'd have any airboats—and then ride like the wind back to the Temple of Delia.

If everything went as ordered we'd catch the worshipers of the Black Feathers. I wondered what they did for a statue here. If Himet the Mak was the priest, as seemed probable, then one of his statues was unavailable.

An elongated black speck darted up against the golden disk of She of the Veils. The swirls of limpid color over the larger moons, evidences of some atmosphere there, confused sight for a moment. Then the golden gleam pulsed clear and I saw the hard black shape of an airboat lifting. It flicked past the limb of the moon and vanished among the stars.

I frowned.

I craned my head back to look along the way I had come. Roads in Vallia are usually atrocious, by reason of the superb canal system, but all country districts must have their roads for the quoffa and krahnik carts. Dust hung glittering in the light of the moon, raised by my hirvel's hooves. I could see no pursuit. Airboats taking off, at night, close to me, always make me reach a hand down to the hilt of my sword.

I nudged Whitefoot along and we trended down past the edge of a cornfield with the somber mass of a wood on the far side. I'd have to get off and walk to rest Whitefoot in a moment or two, for the hirvel, although looking nothing like a horse, with his round head and cup-shaped ears and twitching snout, has a performance not unlike a good quality waler.

Dark figures showed at the edge of the wood.

Instantly I slowed the hirvel down. He had been pushed hard and now, at the time when I wished to walk him, he was faced with the imminent prospect of hard running.

The figures were mounted on zorcas. There was no mistaking those glorious close-coupled animals with their fire and spirit and energy. So even if Whitefoot had been fresh and in tip-top condition, the zorcas would have overtaken him as a cheetah overtakes a deer.

"By Zair!" I said to myself. "Phu-Si-Yantong, a week's wages against a sucked orange!"

I kept on. There are tricks and strategems in encounters like this.

We met as the dusty roadway curved up at the end of the cornfield to give way to a field of gregarians. I came over the slight ridge past a tumbledown fence and the zorcamen spurred out to stop me, very fierce, the moonlight glistening on their blades.

They wore the black and leather, and there were black feathers in their helmets. They were Rapas. The vulturine-headed diffs leered on me, completely confident. Mercenaries, like those apim mercenaries at the Temple of Delia, these Rapas with their predatory beaked faces were masichieri, without a doubt. I was absolutely convinced that they had been sent against me by Phu-Si-Yantong after his apparition had spied on me. Now this puzzled me, before I reasoned that the Rapas would almost certainly have orders to take me alive.

I knew from an overheard conversation that the wizard with his maniacal and ludicrous ambitions wished to rule all Vallia through me acting as his puppet. Well, he might try. The effect of this was that I knew he had given orders that I was not to be assassinated, not to be slain.

I spurred forward, yelling, whirling the bamboo stick about my head.

A good rousing charge might carry me through, and I might knock one or two over and leave perhaps three to deal with.

They opened out, very prettily. The light grew as the Maiden with the Many Smiles rose over the horizon. Now there was no escape in the shadows.

The first blows struck down, the thraxters held so the flat of the blades smashed in at me. The bamboo stick could parry that kind of blow without being cut through, or not, given the nature of that stick.

I stuck the end of the bamboo into a beak, heard the Rapa shrill his agony. I swirled around, chunked the stick into the guts of a second, ducked as the swish of a blade passed close over my bare head. The hirvel nudged up into the forequarters of a zorca and the rider swung back, for a moment off balance. Before he could recover my left hand gripped his arm and pulled and he came out of the saddle in a gyrating heap of black feathers and black cloak. He fell under the hooves.

From nowhere a parrying-stick slashed at my shoulder. The jolt numbed my left arm. I kicked Whitefoot and he blundered ahead. Swords and parrying-sticks laced about me and I knew I'd have to unlimber the stick when a magnificent bellow roared out over our heads.

"Hold, you cramphs! Take on a man with a sword, you moldy villains!"

A glimpse I caught, a fragmentary glimpse of a man riding a zorca charging into the midst of the Rapas. He wore metal armor and a metal helmet, all burnished bright as gold in the radiance of the moons. He swung a thick straight sword, a clanxer of Vallia, and he cut the first Rapa down in a smother of blood.

The Rapa nearest me let go of Whitefoot's bridle and swung his mount away. He babbled something about: "You are not supposed—" And the clanxer curved down and went chunk into the leather armor over his shoulder. The man—he was a numim with golden fur under the armor and a bright golden mane—bellowed, "I'm not supposed to beat off footpads, is that it, you tapo! I'll have your tripes, every last one!"

I slashed the bamboo, and a Rapa collapsed over his zorca.

The numim, his lion-face snarling and his whiskers bristling, smashed his sword down onto the leather helmet of another Rapa. The vulturine-headed diffs had had enough. They reined away and set spurs to their mounts and galloped off. Two rode as though drunk, just managing to cling to their seats and rolling in their saddles.

The numim glared after them, golden, glorious, swearing that, by Vox! they were a poxy lot of scum.

"I must thank you," I began, in the proper form.

He flicked blooddrops from his sword.

"Think nothing of it, my man! A wayfarer is entitled to the protection of a koter of Vallia."

He used the word *koter* in its meaning of gentleman, rather than of mister.

He reached out and grasped the reins of a zorca from which a dead Rapa hung tangled in the stirrups.

"Llahal and Lahal," I said in one of the prescribed forms for making pappattu, the first Llahal with that strong Welsh double-L sound, used in greeting strangers, the second with the softer single L, used for greeting friends. "I am Nath the Gnat." I said this promptly, almost without thought. My cover as a poor old wandering laborer seemed valuable enough to maintain for the moment.

"Llahal and Lahal. I am Koter Rafik Avandil." He appended no further information, but I did not mistake his deliberate use of the title. For a poor laborer koter was a gentlemanly rank that should impress.

Moving slowly yet with sureness I dismounted from Whitefoot. The hirvel had served as well as he was able, not unlike a nightmare version of a llama, with that tall round neck and shaggy body. I took up the reins of the only other zorca left by the Rapas. Koter Rafik looked on.

If he wished to claim both animals as his own he would have a fight on his hands. But he offered no comment.

Numims are loud and boisterous, with their golden fur and golden manes and fierce bristly mustaches. Lion-folk are numims, and the lion-maidens are glorious under the rays of the suns. They are also extraordinarily seductive under the moons, or so I am told.

I mounted up with a sack and my bamboo stick. I took up the reins. "I am for Arkadon, Koter Avandil. I am in a hurry. I give you my thanks again for your assistance." He was not to know that I'd been in no real danger. If the Rapa masichieri had turned nasty and attempted to use the edges of their swords I'd have been forced to unlimber the bamboo stick and settle their business. But he had come charging in like a knight errant and so deserved his due of praise and thanks. "I ride fast, Koter, so will bid you Remberee. May Opaz the All-Glorious have you in his keeping."

"Eh?" he said, a little put out. Then, with a real numim bellow, "Oh, yes! By Vox! I don't hold with religion! A man's right arm and his sword, they are the gods of Vallia."

He wore a rapier and a dagger, I noticed, but the clanxer, the cutlass-like weapon of Vallia that is so often derided had proved a good choice against the thraxters of the Rapas.

I set spurs to the zorca and took off.

He followed, keeping pace, but made no attempt to engage in conversation which was, in any event, not too easy as we galloped along the dusty road.

There was an odd, eerie sensation about that wild nighttime ride across Vallia under the moons of Kregen. Only the sounds of the zorcas' hooves and the wind in our ears and the thumping feel of our onward passage kept us in touch with reality. With some thankfulness I saw the sharp-cut outlines of the fortress of Arkadon rising up against the star glitter, and soon made out the circuit of the walls and a few scattered lights from tower and window within.

We made enough hullabaloo at the arched gate to arouse the sleepy sentry. My Delia's Delphond is a quiet, lazy place, but any town near the coast must needs stand a watch. This is one of the ways of Kregen that can never be forgotten, if you wish to keep your head on your shoulders or your wrists and ankles free of chains. The slavers and the aragorn prowl many lands and seek to snatch away slaves where they can. Even here, in civilized Vallia, in sweet Delphond, the slavers sought to carry on their foul trade.

The response was quick enough to surprise me.

A yell and a curse from the ramparts, and then: "What's all the noise! Quiet down, you great villains, you'll wake the town!"

We managed to convince the sentry and the ob-deldar guard-commander he called that we were not slavers or bandits, those drikingers of the wild places unknown in Delphond. The ob-deldar was surprisingly suspicious. My few experiences of Delphond had led me to believe the easygoing people would have welcomed a pack of rascally kataki slavers with a proffered flask of ale.

Rafik Avandil bellowed out in his numim way, quite out of patience.

"Open the gates, you onker! Jump to it! *Bratch*! Or I'll have your deldar rank torn off and burned!"

Bratch is not as ugly a word as the terrible *Grak*! shouted at slaves to make them work until they drop, but it is still a powerful word of command, implying move, jump or you know what will happen! The ob-deldar jumped.

The gates swung open, well-oiled and uncreaking, admitting us to the cobbled street.

"I need a bath and a meal and a bed," bellowed Rafik. "I'll stand the same for you, old man, and you will."

This was munificence.

"I thank you, Koter Avandil. But I think it best for me to finish what I must do. Perhaps—"

"Aye! That will serve admirably." He waved a violent hand at the guards sulkily trailing their spears back to the guardroom under the archway. "These southerners are a puny lot! By Vox! I'd smarten 'em up!" These sentiments appeared to put him in a better humor, for he finished in a roar: "We'll meet on the morrow at an inn that has some pretence to fashion. I'll see you at Larghos's Running Sleeth."

"Until tomorrow, Koter Avandil, at the Running Sleeth."

He cantered off and he began to sing, one of those rollicking numim songs that always bring back memories of Rees and Chido and wild days rioting as a Bladesman in

Ruathytu. I took myself off to rout out men and mounts and weapons for the rest of my night's work.

I had to reveal my identity to the town governer before I got any sense out of him, sleepy-eyed in his night attire, tousled of hair, roused from bed. He held the title of rango and was your usual plump, easygoing, smiling, lazy Delphondian. But I impressed on him, this Rango Insur na Arkadon, the importance and the urgency of the night's business, and soon thereafter I rode out on a fresh zorca at the head of all the zorcamen he could spare, a miserable thirty of them, all sleepy-eyed and cursing away and rolling about in their saddles trying to ride off the fumes of the evening's wine.

She of the Veils vanished beyond the horizon and the Maiden with the Many Smiles would follow and then the suns would rise and a new day would dawn over Kregen. By that time we reached the Temple of Delia. Harshly I ordered the party to dismount and giving them no time to rest their aching backsides gave instructions in a cutting voice to their hikdar and the deldars to spread out and surround the central roofed area, which gleamed in the first chinks of morning light, ominously silent.

Birds were chirping merrily away in the trees, and the dew sparkled everywhere, fresh and sweet. The air tasted like the best Jholaix. But, I, Dray Prescot, took no comfort from all that beauty.

We crept in, and I held a rapier borrowed from Rango Insur, and we stole between the pillars ready to leap upon the congregation engaged in their blasphemous rites to the Black Feathers of the Great Chyyan.

I knew, I supposed, when I heard the birds singing.

We burst in, and the place was empty. We scoured all the tumbled ruins, peering and prying, prodding with our swords. Nothing. Not a single thing gave any evidence of a soul having been there for a thousand years.

"It seems, Prince, we have had a wasted ride."

The hikdar spoke a little sourly. His head was still ringing, I judged, from the party of the previous evening.

"The birds have flown, hikdar. I'll grant you that. But as to a wasted ride, I think you'll eat a better breakfast this morning than you would otherwise have done."

He made a face, but bellowed out, "Too right, Prince!"

It was so, of course.

There was nothing here. I had failed in this night's

business. Then I walked quietly around to that crumbled corner of masonry and bent among the dew-bright ferns.

The hikdar stared at me curiously, hands on the hilts of his weapons, his booted feet thrust wide. I straightened up. In my hand I held the scrap of rusty black feather.

"Not altogether wasted for me, hikdar, either."

Then we mounted up and I shook the reins and turned my zorca's head for Arkadon and the Running Sleeth and this Rafik.

Chapter Eight

A disrobing at the Running Sleeth

Sleep would have to take its turn. I'd been up all night haring about Delphond. If I bothered to ask myself why I should care tuppence about this Koter Rafik Avandil, I suppose, then, I would have answered that the fellows had conceived he was saving my life. And a lone koter against a rascally gang of Rapa masichieri demanded a high brand of courage. So I banished the idea of sleep and rode up to the inn run by Larghos, the inn with the revolting name of the Running Sleeth.

One positive thought I had. I would question Rafik about the airboat that had taken off just before the Rapas attacked. It seemed perfectly clear to me that Phu-Si-Yantong had observed me in his trancelike state of lupu and had then whistled up his gang of bully boys to take me. The airboat had dropped them to lie in wait. Rafik might have seen something useful.

All the same, although I kept my usual careful lookout as I rode, I remained firmly convinced that the wizard's orders that I was not to be killed remained in force. His ludicrous desire to rule, physically and in person, vast expanses of Kregen and to set up puppets to carry out his orders told most eloquently that he must be mad. Mad in that special sense, of course, a kind of madness which afflicts people in certain ways. He was clever, brilliantly clever, and fiendishly ruthless, as I knew. He was an opponent to reckon with. Apart from anything else, his sorcerous skills gave him an advantage almost impossible to conceive of on this Earth. I must look to my own defenses within the mystic realms, that was for sure, and get Khe-

Hi-Bjanching to earn his keep, although that was hardly fair. Khe-Hi had done wonders. His own powers had grown over the years. He would, if he lived, prove a most potent ally to me and adversary to Phu-Si-Yantong.

Thus thinking, I dismounted from the zorca and tied him to the hitching rail. Pulling my tattered brown cloak around my shoulders and with a touch of the fingertips to the bamboo stick, I went into the Running Sleeth.

The brightly painted wooden sign over the lintel had been carved in the round and showed a sleeth running, the reptile's powerful back legs fully extended, its silly front claws curled, its dinosaur-head thrust out, the forked tongue—a strip formed of brass wires—twitching out most realistically. The craze among the young bloods of Hyrklana and Hamal for owning and racing sleeths had not yet extended to Vallia, I had thought. In this I was clearly wrong. The reptilian sleeth can run reasonably fast, not as fast as a zorca, but it is a damned uncomfortable ride, waddling along on those two massive hind legs, with its tail stuck out aft to balance itself.

So the name told me the kind of inn this would be.

The place had been tarted up. Smoky old beams had been painted over. Garish pictures filled every corner. Instead of quaffing ale from jacks or flagons, the customers were drinking parclear or sazz from thin glass goblets. The smells of cooking told me that the over-refined food served here would be all fashionable rubbish, not fit to last half a bur in a man's stomach. Still, it takes all kinds to make a world.

Small round tables on spindly legs, elegant chairs with needlepoint covers, flowers in pots of chunky ceramic—well, flowers are a boon to tired eyes—all gave the impression that this Larghos who owned the place must be a man of taste, well able to satisfy his provincial clientele that they were being entertained in the best fashion of the capital.

Mind you, there is nothing wrong with sazz or parclear or elegant chairs and furnishings. It is when these appurtenances to gracious living are pushed blatantly forward as an end in themselves, catering for empty-headed gadflies, that the ordinary man must recoil. I say must. Some do not see things in this light, and as I went in and sat down in a chair with my back to a wall facing the door—an instinctive action, this, done without thought—I was prepared to let any man enjoy whatsoever he wished within reason. So I scanned the people there and then prepared to ignore them. Farmers, stockholders, breeders, they were unlikely to be found here. Here in the Running Sleeth would be found those men's sons, eating up the family wealth. One or two soldiers of the garrison who fancied themselves men of culture, an artist and poet or two, if they had little talent but large incomes, light ladies and fashionable damsels, the would-be cultured layer of provincial life would come here to ape the ways they imagined to go on in Vondium.

And then, well, I admit it fully and freely, I could not find it in my heart to blame Larghos, the owner and landlord. After all, into this place of conscious refinement and culture stumbles an unshaven common fellow, a wandering laborer, with a raggedy old brown blanket cast over his shoulders and a mop of untamed hair, and puts his odiferous sack on the beautiful embroidered tablecloth and sticks his naked feet out over the charming rugs woven in imitation of Walfarg Weave. Well!

Larghos, slender, oily, charming, with wavy hair, trotted over and his face showed such outraged fury that I almost laughed. I couldn't see what was setting him going.

"Out, fellow! What do you think you're at! Schtump!"

"I only wanted—" I began, beginning to understand.

"You'll have a broomstick over your head! Schtump!"

I made a solemn promise to myself. I would not allow myself to become angry. No. No, this Larghos was right. I had no business bringing my old blanket cloak and my sack into this temple to culture and gracious living.

I sighed. "Is Koter Rafik Avandil here? I am supposed to meet him."

"He is gone out! Paid his bill and gone. Now you go!" Then he lifted his voice and shouted squeakily, "Nath! Cochu! Come running and throw this fellow out, and his verminous sack with him!"

I stood up.

"Thank you for your hospitality, dom, I'm going."

I hefted the sack and put out my hand for the bamboo stick which I'd placed on the table.

Now there are some men who cannot let well alone. Larghos stepped back, his face red, breathing heavily, scandalized at my intrusion into his establishment that had such a good name, but prepared to let me go without further ado. Not so the idler at the adjoining table who had watched all with a bright, birdlike gaze.

He was young, full-fleshed, bright of eye and erect of carriage, and yet about him there were plain to see the old familiar hateful signs of corrupt authority.

"Let Nath and Cochu give him a beating before you let him go, Larghos. The rast deserves a lesson, forcing his filthy self in here among decent people."

Before I could stop myself, I'd said, "I'm not filthy, dom."

He levered himself up from the chair. He wore foppish clothes, not of decent Vallian buff, but of a mixture of bright colors among which the black and white predominated. His rapier was overlong and the hilt was ornately set with jewels. Whoever he was, he was not a citizen of Arkadon.

Larghos began to wring his hands.

"Please, jen, my men will throw him out without fuss—"

"Silence, cramph!" This young lord—for Larghos called him *jen*, which is the Vallian form of addressing a lord—pushed himself up from the table. I saw by the glasses and bottles on the table that he had been drinking wine this early in the morning. So he had that problem as well.

His full-fleshed face flushed with blood. A vein beat in his forehead. His two companions at the table with him rocked back in their elegant chairs, thrusting out their boots, and egged him on with comments that suggested a little workout would do him good and a thrashing would do me good.

Larghos was wringing his hands. I could guess in his mind's eye he saw spindly-legged chairs and tables smashing into costly ruin all over his inn.

There would be no profit in my telling this young bully that I was the Prince Majister of Vallia, for he was a racter and would joy in having the excuse to get his rapier between my ribs, claiming afterward that this filthy tramp could not possibly have been the Prince Majister. How was a loyal jen supposed to know that?

Nath and Cochu appeared, beefy apims in blue-striped aprons, bare-armed. Larghos started to say something and the young lord waved him down. "I shall deal with the cramph myself. I do not care for his manners. You, rast!" he shouted at me. "I shall teach you manners!"

With that, confident in his own limber strength against

this bent-over fellow in his brown blanket cloak, he took a couple of dancing steps forward and struck out, with more power than skill. I slid the blow and stepped away from the table calmly. The bamboo stick was in my right hand, held by the end, the thick, ridged end.

The young coxcomb went mad with fury. He shook with rage. "Do you see that!" he yelled. "The calsany! He threatens me with his stick! A filthy tapo daring to lift a stick against me, against the Trylon of Tremi! I'll prick a little blood from his mangy hide!" With that he ripped out his rapier and flung himself into a fighting crouch.

I sighed again, this time with real regret.

He lunged for me. I used the old bamboo stick to parry him off. I judged him to be reasonably skilled with the rapier, well able to take care of himself in an inn fracas, swishing and swashing; as to his caliber against real opposition, I was still unsure.

When he couldn't quite get his rapier to cut me up, as he expected to do just as he expected the twin suns to rise each day, he grew even more angry. His face was blotched. His eyes glared. His lips twisted with rage and frustration.

His cronies at the table, laughing and hawking, did not help him with their crude advice and mocking injunctions to spit the old fellow and have done.

Here in my Delia's Delphond, I knew, a murder would merit the strictest investigation. Delphond was civilized.

He blundered toward me and caught his foot in one of the elegant chairs and sprawled forward. His left hand raked up instinctively. He caught the bamboo stick. His face went mean.

"I've got you now, you cramph!"

He tried to wrench the stick aside and so slice me down the face, as a nice preliminary to what he intended to do to my carcass.

He twisted the bamboo, hauling back.

He was an onker, right enough. He twisted the bamboo. I felt the click and the sweet sliding of oiled metal. He staggered back clasping the hollow bamboo. All the people watching gasped, as this foolish young trylon fell back, pulling the bamboo free of the blade.

In my right fist I held the ridged wooden hilt. Two feet of oiled steel blade glimmered in the lights from the windows. That blade had been forged by Naghan the Gnat in the armory of Esser Rarioch. I had designed it with Naghan, and we had laughed as we'd mounted its slender length into the bamboo hilt, covering the murderous brand with the rest of the hollow bamboo. I keep calling this wood bamboo; it is not real bamboo. It is of a deep orange luster, ridged and grows in the marshes. Kregans call it pipewood, for it is often used for tubing work in plumbing and the like.

The blade glistened. The Trylon of Tremi stared and his face assumed a caricature of enraged fury, black with passion.

"You murderous rast! Now I'll spit you lean through your filthy guts!"

And he set to, swirling his blade, thrusting and slashing like one demented.

His companions stumbled up from the table, their chairs going over with a smash. They ripped their own weapons free.

One came in from one side, the second from the other.

If I was in for a little exercise then I'd make it reasonably entertaining.

As I fought, foining off the two from the sides and beginning an amusing disrobing of the trylon, I reflected that this Rafik Avandil possessed a rare sense of humor. He had arranged to meet me here in this pseudo-cultural Running Sleeth knowing damn well what would follow. So I felt a double amusement as I cut the laces of the trylon's fancy tunic and so stripped his clothes from him, garment by garment. When his two cronies pressed too close one was sent staggering and yelling away with a slit ear and the other with a punctured right forearm. The good old over and under stop-thrust worked beautifully.

This idiot trylon's overlong rapier most often pointed at the ceiling or the floor, or angled toward one of the garish pictures along the walls, more often than it aimed at my guts. I played him long enough to cut away his clothes down to his breechclout—bright pink, would you believe?—and then I had had enough.

Disgust filled me.

This kind of petty mindless brawl leaves a foul taste in a man's mouth. This kind of bestiality is for the morons of the world, for the morons of two worlds.

Once they had seen how they thought the fight would now go, the rest of the patrons began to laugh. In their stupid heartless way they laughed at the Trylon of Tremi. He, poor fool, gagged on his own spit. His face was now whey-colored, gray and green, his eyes staring, his mouth slobbering. His beautiful pink breechclout with the embroidered chavonths and zhantils looked pathetic. It had blue lace edging. I stripped a little away and then he jumped at the wrong moment and the blade nicked his flesh in a tender spot.

He screamed.

So, wishing to have done, I snaked his blade away and stepped in. I took him by the throat with my left hand. I choked him only a little.

"The next time you seek to bully and thrash a defenseless old man, think, rast. Think, you brainless cramph, and remember this day."

Then I turned him around and gave him a hard toe up the backside and so kicked him staggering across the floor.

His cronies stood back, furious but cowed, unwilling to reopen the fray.

Blood had been drawn from both of them, splattering their finery and the black and white favors, but they had come out of this less injured than their lord. His hurts did not show on his skin. His hurts would not mend as fast as the scratches they had suffered.

The contrast between the conduct of this spoiled lordly brat and that of Rafik toward an old man was to me at the time most edifying. I felt an amusement toward Rafik, engendered as much by his trick as by the circumstances of his supposed rescue.

Larghos was visibly recovering his composure, seeing that no real damage had been done to his establishment. He began to flutter about. So I wiped my blade tip on the corner of my old brown cloak, picked up my sack, cast a last look upon the assembled gaping patrons—remembering to bend over as I did so—and bid them all a pleasant Remberee.

Then I stepped out of the Running Sleeth into the clean air and luminous suns-shine of Kregen.

Chapter Nine

Nath the Gnat misses the Princess Majestrix

Delphond is not as well served by the intricate canal system of Vallia as it might be, especially as it is an imperial province, descending in the imperial female line. This has served in the past as a distinct advantage and goes some way to explaining the surprising remoteness of much of the province, situated as it is relatively close to the capital. This fact, too, I suppose, does explain, as Delia maintains, why so many tides of conquest in the troubled history of Vallia have passed Delphond by with little destruction.

The zorca ambled along the dusty road, kicking the thick white powder into a floating trail, and I jogged along, sunk in thought, yet still keeping that old sailorman's weather eye open. The oiled steel blade was snicked back into its bamboo scabbard and now looked like any wandering laborer's stick.

Making no attempt to discover the whereabouts of Rafik, I had simply ridden out of Arkadon. I could feel the muzziness clouding my head a trifle and a light-heaviness about my limbs; but, if necessary, I could go on swashing and fighting and drinking for another night or two without sleep yet. It is a knack. The rendezvous with Delia drew me on. The moment I reached Deliasmot where a canal trunk system terminated I would transfer to a narrow boat and be rapidly hauled all the way in first-class comfort.

If Rafik was headed this way we would meet. I fancied I'd not seen the last of that golden numim with the sense of humor.

The white road wound between cornfields, with orchards all green and shining beyond, rising and falling over the gentle countryside. The road remained deserted until a cloud of dust heralded a considerable party of country folk taking their produce into Arkadon. I was surprised. The quoffa carts trundled along. Men thwacked on krahniks loaded with bales and baskets. The calsanys trotted along in their strings of patient bearing. Women and children perched on the carts or walked together in the intervals. The men marched, I could swear, almost in the form of a guard, with a scouting party ahead riding preysanys, superior forms of calsanys, and carrying not only their sticks but spears and long-knives.

They gave me highly suspicious looks. But I was alone, and so we exchanged Llahals and parted, and I spat dust until free of their trail.

Logic told me that I did, indeed, look highly suspicious.

Here I was, a raggedy old laborer with a tattered brown blanket cloak, bareheaded and barefoot, riding a well-groomed and, if not first water, then reasonably high-quality zorca. Yes. Logic told me the country people might well have thought it their business to stop me and question me. There would be a reward for the return of the zorca to its owner. They were not to know the Rapa masichieri lay with his blood spilling out into the Kregan dirt.

But they had not stopped me. If anything, they had displayed so extreme a caution that it could be construed as fear.

And this, in Sweet Delphond, Delphond the Blessed, the Garden of Vallia!

The other interesting fact I had observed was simply that these country folk appeared to have shed their fat and lazy indifference. The men—abruptly, it seemed to me—presented an altogether new and different aspect. They had held their spears and long-knives with the firm determination of men intending to fight if they had to. This was remarkably unlike the usual attitudes I had encountered in Delphond.

Ahead along the road the lath and plaster walls of a country inn came in sight, the red tile roofs shallowly peaked, the twisted chimneys lifting in welcome. No smoke rose from the chimneys. A window pane caught the red light of Zim and flashed. I perked up. Here was where

I would repair the deficiencies missing breakfast was causing my stomach.

I rode up, feeling cheerful, and the damned place was empty, deserted, with windows smashed and doors hanging loose and weeds choking the neat fenced gardens. I cursed. Just my luck to encounter a wayside inn that was derelict.

"By Vox!" I said, aloud, thoroughly miffed. "By the disgusting bloated swag belly of Makki-Grodno! My throat is like the Ocher Limits."

A voice spoke from the corner of the inn and I was off the zorca and under the eaves before the last words were uttered.

"Temper, temper!" said this light voice. "If you would accept a Llahal and a drink of wine from a stranger, they are here for the asking."

Cautiously, the hilt of bamboo in my right hand and the rest of the stick in my left, ready for emergencies, I peered around the corner. A man sat there on a pile of old sacks holding out a leather wine bottle. The spout was formed of balass, black and shining, stoppered with silver-wound ivory.

"Wine, dom," said this young fellow, smiling.

"It is too early for wine," I said, somewhat surlily. "But Llahal, I thank you and I will take a sip."

I took the bottle. It was deliciously cool. I moistened my mouth—a light white Yellow Unction; so this fellow had a few silver coins to rattle in his pouch—and then took two measured swallows. I looked hard at this purveyor of wine. Young, in that way the Kregans, with their better than two-hundred-year life span look young, he had a peaked, cheerful face, with merry eyes and a droll mouth. He was dressed in a simple open-necked buff tunic and decent breeches. His boots were not black, being of a tan color, well-splashed with the white dust of the road. He had a scrip and a staff, and at his belt hung a strong lesten-hide satchel.

I handed the wine bottle back. "My thanks, dom."

"Oh, I am Covell. Men call me Covell of the Golden Tongue."

"I have heard of you," I said, pleased. "All Vondium rings with praises for your latest, 'Time Lost is Time Gained Hereafter,' I believe. A fine poem."

He laughed easily and drank wine himself, moderately.

This Covell was by way of being a poet. I saw that he

favored the unconventional life, in order to gain the experiences he distilled into his verses. Some of the older and sterner critics of Vallia condemned his work as trifling, but they were a trifle ossified, or so his supporters said.

"What brings you here? Is Vondium too hot for you again?"

"You know me then? Yes, a tavern brawl and an onker with a knife in his guts, he did not die. But the guards thought to lay me by the heels and question me, and I do not fancy mewing up. So I took to my travels again."

"Who does? I am Nath the Gnat and—"

"And," he said easily, laughing, standing up, "and you are no laborer or farmworker, not even a cattleman. Whoever you are, Gnat is not the appellation for you, dom."

I remembered to bend over at that, whereat he laughed again.

"I have my hirvel tethered in the shade. Should we ride together? I heard uncommon evil stories of Blessed Delphond in these latter days."

I fired up at this. If my Delia did not know what was going on in her estates, then it behooved me to find out.

"Right willingly, Covell. But I am a laborer. That is true."

I meant I labored for a living, not that I was a laborer who dug ditches or built walls. I fancied this Covell of the Golden Tongue understood.

"There are fields of labor that demand other skills than brawny shoulders." He picked up his satchel. "I labor with words, and damned intractable beasts they can be, as well as singing with golden wonder. Why I do so is beyond my limited understanding."

He mounted up on his hirvel. The animal was a fine beast, superior to Whitefoot, whom I had slapped on the rump and sent off, knowing he would find his own way back to his owner. Covell eyed the zorca.

"You are well mounted for a laboring man, Nath the Gnat."

"The zorca came to me by way of a bequest from a dead man."

He laughed again at this and shook his reins; together we rode gently along the dusty white road. He carried a long-knife like Oby's and, as far as I could see, no other weapon on his person, although a short blade mounted on a shaft some six feet in length was stuck down into a boot on his stirrup. His scrip and staff were slung onto the hindquarters of the hirvel, and rode a trifle awkwardly.

So we rode along talking. It is not my intention to regale you with all we spoke of, but you may be very sure I soaked up all the information he gave, and as it bears on this my narrative I will tell you, all in due time.

Covell mentioned the concern felt in Vondium over the continual unrest in the northeast of Vallia. Up there the folk were of altogether a more down-to-earth character, blunt, hardheaded, out for red gold and self-determination.

Using some little skill I introduced a query about black feathers into our talk.

He replied as an educated man interested in literature would reply, quoting *The Black Feathers of Ulbereth the Dark Reiver*, giving a stanza or two of that old epic fashioned from the legends of olden time. But that is another story.

I judged that he did not dissemble and had not encountered the Black Feathers of the Great Chyyan. But I would not completely trust anyone in this thing.

So, later, I mentioned the craze for flying fluttrells in Vondium, and suggested that flying a chyyan might be interesting. Whereat he said: "I have flown a fluttrell owned by a comrade, Nath ti Havring—and an experience it was, too!—but I am told by those who know about these things that chyyans are unridable. Surely, Nath the Gnat, it is zhyans you mean?"

"Perhaps it is," I said, "They are all foreign, out of Hamal. Give me a zorca."

"Aye. But one day these great soldiers of ours will go up against Hamal, and we poets will be forced to sing their praises. I prefer to tune my songs to sweeter themes."

"Amen to that."

I pressed him to recite a line or two of his own, and nothing loath, for he loved an audience, he declaimed his "Ode to Dawning," in which the red sun Zim and the green sun Genodras are apostrophized as mere balls of colored fire, without sentience, marvels of nature, bringing light to all men over the whole of Kregen. He added, when he had finished, that translating Zim to Far and Genodras to Havil ruined the feel of the piece. "I have a large contempt for religiosity in pious hypocrites. Opaz is well enough, I suppose, given as a sop. But a man's heart is his true religion."

I made no direct answer. Rafik trusted in a right arm and a sword, and Covell in a man's heart. What, then, did I trust in? Anything at all apart from my Delia and the Krozairs of Zy?

When I had first returned to Kregen after that hideous expanse of twenty-one years on Earth I had fancied Kregen had not changed. The more I learned the more I discovered that this marvelous world had changed, was changing and was like to change even faster as the days wore on.

When Covell spoke of the emperor he simply laughed and made witty jokes. He did say that the taverns reeked with plots, and then contemptuously dismissed them as wine-soaked dreams. "Trouble is coming to Vallia, Nath the Gnat, and all men can see that plain. There is the northeast. There are the racters. There are other parties and plots. I want none of them! By Vox! I am a poet and as a poet will I live and die a happy man. All else is illusion."

"You do not share the fear of the locals to travel alone?"

"Do you?"

"Ah, well, I was not fully aware of the situation, being a simple wandering laborer. If there is no work here by reason of the troubles—"

"There are no troubles in Delphond, at least not yet. That is why I chose to travel here. But the lonely traveler is not as safe as he once was and isolated houses, like the inn where we met, are no longer little fortresses of peace. The damned aragorn prowl all the land—aye, and the racters aid and abet them. That is where their money comes from."

"You do not like the racters?"

"I dislike all political parties. I am an individual."

"The people take precautions against drikinger."

"Yes, but Delphond is not an easy province for bandits."

"So it is the slavers they fear?"

"If the emperor and the Presidio do not act soon no one will be safe. Vallia is like to be torn asunder."

Deliasmot was its usual charming, smiling self, a typically beautiful, easygoing, life-loving Delphondian town.

Yet even here the new edginess was apparent, the more anxious demeanor, the stricter controls at the gates. Here Covell of the Golden Tongue and I parted, for he was contracted to give a recitation of his poetry, a declamation, he called it, and I was for the canal and for pressing on to Drakanium where I would meet Delia.

We made our Remberees and I expressed my disappointment at missing his declamation, for he was truly a golden voice, and then I hurried to the canal to make travel arrangements. The zorca ensured a ticket in a narrow boat. I found a quiet seat where I might watch the passing banks, sliding along all green and golden under the suns, and I dozed and took my meals with the best of them and kept to myself, tolerated here in Delphond, and so came at last gliding with the canalfolk all hauling lustily away under the stone vaulted archways of Drakanium's watergate.

As a city, Drakanium was simply a larger edition of a Delphondian town, clean, neat, sparkling, bowered in vegetation, filled with the prosperous bustle of a contented folk—at least it had been. The city was just as clean and neat and the flowers bloomed magnificently and the fountains played. But the people hurried about their tasks with worried looks. A regiment of totrixmen were exercising on the parade ground and I judged by their antics they were newly formed. The jiktar was near to apoplexy as he bellowed orders, and the awkward six-legged totrixes tangled up and squealed and the lances all slanted at odd angles. But they flew nice banners and flags.

I had agreed to meet Delia at the best inn, instead of her villa here, to keep my cover. A hostler took in my message, giving me a sharp look as he went in through the lenken door under the glowing tiles, where the moonblooms clustered thickly. Bees droned and the shadows lay across the stone-flagged court. I sat down on a bench and a serving wench brought out a flagon of best Delphondian ale. I quaffed it gratefully.

To these people I was a mere wanderer, a tramp, and if the Princess Majestrix wished to speak with me she would, and that was her business, and if she did not, then I would be told and seen off the premises. They are civilized in Delphond.

The hostler came back. He wore a frown.

"I gave your message to the landlord, dom. He says to tell you the Princess Majestrix is not here."

"When is she expected? Maybe I am early."

"Oh, she's been here. You were expected." He did not add that he couldn't for the life of him understand why a great and glorious princess should worry her beautiful head over a dingy tramp. He went on, almost casually, imparting his news: "She has had to return posthaste to Vondium."

I stood up.

"Did she say why?"

He took a step back. His coarse sacking apron rustled as he switched his arms out. "No. She did not say. Just that she had to go to Vondium on a matter of extreme urgency. A courier came in an airboat. From the emperor, it was said. The princess went with him and her suite with her." He rolled his eyes with the memory of a great dread removed. "She had a ghastly creature with her, a most bloodthirsty monster, all claws and fangs and hair, but they all went in the airboat to Vondium."

That monster was Melow the Supple, and I felt relief.

Relief that Delia was safe. But what could have caused her to dash back to Vondium? What disaster had struck now?

Chapter Ten

Of an independent girl of Vallia

The airboat flew swiftly toward Vondium.

Once I had received Delia's message I had wasted no time. A quick trip to our villa in Drakanium, a change of clothes, with a flustered majordomo and flunkies running in circles, a hamper of food and drink, weapons, money, and I was away in one of the small fliers we kept at the villa, as we tried to keep a voller or two at all our places.

I did not think my cover had been broken, but then, I didn't give a damn if it had. What had happened in Vondium to drag Delia away? Was the emperor dead? But everyone would have known—no. No, perhaps not. It paid very often to keep news of the deaths of kings and emperors secret for as long as possible.

The voller was a fleet craft, for its stabling at the villa envisaged its emergency use, and we made a good thirteen and a half to fourteen dbs.*

At this headlong speed I would reach Vondium in a couple of hours. So, composing myself as best I could, I sat down and raided the hamper. Of the details of that meal I remain vague, save that I ate and drank and looked continually ahead for the fantastic sight of Vondium, the capital city of the Empire of Vallia, to rear over the distant horizon.

Once again I was entering Vondium at breakneck speed and with a single definite goal in mind. I flashed over the broad expanse of pastureland and agricultural activity sur-

*dbs. Dwaburs per bur. A dwabur is five miles. A bur is forty minutes.

rounding the city. The waters of She of the Fecundity, the Great River of Vallia, sparkled ahead. There were the Hills, spread out and bowered in greenery, with the flash and gleam of white villas and red roofs. There were the sky-spanning aqueducts. There the grim gray walls and the higher battlements in gleaming yellow and sapphire, the flagstaffs, the conical tower roofs, the long, incredibly thin extensions of archways beneath the suns. Other fliers circled in landing and ascending patterns. The broad swaths of the major canals and ornate boulevards crisscrossed the city, creating islands of stone or brick, the timber and stucco, island given over to parks and preserves, islands covered with barracks and factories, island for sport, islands for all the devoted pursuits that obsessed the citizens of Vondium.

Of it all I fastened my eager gaze on the enormous Palace of the Emperors.

Over wide colonnaded streets parallel to the canals we flew, this speedy little voller and I, seeing below the broad wharfside avenues thronged with busy people. Over a cluster of temples, built to foreign tolerated gods, over an arm of a canal leading directly to the Great River where shipbuilders worked on the skeletons of galleons of Vallia, bare and ribby in the light. On, and now I slanted down, aiming for the palace. The majestically architectured kyro before the main facade showed its usual hectic activity and few people bothered to look up at a single small airboat.

Chafferings in the marketplaces would not be interrupted for so small an event. But what events were taking place within the glowing walls of the Palace of the Emperors?

The instant I touched down on the landing platform above the small garden of the palace wing reserved for the Prince Majister, I leaped out. Delia's old apartments had been enlarged and improved and when we stayed in the capital we stayed in our own private wing of the palace. I raced inside, seeing servitors running. Delia and I kept no slaves; there were many thousands of slaves in Vondium, aye, and many in the great palace of the Emperors.

Normally we kept only a skeleton staff in our wing of the palace for, to be honest, we spent little time there. Now the place hummed with activity and very soon I had made my way, followed by various flunkies who conceived it their duty to run with me, just in case I might drop something, or require a service—Zair knows why servants will fuss so—through to our inner and truly private apartments. The jiktar of the guard detail, a Pachak called Lake Pa-Re, bellowed his men to attention.

"The princess?" I asked, not stopping.

"In her apartments and all well, my prince, may Opaz shine the light of his countenance upon her." Then he added, quite outside the usual military formula: "By Papachak the All Powerful, my Prince, it is good to see you!"

"And to see you also, Laka Pa-Re."

His men bashed open the balass door smothered with the gold zhantils with diamond eyes, and I went hurrying through. Laka stood back, still remaining at attention, his tailhand upthrust with that wicked steel blade glistening. He had retained his Pachak name for he was a mercenary, a paktun—the silver mortil-head on its silken cord looped over the shoulder of his armor proved that—and perhaps a greater contrast could not be imagined than between his loyal service as a paktun and the thieving deviltry of those masichieri I had been stumbling over lately.

The tail balass doors closed and I looked down the carpeted corridor with the golden lamps and the ivory ornaments, the great Pandahem jars filled with flowers, the silver mirrors, and the doors at the far end opened and a trim figure clad in hunting leathers stepped through. At her heels a prowling, incredibly ferocious Manhound trotted, tail lashing, fanged jaws opened, saying in that growly, spitting, menacing way of jiklas: ". . . Deserves to be spanked, the hussy."

They saw me.

Delia simply flew at me, wrapping her arms about me, kissing me, laughing and sobbing, saying breathlessly, "I know, my heart! I know what you will say! But this cannot wait!"

I held her close, feeling her heart beating against mine, holding her, the dizzying scent of her in my nostrils, twining around me, making me wonder why I ever was fool enough to leave her. I forced myself to regain my senses. I took her by the shoulders and held her off, looking at her, at her face, her eyes, her mouth, her hair. "Delia! What cannot wait?"

"I am forbidden to tell you."

I felt outrage.

"Who can forbid the Princess Majestrix of Vallia? Your father—?"

"No." She looked gorgeously lovely, yet filled with a distress I could not hope to understand then.

"All I can say is that I love you, that I must go, that—by Vox!" she cried, which made me realize how serious a matter this really was. "By all that I hold dear I will tell you as much as I may—and more, I dare say, if you hold me so and look at me like that."

My ugly old face must have been a sight, by Zair!

"Well?"

She spoke more calmly. "I must hurry. You know I am of the Sisters of the Rose. . . ."

"Yes." I began to have an inkling now.

"I dare not tell you, even though you mean all there is in the world to me. But, but, dear heart, you are a man."

"And you are a woman and, to pile the cliché upon the banal, I give thanks every day to Zair that it is so."

"Do not laugh at me, my darling! This is women's business. The Sisters of the Rose, we hold our secrets . . . well!" She flared up as her thoughts sought utterance. "Do I question you too closely about your precious Korzairs of Zy?"

I felt only a small shock.

"No, my love, you do not. For you know I am under vows."

"And may not a woman, even if she is your wife, also be under vows?"

Instantly I felt the biggest boor in two worlds. I felt an onker, a calsany. What right had I to pry into exactly those areas of my Delia's life that were, through other forces, denied her enquiry in mine?

I drew her to me and kissed her. The kiss was long and passionate and if she was in a hurry to be about this mysterious business of the Sisters of the Rose she was in no hurry to end the kiss.

At last I stepped back and released her.

"You have everything for the journey? Melow will go with you? Weapons, clothes, money, food, the fastest voller?"

"Yes, yes, my heart!" She laughed. "Do not take on so!"

"When you go venturing out into Kregen, my love, you must take all the protection you may."

"That is true. But the Sisters of the Rose take care of their own. We do a great deal of good, in a quiet way. We have opened two new hospitals for sick slaves in the past year. And when there is a war . . . well, you know."

"Yes. I did know. The Sisters were invaluable. There were other feminine orders, of course, notably the Sisters of Samphron and the Order of Little Mothers and the like. Delia often abbreviated in the Kregen way, calling the Sisters of the Rose the SoR, as I abbreviated the Krozairs of Zy to Krzy. This was important, truly important.

So I contented myself with making sure she had everything I could think of—save myself—upon her journey. Melow would go, and a female Manhound, a jikla, can rip up a wersting or a neemu and the chances of a strigicaw are not all that bright.

Melow the Supple jagged her fangs and said in her hissing voice, "Do not fret, Dray Prescot. The princess is a canny girl and knows her way about. I can but wish you had eased two more sets of twins into the world for me."

"Hush, Melow!" said Delia.

The Manhounds of Kregen are indeed a fearsome sight. Artificially bred to run on all four like hunting cats, ferocious of aspect, deadly in killing skills, superbly muscled, they can strike terror into the stoutest heart. Yet this Melow the Supple, for whom I have a great fondness, savage and vicious as she was, was a kindhearted mother of twins. She was dressed in bright clothes, for she loved brilliance in dress, with neatly groomed hair and wearing sandals over those gut-ripping claws. I put out my hand and touched her cheek.

"Take care of her, Melow."

She grimaced and hissed, as much as to say what an onker I was and I ought to know better than even to mention so obvious a thing.

Then I said another stupid thing.

"Thelda?" I said to Delia.

Well Thelda, Seg's wife, had been companion to Delia in some fraught moments in our lives, and she always meant well, and she always said that she was Delia's best friend. I knew Thelda belonged to the Order of Sisters of Patience—I invariably found a high amusement at that particular trifle of appositeness—so I couldn't be surprised when Delia very calmly said, "This is a matter for the

SoR, my love. Now you have delayed me long enough. Come on, Melow."

She kissed me again and I let her go reluctantly, saying, "But you haven't said when you'll be back."

"When you see me." Then she relented, and said, "I'll be as quick as I can, I promise."

I saw her to the voller. And it was no joke; she'd selected our fastest four-place craft. I saw the way she solemnly observed the fantamyrrh as she stepped aboard.

I stook back. The guards and the retainers stood in a ring, all looking up.

The voller sprang away, with Melow looking over the side like some frightful gargoyle, and rose up into the limpid air with the streaming mingled lights from the Suns of Scorpio lighting up her side and blazing like a beacon.

"Remberee, my love!"

"Remberee, my heart!"

And the flier spun up and away and soared over the glittering rooftops of Vondium.

Damned independent in their ways are the girls of Kregen.

But, then, that is just as it ought to be.

Chapter Eleven

We sing the songs of Kregen

"All praise to Papachuk of the Tail!" said Laka Pa-Re, and he thumped his empty flagon back onto the stained sturmwood table with a crash. All around the low-ceiled room of the tavern men were drinking and shouting, a few were brawling, some were trying to play Jikalla and being continually interrupted. The clatter of dice sounded from the corner and on the opposite side a Pachak was tail-wrestling a comrade amid spilling wine bottles and toppling ale flagons.

This was the famous tavern The Savage Woflo, an example of the warped Kregan humor that either amuses or infuriates, for the woflo is a wee creature of extremely timid nature, overfond of cheese.

Among the tables ran remarkably pretty girls of various races carrying wide wooden trays stacked with foaming jugs or exotically shaped bottles. These serving wenches were, unfortunately, slaves. They were clad in transparent draperies, with tawdry bangles and beads, with colored feathers, all designed to enhance their natural beauties. Well, I suppose that in some cases they did. But generally cunning old Urnu the Flagon, landlord of The Savage Woflo, had an eye for female beauty and his wenches—I dislike the commonly used word *shif* for these serving girls for it indicates a contempt I do not feel—were every one carefully chosen at the auctions and paid for above the standard price.

Normally I avoided places like this and when in Vondium and in need of a quiet drink I would go down to Bargom's Rose of Valka by the Great Northern Cut. Bargom, a Valkan, did not employ slaves and aroused some bemused envy that he managed so well without their unwilling aid.

Now the Pachak paktun, Laka Pa-Re, yelling for more ale, handled these slaves girls with a courtesy I fancied was not assumed for my benefit. This tavern, the famous Savage Woflo, was much patronized by the guardsmen. No female customers were allowed. Such a thing was still possible in Vondium. This was a male preserve and, I suppose, on Earth would have been choking with smoke as well as the fumes of alcohol.

"By Mother Zinzu the Blessed!" I said, lowering my flagon. "I needed that!"

Saying that little aphorism cheered me up, although Laka had never heard of Mother Zinzu the Blessed, the patron saint of the drinking classes of Sanurkazz.

"You do me great honor, my Prince, in drinking with—" he said, until I shushed him.

I wore simple buff tunic and breeches and swung a rapier, as we all did here, where brawls and good-humored swishings of blades were common occurrences. I wish to look inconspicuous. Laka also wore plain buff, out of uniform.

"If you must call me anything, let it not be prince," I said. "Rather, merely call me Nath and have done."

"Aye, my Pri—Nath!" he bellowed, and used that cunning tailhand to whip a fresh flagon from a passing girl's tray. She squeaked and laughed—all simulated, for that was how the customers liked to think these girls behaved—and ran on with slender flashing legs to fetch more ale. There were Fristle fifis, and sylvies, and shishis here, as well as other races of beautiful girls. There were no Rapa girls or Och maidens, but then there were few of their menfolk in the tavern either.

A parcel of Chuliks sat glowering at a table, steadily drinking. When the singing began the Chuliks would depart to find a place where a fighting man might drink without having to sing. That is the way of Chuliks.

I had come here because—and then to admit the true reason would be to betray more, perhaps, than I cared to. I knew that I would hear gossip here that might be overlooked in the echoing corridors of the palace. Also, I felt sure that one of the emperor's agents would be here listening. What he would report might not tally with what he heard.

For the emperor's position had been steadily eroded.

Covell of the Golden Tongue had said the tavern plots were all moonshine. Maybe they were. But I felt the need for a drink and a song in masculine company.

Most great nobles of Vallia kept up their villas in Vondium even if they only visited them once or twice a year, and their guards patronized establishments like this, so there were many varieties of uniform and colors among the civilian dress. The Vallian Air Service was notable by its absence. Also, Laka was one of the few high-ranking officers present. I noticed three other jiktars and quite a few hikdars, but the majority of the drinking, gambling, shouting men were deldars and swods.

When I had quizzed the Pachak paktun as to why he had said he was pleased to see me, he had answered evasively, even defensively, but now he was thawing out and eventually he said: "It's like this, my Pri—Nath. I drew guard duty on the Prince Majister's wing of the palace. I do not grumble at that. But I see things. I hear things. There are men among the guards—aye! Men I have known! Men who speak behind their hands. They have been bought by gold."

"Who is doing the buying? And to what end?"

He took a swig and wiped his mouth. "For one, the Racter Party. Oh, yes, they have a hand in everything in Vallia. But why should Naghan Nadler, who has been a paktun for twenty seasons and will make ob-deldar soon, take gold?"

"Why?"

"Why, because they want to buy his sword! And others like him. There are plots against the emperor. Everyone knows that. A little gold spread around now will buy loyalty when the plots hatch. That is my opinion."

"And you have reported this?"

He opened and shut his lower left hand, and his right hand gripped and tugged at the pakmort around his neck on its silken cord. "I wanted to speak to you."

I was not sure if he had done right. But this was no time to suggest he might better have taken another course. What struck me, forcibly and with a chill of foreboding, was the frightening thought that whichever of the parties—or perhaps all of them—that were bribing guards to fight for them had reached the swods. A simple swod may well be a terrible fighting man, but it is the captains and generals who carry the say when bribery is in the wind. I felt pretty confident that Laka had not been approached because all men knew once a Pachak had given his nikobi to serve an employer his loyalty remained steadfast. But a swod in the ranks, being given gold, told to obey orders that would not come from his employer, this typified the destruction of values, the end of one way of life and, if a new began, a system barely nameable as life.

So, as you can see, I was in a highly wrought state.

Hadn't I suborned guardsmen before, to fight for me against their employer, and, by Vox, wouldn't I do so again? But at the least, no mere petty ambition had driven me, to topple a throne for the sake of the power.

So we drank and talked and I watched the clientele, seeing the many different patterns of banded sleeves, each set of colors denoting a man belonging to a noble house. Even among these soldiers and guardsmen the white and black favors were flaunted openly, along with the white and green of the panvals and other color combinations. A Pachak hikdar, squat, leather-faced, roaring his good humor and slopping ale, plunked himself down on the bench opposite Laka and bellowed a greeting.

When the confusion died down Laka introduced him as Nidar De-Fra, an old mercenary comrade newly arrived in Vondium with his master. This Nidar wore banded sleeves, for he was in uniform, the banded colors of unequal widths of blue and green and yellow, with two thin vertical stripes of white. It must not be taken that these color-banded sleeves of Vallia are like the tartans of the Scottish clans; but with their color-coding, once a man saw a combination of shapes and colors he would know it again and know the owner. This Pachak, Nidar De-Fra, had given his nikobi and his sword to Kwasim Barkwa, the Vad of Urn Stackwamor. He was in the capital because his master wished it. Anyway, as all men knew, the emperor was due to return from his journey around the far southwest. Here the Pachak laughed and said that the southwest was a joke and all men knew the future of Vallia lay with the northeast.

There is good comradeship among the Pachak mercenaries, and their intricate system of nikobi can sort out the rights and wrongs of employment and the puzzles of when a man may in honor fight a comrade under employment. Now these two talked of old days. I looked for a moment at Nidar. He did not wear the pakmort, but he was wholly convinced that northeast Vallia must demand self-determination and break away from the empire. This astounded me. I clamped my ugly old mouth shut and listened.

When Nadar's term of service with Kwasim Barkwa ended he might take employment with a noble of the south, and then he would be as vociferous that the empire should stay in one piece. A mercenary may not have to believe in his master's cause to fight for him, but the Pachaks are deadly serious when they hire out as paktuns, and give their loyalty.

A couple of brilliant Fristle fifis came out with streaming silks and started to dance; they were soon chased off and then the swods began to sing.

So, as you may imagine, I let all my problems slide away for a space and gave myself up to hoggish relaxation. There are many finer things in two worlds than sitting in a tavern singing with swods, and this is so. But all the same, when you are singing and roaring out the old songs, the world takes on a marvelously brighter hue.

My Delia had gone off and left me at home. The idea intrigued me. I felt no indignation. She was as entitled as I was to her own life. Our shared life was so intense and passionate that nothing could interfere. I was dragged away by a great ghostly representation of a Scorpion, blue and shining, whirling me away to some other part of Kregen to fight for the Star Lords, or hurling me back to Earth in despair. Delia had gone because her vows, vows like mine to the Krozairs of Zy, impelled her. I had discarded at once any notion of following her secretly. That would shame us both. Anyway, with Melow along, she should come to no harm. And she could handle weapons with the best of men. I knew that.

So I, Dray Prescot, left at home with the dishes, sang with swods in a tavern.

We sang the *Lay of Fanli the Fristle and Her Regiment of Admirers* and the *Lay of Faerly the Ponsho Farmer's Daughter* and *Tyr Korgan and the Mermaid.* The Jikalla players stopped pushing their counters around the board and the dice fell silent in the cups. We roared out *King Naghan, his Fall and Rise,* and *Eregoin's Promise.*

Then these hard-living, hoarse-voiced, hairy fighting

men drew on a sudden maudlin melancholy, and led by a fellow with a thin reedy voice we warbled out *The Fall of the Suns.* This is a menacing song, for its cadences and images invite mournfulness. It tells of the last days when the twin suns fall from the sky and drench the world of Kregen in fire and blood, in water and death. I am not overfond of it, for all the deeper truths it expresses in its roundabout way.

So when a flushed fellow, bulging his tunic and wildly slopping his ale, leaped to his feet and started bellowing out the first lines of *Sogandar the Upright and the Sylvie,* I, for one, joined in with a full-throated roar. And the rafters shook as the swods came to those famous lines that always crease them up, and great gusts of laughter swept across the room as we sang out: "No idea at all, at all, no idea at all."

Yes.

We kept that refrain going until we were all well-high bursting. The serving girls scurried in with more flagons and great was the relishment thereof. We quieted down as the tall thin fellow with the reedy voice favored us with a solo, choosing parts of the song cycle composed from fragments of *The Canticles of the Rose City* concerning the doings of the part-man, part-god Drak. Naturally my thoughts winged to what my Delia was doing now, how she was faring, and I offered up a fervent prayer that she would be kept safe.

We did not sing *The Bowmen of Loh,* for almost all the Crimson Bowmen were away with the emperor.

It seemed to me my course was reasonably clear. I would have to discharge all those mercenaries who had become untrustworthy by reason of accepting bribes. I would seek to discover who had paid them; I would make no attempt to match the bribes, gold for gold. If a man takes gold from another when in employment his trust is forfeited. I had experience of that when I'd been a renegade and contracted to Gafard the Sea Zhantil, the King's Striker.

The decision about reporting to the emperor what I had so far discovered about the Chyyanists would have to be taken. There was, in truth, pitifully little to report. A minor religion would appear to offer little danger to the emperor, beset as he was by combinations of powerful nobles. While everyone in Vallia regarded as a foregone conclusion that the conflict with Hamal must reopen at some time in the future, for the present the uneasy state of truce between the two empires offered some hope of continuing peace. The emperor would brush aside any suggestions I might make along those lines, and his Presidio, torn as it was by internecine strife, would greedily pursue the path of individual power.

By Zair! The worst thing of all was how lost, how at sea, empty and forlorn I felt without my Delia. When I'd been dragged away from her before I had struggled always to return to her. I had cursed and raved at the forces keeping us apart. But now well, this was a topsy-turvy situation and one I just did not relish at all, at all, as Sogandar the Upright might say.

The swods were just beginning *The Maid with the Single Veil* and the serving wenches were giggling and laughing as is their wont when that song is sung, when a fellow at the adjoining table, leaning across, began to make directly offensive remarks. He was getting at me. There is no mistaking the idiot who intends to pick a quarrel.

I felt a hot resentment. I'd come out for a quiet evening bellowing out the old songs and this rast wanted to stir up trouble and spoil it all. I determined, mean and vicious, that I'd spoil his fun, that I'd not react, that he could cuss until he was blue in the face and I'd give him no satisfaction. I'd ruin his enjoyment and he could jibe and mock and insult all he liked.

I said to Laka and Nidar, "I'll play the cramph along. Take no notice."

Laka knew me and so laughed, falling in with the ploy. Nidar favored me with an old-fashioned look, but said nothing.

The fellow who got his kicks from being unpleasant wore too much gold lace about his buff. His face was lean and marked by a scar, and his mustaches had been clipped. I noticed the emblem he wore at his throat, a little gold strigicaw and swords, swung on a golden chain.

He did not speak directly to me but insulted me through his cronies, in the way of these fellows.

"He perhaps thinks we are woflos who come here. His senses probably do not even understand that small thing."

Nidar leaned across fiercely and said under his breath to me: "Let me blatter the fellow, Nath."

"Tsleetha-tsleethi," I said, which is to say, "softly-softly." Nidar's offer to bash the fellow in for me amused me. Normally quick to avenge an insult, on this night I wanted to bash this insulting fellow with more subtle weapons than a set of knuckles or a rapier in his guts.

He persevered. His cronies tried to help his game. They called him Rumil the Point. I turned my back on them and bellowed for more ale. The song had changed and so we could all sing *The Worm-eaten Swordship Gull-i-mo* which is a Vallian sailor's song, for a few swordships are employed in sheltered waters. That song is known in many anchorages in Kregen, and I'd sung it as a render up in the Hoboling Islands.

A hand touched me on the shoulder. I turned. I stopped singing.

Rumil the Point stood up, leaning over me, his lean face black with his sense of insult, because I took no notice of him whatsoever.

"Rast!" he shouted, thumping my shoulder, speaking thickly, either drunk or pretending to be drunk. "You do not insult me and stand on your own stinking feet!"

I shook his hand off and started to turn back to the two Pachaks, determined to play my part out to the end. By Zair! But he was in a paddy! He just couldn't believe that I didn't consider him important enough to worry over. He felt at a loss, puzzled, reduced in dignity, his pride shredded.

"Then I'll settle you, you zigging cramph!"

I saw Laka's face go hard and I heard the scrape of steel and so knew I had miscalculated.

With a motion I trusted would be quick and fluid enough I slid aside and turned back.

This Rumil the Point stood glaring at me. His eyes protruded. The tip of his tongue stuck out, and his face was contorted back, ricked, stamped with an awful terror.

Around his neck clamped a buff-clad arm, and the paw-hand gleamed with golden fur.

"Lahal, Nath the Gnat," said Rafik Avandil. "I see I may be of service to you once more.

Chapter Twelve

A message via the Sisters of the Rose

If I thought that because Delia and I were parted and I was alone in Vondium life would be flat and insipid, I was only partly wrong. Of course, life lacks its deep brilliance and color when Delia is away and I turn to fripperies, but sometimes the trifles turn into matters of more profound importance. The time when I made myself King of Djanduin serves as an example. So life helter-skeltered along in Vondium as I sought to think out the best way of facing the various dangers that threatened.

Rafik Avandil, quite enchanted at his opportunity to rescue me for the second time, as he thought, had spent the rest of the evening with us. Laka kept up my disguise as Nath the Gnat, and for this I was grateful. We saw a deal of each other in the days that followed and eventually I was persuaded to move into the inn at which Rafik stayed. I told Turko the Shield, Balass the Hawk, Naghan the Gnat and whoever else absolutely needed to know. Turko and the others grumbled about having to stay in our wing of the palace while I was off roistering in inns, but I explained that I was on to a lead. They were to call me Nath the Gnat. Here Naghan pulled a face, and I chided him, saying, "A great name, Naghan! And one I am proud to borrow."

"Just let me have it back, Dray. I shall be Naghan the Arm, I think, if we two chance to meet, in remembrance of that hyr-kaidur."

"Aye," I said. "So far I have had no word of a single Black Feather in all of Vondium, and this is strange."

"Maybe not so strange," offered Khe-Hi-Bjanching, putting a finger in his book to mark the place. "The signomant held only an empty space for Vondium, remember."

"I still think that the true reading. By Vox! If only we knew where they would strike next!"

"Agents are out, asking questions. Vallia is being scoured."

"And," said Naghan with the old armorer's shrewdness strong on him, "that is costing a deal of money."

"If the Opaz-forsaken Chyyanists win, we'll have no money, you may be sure. And we, along with our people, will hang by our heels."

"They'll have to catch us first," said Turko ominously.

This wing of her father's palace had been furnished under the supervision of Delia, and I relished that. Even so, I was not enamored of the great palace of Vondium. Delia's vision had created apartments of great beauty, but still the chill of the imperial presence came through. Rafik's inn offered a change, at the very least. I just hoped Bargom at the Rose of Valka did not hear I had stayed at some other hostelry than his own. But, then, a few words and he would understand.

The capital city hummed with news. The emperor was returning in state and bringing with him as an honored guest to the Empire of Vallia none other than the famous Queen of Lome. Everyone was agog to see this fabled woman. The reports of her beauty and wealth had spread over this part of the world, dazzling men with impossible dreams. Everyone gave a curse and said how fortunate the emperor was, and how they'd like to be in his shoes. And some of them, saying that, would laugh and add words to the effect that his shoes would be fine and dandy—*for now*.

One item of encouragement, and of alarm too, we had in those days. Balass received a report that among a group of his countrymen from Xuntal, traders and merchants down in the wharfside area of the city, a man had been heard to speak of the Black Feathers when he'd been drunk.

I said, "Then it is up to you, Balass. You are Xuntalese. You can mingle. May the Curved Sword of Xurrhuk guard you."

"Amen to that, my Prince. By my hopes of entering Xanachang! My people are a fearsome people if they think they are spied upon."

"It's of little comfort to tell you that almost any people

resent spying. But look at it in a different light. You go to root out evil. Make no mistake, Xurrhuk of the Curved Sword finds no favor in the hearts of the Chyyanists."

Balass's firmly muscled body glistened black and silver in the light of the suns streaming in through the high windows, for we met and talked in this small enclosed arena set up within our part of the palace. The silver-sanded floor slid and shushed to the quick scrape of feet as we foined and parried with wooden swords. Turko, I knew, had put in a good many burs of practice with his new parrying-stick, and he handled the klattar now with a sureness that pleased me. Mind you, I'd be the last to suggest it was but a small step to go on to handling a weapon very much like a parrying-stick with one blade and with sharp edges. Its name would be a sword. And Turko, the High Kham, would have none of them.

Oby came in, throwing off his tunic, getting ready to have a bout with anyone willing to stand against the liquid cunning of his long-knife. He left the lenken door partly open and Naghan, about to shout out about people being born in bars, stopped. A flunky sailed in through the door. He wore the fancy and immodestly ridiculous court dress for servitors, for we were forced to accept the services of other servants than our own from Valka. He was not a slave. His red and silver and yellow clothes billowed about him as he flew through the air.

I turned to make sure Turko really stood by me. If he had not been I'd have sworn he was the fellow outside thus casually hurling importunate servitors about.

But it was no man.

Through the pushed-open door strode a strappingly handsome girl. Her face was only lightly stained with a flush of blood under the tanned skin from her little exercise. She was clad in tights, with a body-hugging tan tunic strapped about with a lesten-hide belt from which swung rapier and dagger, buckled up in a way which showed she was ready to draw in a twinkling. Her weapons swung in that cunning way I had seen an infinitely more glorious girl scabbard her own rapier and dagger.

So, forewarned by the weaponry and the demeanor of this girl, I knew from whom she came.

She wore her light brown hair cut short. Her face held that open, frank look of the girl who knows she is a girl and is prepared to treat men as men because that is their misfortune. I liked the look of her. Over her heart an embroidered red rose, twined about with gold threads, resembled very much the little red and gold brooch, fashioned in the shape of a rose, Delia had given me in return for the brooch like a hubless spoked wheel I had given her.

"Llahal and Lahal, Prince Majister," said this girl, marching straight up to me with a swing of the hips and a lithe and limber step. "You are well met. Here, my Prince." And she hauled a letter from the small script at her waist.

The letter was written on yellow paper and carried a faint and fragrant perfume to my nostrils. The writing, firm and rounded and yet girlish, in that beautiful running Kregish script, is very dear to me.

My comrades stood back. The girl touched the rose embroidered upon her breast. "I have a letter for the Princess Katri. But yours, my Prince, I was instructed to deliver first." She laughed, a clear tinkling sound. "And the letter for the emperor the last of the three."

So I, being intoxicated on emotion, laughed too.

"I cannot wait, for no reply is expected." She turned to leave, her legs in the tights very long and lovely. "But there is one lie I shall no longer believe."

With the letter burning my hands I said, "Will you not stop to take refreshment? And what is this lie?"

She halted at the door and smiled back. "I thank you, my Prince, but I must hurry. As to the lie, all women say the Prince Majister of Vallia never laughs."

And she went out, swinging, jaunty, laughing, the rapier and dagger swinging at her sides. She was a woman, like my Delia, all woman.

I banished her from my mind and opened the letter.

I know the words by heart, but many of them are private so I will simply say that Delia said all was well, she was in good health, Melow sent her love, the task was proving more difficult than she'd expected and she was like to be away longer than she had hoped. There was more, but that is for Delia and me. She finished by saying that the letter to Aunt Katri requested the emperor's sister to go to Valka to see after Didi, and that the letters were being entrusted to Jikmer Sosie ti Drakanium.

The word jikmer had been crossed through, but Delia had been in a hurry and so I could read it beneath the quickly scrawled scribble. Jikmer. That would be the Sisters of the Rose equivalent to Jiktar. Hmm.

These girls had their chukmers, their jikmers, their hikmers and their delmers too, without doubt. The notion charmed me. It all added up, without the shadow of a doubt, to a powerful and secret organization of women who, from my knowledge of Delia, were dedicated to philanthropic and chivalrous ends. What the mysticism might be I, of course, could not know.

I think it was the delivery of this letter with its evidence of an efficient organization of women devoted to purposes with which, from the little I knew of them, I could sympathize, that made me finally put into practice a scheme I had been harboring for some long time. As the scheme developed—and I worked on it with some intensity—I will tell you as it impinges on my story. For now, I would have to wait for the first fruits until Seg and Inch were available.

Also, I must make it clear that I am concentrating here very much of the Chyyanists. A great deal happened in Vondium during this time. Instead of being an idle layabout, I found myself hard at work. As the Prince Majister in the capital with the emperor absent I had many official functions to perform. I performed them. Most were very little of a laugh. I sat in the courts for a time and handed down judgments. I canceled work on a new slave bagnio, letting the slave masters see my scathing contempt, and set the laborers and masons into constructing a building to plans I laid out for them. They couldn't really understand what the building was for. A visit to anywhere in Kregen where men and women flew saddle-birds through the air would have told them. It was accommodation for a thousand flyers. One day, and alarmingly soon, I fancied, Vallia would have need of them.

So life was not all dressing up inconspicuously and sliding off as Nath the Gnat. Often one or another of my boon companions would accompany me, but we made a compact that we kept apart. Turko, as usual, grumbled. But he saw the sense of it. My cover, if it was to be kept, would not be served by my suddenly appearing with friends. In a tavern, Turko could sit drinking quietly and keep an eye on me. We all chuckled over the episode of Rafik rescuing me.

That was a strange time. Here I was in Vondium, the

capital of the puissant Empire of Vallia, and my Delia not with me. By Zair! I had fought and struggled to reach this place, and had been dragged here in chains, and never had I thought I'd live here without Delia. It was unnerving.

I had all preparations made for the society I formed. There are many secret societies on Kregen. This seems to be a part and parcel of the makeup of all cultures. In the most simple terms, I wanted to instill some of the superb qualities in the teachings of the Krozairs of Zy into Valka and Vallia. But I had no intention of limiting the new order to the island of Vallia. If I could bring Pandahem in and Zenicce and the Hoboling Islands, perhaps even Seg's Erthyrdrin, that would be even better. I would find men I could trust, men of good heart, of good character yet lusty rogues withal, men who could see evil and stare back at it unflinchingly and do what they might to root out evil and plant the good. Of course, these terms are all relative. Good to one man is a mere matter of decency to another; evil to one man is normal human behavior to another. But there are basics on which men of goodwill may agree. The women had found them, it seemed. Of the various secret societies of Vallia none had asked me to join up. I had felt vast relief at this, for I had taken a firm vow to join none, assuming that the others would regard me as an enemy or, at the best, cold toward them. As the Prince Majister I had to remain aloof, if I could.

So do not think I organized the new order out of pique. If they don't want me to join I'll start my own club—no. That was not the case. This I believe. I had heard of no order in Vallia that sought to do what I sought. . . .

As a starting point the Black Feathers of the Great Chyyan would serve.

Balass reported back that the drunk—muttering darkly that when the Black Day dawned the Black Feathers would tear down the koters of Vallia and take all their goods—was a newly arrived trader, due to return to Xuntal. Balass looked worried. Perhaps Xuntal was already infected? I said, "I think not. If it is Hamal behind this, then their quarrel is with Vallia. If it is Phu-Si-Yantong, then—"

"Then," said Balass, very grimly, "it is very possible."

I could not argue. Yantong sought his maniacal ambition's culmination in the domination of all Paz. The man was mad. Anyone who wanted to take on trying to rule these wayward folk must be mad. I'd had a bellyful, I knew, of just a very few of them.

"The ship he traveled in," I said.

Balass nodded. "I will ask."

Again I said nothing to indicate that Balass should have already asked. He was a hyr-kaidur, used to the arena; spying would have to be taught him.

So my days passed, gathering scraps of information, working at being Prince Majister, organizing the new order. Among the many patheons of Kregen there is a plethora of minor godlings and spirits. One minor spirit of deviltry had, with assistance from others of his ilk, plagued me in Djanduin. I had allowed the miasmic presence of Khokkak the Meddler to influence me out of boredom and screaming helpless frustration to make myself King of Djanduin. Although, as I say, I do not think Sly the Ambitious or Gleen the Envious had a hand, there were undoubted traces of Hoko the Amusingly Malicious and Yurncra the Mischievous. These devils plague a man. There was no time during that period in Vondium without Delia for them to gain a lodgment in my thick old vosk skull. I was just too busy.

One very good reason for my adopting the disquise of Nath the Gnat was to escape unpleasantness from those who sought to oust me. There were more than just the racters. Although Rafik Avandil had said, "You have come up in the world, dom, since first we met," and I had replied casually that I'd come into money, he provided me with a useful cloak. As Nath the Gnat I could wander freely in the city and mingle with all kinds of people in the taverns. By doing this I know I escaped many an unwanted brawl or duel. And I was learning.

So the day dawned in Opaz-brilliance when the emperor would return to Vondium. He would arrive in his imposing procession of narrow boats, drawn along the canals and through the water gate into the city. On that day I had to dress myself up and be the Prince Majister, and go down to the canal to welcome him.

Among a glittering group of high nobles and koters, all of whom—or nearly all—hated my guts, I stood, glittering in the suns-shine, watching as the haulers guided the emperor's narrow state boat into the jetty. When all was ready and the trumpets pealed and the guard snapped to attention, he stepped ashore onto the crimson carpet.

There was, as usual, a little undignified shoving to get forward—and to hell with protocol! I hung back, my left hand on my rapier hilt, watching.

How the men with the white and black favors fawned about him! Yet each one would sooner see him floating facedown in the canal. The factions vied to be seen in his company. I waited as they advanced down the jetty toward the zorca chariot that would carry him through the streets so the people might see him there as well as along the canals. I saw the woman at his side.

This was the fabled Queen of Lome.

Banners flew, birds screeched up from the water, zorcas and totrixes scraped their hooves, officers barked orders, the crack and smash of sword and rapier as the drills were gone through, the tramp of marching feet—and over all the high shrilling yells of the crowd, welcoming their emperor back to his capital. Yes, this was a day to remember!

He saw me, standing alone, isolated, shunned by the nobles. Oh, yes, there were many nobles loyal to him, but these had gone pushing down with the rest to show that their loyalty, at any rate, was not feigned.

Standing there in all my foppish finery, for I had dressed up with the explicit intention of demonstrating my feelings for this kind of occasion, I refused to budge. Let the old devil walk past me and offer his hand, and then I would welcome him. He and I had had our moments.

Slave girls sprinkled flower petals before the feet of the emperor and this Queen of Lome. She walked with a swaying, gliding gait and she was heavily veiled, whereat a groan of dismay went up from all the assembly. I looked at her. I'd find out about her, that was for sure.

So the emperor, the most powerful man in this part of Kregen, walked past on the crimson carpets. He was between me and the queen. He turned his head. He looked just the same, big and tough with that powerful head, that merciless and demanding expression. He stared at me.

"Lahal, Dray Prescot. And where is my daughter?"

"She is not here, Emperor."

He frowned. He didn't like me calling him emperor.

"I have heard stories concerning your misdeeds. Attend me tonight. I shall demand a strict accounting from you, by Vox!"

Chapter Thirteen

I displease the Emperor of Vallia

The interview with Delia's father was short and sharp.

"Where is my daughter?"

"She has gone about her own affairs for a space."

"That will be the Sisters of the Rose. She's worse than her mother. I shall have this monstrosity you are building torn down. It means nothing and wastes resources and slaves. The new bagnios will be built."

"More slaves!" I shouted at him.

"Aye, son-in-law! You have served me well in the past, I own that. I don't damned well like you, at least not much, and—"

"And you can believe that sentiment returned!"

"Do you forget I am emperor?"

He sat up in his lenken chair with the gold and scarlet cushions, and the gold cup shook and spilled his wine. It was his purple wine of Wenhartdrin. We were alone in that chamber where I had bargained before, where we could speak our minds—well, as much as we'd ever reveal them to each other.

"No. I don't forget. I saw the disgusting display by these damned racter nobles. You know the plots against you? You are aware of the troubles in the northeast? Do you know your own daughter's Delphond is growing surly and suspicious because of your stinking slavers, your foul aragorn?"

"I have to rule as best I can. By Vox, it is not an easy thing to rule an empire."

"I know. You'll have need of proper stabling for the flyers we must have to meet the Hamalian aerial cavalry. Yet you build more slave barracks. Your agents steal away slaves—"

"Not mine! The business is in the hands of Companies of Friends—"

"In which you have damed high stakes!"

"And if I have, do I not have enormous expenses?"

I breathed in hard. Like the scorpion said, it is in a being's nature to be himself. Vallia had always been like this since he could remember, so why should he change it now because some wild clansman roared in to marry his daughter and shout around impossible ideas?

To get away from the explosion I saw was imminent, I said, "And this queen, this Queen of Lome, this Queen Lush?"

He fired up at this.

"The queen's name is Queen Lushfymi! I will not have her called Queen Lush. It is an insult and I'll have the head off the next cramph who calls her that! She is a remarkable woman."

So wrought up was I that I did not look at him, and so must have missed the first signs.

"Since we knocked the damned Hamalese out of Pandahem," I went on, ignoring his outburst, "it makes good sense to improve our relations with all the nations of Pandahem. I have been away—"

"Indeed, son-in-law, you have been away! And no man knows where." I looked at him and he leaned forward, resting his elbow on the carved arm of the chair. "Mayhap you have been in Hamal again, only this time hatching up plots against me?"

I gaped at him.

Then: "You stupid onker!" I brayed it out, brayed it out to this powerful man, the emperor. "I've told you and told you, you are Delia's father and therefore sacrosanct. I'd as soon skewer a Todalpheme as touch you!"

He reared up, opening his mouth, bellowing at me. He did not offer to strike the golden gong. He could deal with this himself.

"You call me onker!"

"Yes, well, if you deserve it by reason of your stupid remarks, you will get it from me."

He lifted a lace kerchief and wiped his mouth. His hand was shaking. "You had best leave Vondium, leave at once.

And, Dray Prescot, do not attempt to return until I send for you."

I glared at him. "I'll go and willingly. If you wake up one morning with a knife in your back of your head looking over your shoulders, don't blame me. I have warned you." He tried to interrupt, but I went on, and I confess I shouted louder as I said: "And if my Delia is in Vondium and I wish to return here I'll come back whether you say so or not, by Zim-Zair!"

He lifted his finger, his hand clutching the scrap of laced kerchief. His finger shook, pointing at me.

"Get out! Get out, Dray Prescot, before I have my guards take your head off your shoulders!"

"I'm going, Majister, but remember you tried that once before, and it did not get you far. Remberee, Emperor, Remberee, and I trust you sleep well in your bed o' nights."

With that petty remark I took myself off, not well pleased. I didn't care a fig about being banished from Vondium. The city is marvelous, without doubt, but I'd seen only a tithe of it and had worked and kept to the Savage Woflo and felt miserable. Now I'd find some better mischief.

I dug my heels into the polished marble as I walked down the long corridor. Crimson Bowmen of Loh, standing guard at the tall double-leaved doors each with its freight of gilded ornamentation, took one look at my face and stiffened into ramrod attention, mute, unmoving, and such was my vicious frame of mind I thought the thought without compunction, trembling in their boots lest I bawl them out.

Into my own apartment I stormed and kicked an overstuffed chair across the room. That was mere petty foolishness. If the stupid onker couldn't see what was going on! He let the racters fawn on him. Well, he was playing their game in that, I suppose, and appeared to be shutting a very blind eye on the other parties out to topple him from his throne and place the crown upon the head of their own puppets.

I removed my court clothes and selected a length of scarlet cloth of good quality. I wrapped it around my waist and drew the end up between my legs and tucked it in firmly. A broad lesten-hide belt with a dulled silver buckle held the breechclout in place. A rapier and main gauche each swung from its own swordbelt went over that. The jiktar and the hikdar were a matched pair, given me by Delia, superb weapons. My old sailor knife went into the sheath over my right hip. I fastened a neat quiver of terchiks over my right shoulder, the swatch of throwing knives snuggling flat and out of the way. I filled a purse with golden talens and silver coins of various countries. A small scrip on the other side held a few necessaries. I was feeling mad clean through. The great Krozair longsword I slung down over my back, the cunningly fashioned double-handed handle raking up to just the right height for me to take a quick snatch and draw the whole gleaming blade free in a single action. That is a knack and a damned useful one on Kregen. I swirled a medium-length crimson cape-cloak about my shoulders and fastened off the golden zhantil-head bosses with golden chains. This was a trifle foppish, but it was worn with a reason. Then, still feeling murderous, I hung a djangir on another belt about my waist, the very short, very broad sword of Djanduin holding a special significance. Finally a great Lohvian longbow and a quiver of arrows all fletched with the blazing blue feathers from the crested korf of the Blue Mountains joined my array of weaponry and I could feel a little better.

What a get-onker I am! But resuming this familiar rig did, without doubt, serve to calm me.

Where Delia was I did not know. I could not, in all honesty, make an attempt, a deliberate attempt, to seek her out. But if I went out of Vondium and trusted to Five-handed Eos-Bakchi, that chuckling Vallian spirit of luck and good fortune, might I not find her? No, I did not really think I would, for Eos-Bakchi does not favor grim faces and hard hearts. But I wanted to rid myself of the feel of Vondium, and I wanted the swift rush of air in my face and the sense of the clean onward surge of life upon Kregen to fill me and drive out the black devils clawing at me like the Imps of Sicce.

It was necessary for me, dressed as I liked to be dressed, to remember to pull on a pair of black Vallian boots.

Now, over all, a massive buff Vallian cloak would conceal all, and one of those peculiar Vallian hats, wide brimmed and with two oblong slots in the front brim, could be jammed down on my hair. The feather in the hat was red and white, the colors of Valka.

Just then Turko came in, beaming, able to walk freely

through into my apartment for I had given orders. He saw my cloak and hat and his face fell. Although it was quite obvious I was dressed for going out, it should be remembered that despite their preference for buff tunics and breeches, the men of Vallian culture habitually don loose lounging robes of many colors in the evening. They are seldom blue, and somewhere on them will the colors of the house or party favor be displayed.

"I had thought to try a few falls with you, Dray, but—"

"That old fool of an emperor!" I burst out. "By Krun! He's banished me from Vondium."

"And you'll go?"

"Oh, aye, I'll go! I can't wait to get away."

"Then we shall—"

"Oh, no, you won't! Some of you will have to stay here and carry on the work. Just because Delia's father is a fambly doesn't mean we have to desert the onker."

"Well—"

"I'll probably go to see Inch or Seg. We'll think of something. I want to know what Balass uncovers. And keep an eye on the Crimson Bowmen. You know half of them betrayed the emperor last time. Trust Jiktar Laka Pa-Re and his men. Discharge at once anyone who accepts a bribe if it can be proved against him. As for me, I'm off."

"Dray!"

"Remberee, my old Turko. I'll think of your great shield, but I doubt it'll be necessary. When the emperor has had time to cool off I'll reappear and this time I'll make the old idiot understand."

"By the time you've had time to cool off, you mean!"

"By Zair! Well spoken!"

"Well, by Morro the Muscle! You take care, you hear?"

"I hear."

"I'll come to the landing platform with you."

"I shall ride a zorca. It is good for the liver."

So we went out and along the ornate corridors. We passed one of the many entranceways to the apartments of the emperor and I saw a man dressed in black and silver abruptly turn and go swiftly into an adjoining passageway past an ivory statue looted from some forgotten city of Chem, I shouldn't wonder.

I could have sworn he was Naghan Vanki, that featureless man who had so sneered at my prentensions for the hand of the emperor's daughter. There was no sign of him as we reached the passage.

Turko remarked offhandedly, "That fellow took off like scorched sleeth. What does he hide?"

"Let it rest. The guards must know him or he wouldn't have got this far without a pass or, if he did reach here, he'd do it with his head under his arm and with chains adangling."

All the same, I was half a mind to go after Naghan Vanki, if it had been him. He'd been one of the party of the airboat *Lorenztone* when I'd been drugged and dumped into a thorny-ivy bush in the hostile territories. Then Oby and Tilly and Naghan the Gnat showed up, all pleased to see me and dismayed that I was leaving. But I slowed them down and went to the zorca stables. Mounted up on Twitchnose, a fine strong zorca with a spiral horn of remarkable length jutting from his chestnut forehead, I looked at my friends.

"Remberee," I said. And then: "By Krun! It is all Remberees for me these days."

One or two of the grooms looked up at the oath, for that is an oath of Hamal and Havilfar. But I didn't care. Let the emperor choke on a little more bile when his spies reported.

Turko and the others offered to ride a ways with me, but the Maiden with the Many Smiles was up and the Twins would shortly follow so I declined their offer and told them to have a party instead. Then I turned Twitchnose's head toward the Mustard Gate, which is a strong battlemented tower set in an angle of the northwest walls of Vondium.

Away to the northeast the monstrous pile of mountains known as Drak's Seat glowered up darkly against the stars, lit by the Maiden with the Many Smiles. I rode on, sunk in odious thoughts, and the zorca riders closed in on each side.

My rapier came out in a moonlit blur of steel under the overhanging balconies where the moonblooms drank up the light. A hulking fellow swathed in a dark cloak husked out. "We mean you no harm, Prince. We are your friends."

"What friends ride up so suddenly from the shadows?"

He lifted his hands. They were empty. The street led to the Boulevard of Grape Pressers which, bordered by an arm of the Vindelka Cut, would bring me to the gate I sought. They had chosen their spot well. The overhanging balconies, the pressing walls, the narrow slot of star glitter—yes, they had waited here for me, knowing I would pass this way. How? The answer to that came more rapidly than I expected.

One of the fellows on my left side, a canny position, reined up. He doffed his hat. The moon showed me a thin face with bright sharp eyes, a narrow face, a hungry face. The jaws were hard and lean. I knew him.

"Strom Luthien!" I said, surprised.

"Aye, Prince. At your service."

He was a racter. The black and white favors showed dark and bright upon his tunic and cloak and pinned to the hat he had doffed. Now he sidled his zorca closer, disregarding my rapier point like a bar of pink and golden light between us.

"There is much to be said, Prince, between the chief party of Vallia which seeks to save the empire, and the Prince Majister who has been disowned and banished by the emperor."

Those damned secret ways in the walls of palaces? Spies had listened to the emperor and me talking privately. With a sudden gush of relief I felt reborn. This, then, was what the night held.

I fancy he was surprised at my tone, for I have, as you know, a certain unsavory reputation with villains.

"Lead on, Strom Luthien. It is I who am at your service. Let us go and talk, by Vox!"

Chapter Fourteen

The racters intrigue with the Prince Majister

The fuzzy pink light from the Maiden with the Many Smiles and the golden glitter from a distant torch bracketed to a wall ran gleaming up my blade as I sheathed the rapier. We rode through the nighted streets of Vondium, this parcel of avowed racters and I. They were all apim. There are many so-called menagerie-men on Kregen, as you know, and you also know that they are men even if they are not carrying their spirits and souls in bodies exactly like those of *Homo sapiens*. To call them menagerie-men is to demean your own sense of your pride in matters of true value. So we rode and if you think I trusted this Strom Luthien then you misread my nature.

Vondium is a large and sprawling city, not occupied by as many inhabitants as the enclave city of Zenicce, perhaps, but large and prosperous and filled with great wealth and luxury.

Up the paved roadway of one of the Hills we rode, the Hill known as the Ban'alar, past dark masses of vegetation and long walls concealing the villas of the rich. The Ban'alar holds a number of the richest houses in Vondium. We halted by a fortified gateway outside a stone wall with bronze spikes where four samphron-oil lamps cast their pleasant mellow gleam upon the guards and the gates and the shimmer weapons. The simple fact of four samphron-oil lamps conveys adequately the wealth of this house.

We were passed through and rode silently along a winding pathway bordered by missals and flowering shrubs. The sweet scent of night-blooming flowers reached me, most soothing. But I kept my senses alert as we dismounted and slaves ran to attend the zorcas. We passed through ornate halls and lushly furnished corridors and so out a glass door into a crystal-walled conservatory. Heat smote me. The walls and ceiling were fashioned of fireglass and the crystal which resists great heat showed the steady beat of furnaces beyond.

The place was crammed with exotic plants, many from the jungles of Chem, and others from Zair knew where upon the face of Kregen.

In a wicker chair stuffed with cushions the Dowager Kovneva Natyzha Famphreon awaited me.

I let her have a half-bow, a small mark to show irony, rather than any mark of respect.

"So you come to see me, Prince Majister."

"The invitation was pressing."

"Strom Luthein had his orders. You would not have been harmed."

I looked at her. She had been carried in her palanquin this morning, joining in the rush to greet the emperor. Now she let go one of her famous barking laughs. Yes, I knew her, this famous old biddy, this Dowager Kovneva of Falkerdrin. She must now be almost a hundred and seventy. Her face contained that nut-brown, cracker-barrel experienced look of iron authority. Her mouth curved down at each corner and deep grooves extended the arc of her rattrap mouth so that all her habitual callous command lay revealed in that dominating face. Her lower lips was upthrust in a perpetual sneer. And as I could see by the way she was dressed all in gauzy silks, that carefully pampered body of hers remained as lushly alluring as ever. She kept her priorities in order, did Natyzha Famphreon.

Standing with his hand on the back of her chair, her son the kov looked at me uncertainly. He was a weak-chinned, spinless nonentity, his every thought and deed ordered by his mother. That was not his fault, but rather the fault of his breeding. He was still the Pallan of the Armory, and through him his mother wielded enormous powers.

Many of the pallans, the high officials, the ministers or secretaries of state, had changed since my absence. But Natyzha Famphreon held onto her power with iron claws.

"You say I would not be harmed. If you wish to talk I will listen for a mur or two."

She didn't like my tone.

"Will you remove your hat, your cloak?"

They could all see the bow stave thrusting up. The hilt of the longsword was hidden by the upstanding jut of the cloak's collar.

It was warm. I said, "I am comfortable. Speak."

"Let us drink a little wine first. I await others who wish to speak with you."

As to drinking wine with these racters, that was another matter. That I had been called in for conversation meant they had a zhantil to saddle, and I fancied the purpose of my presence, alive and without a slit throat, was to make an attempt to seek my alliance. After all, however they had found out about my banishment from Vondium, they knew and therefore counted on that to make me amenable to their proposals. Those proposals must be obvious. So I refused the wine and waited for a space, removed my hat and looked about this luxurious conservatory.

What a wonderful world this planet of Kregen is! What a profusion of life seethes and ferment there! So much there is to know of Kregen, so very much, and so pitifully little have I been able to speak into this microphone. But if you who listen to these tapes have some small inkling of the wonders of Kregen, the marvels, the beauties and the horrors, then you will grasp at the wider reality and the sheer vastness of it all. And I never forget that sheer size, although counting for a considerable amount, is by no means that most important criterion of value. Most assuredly so. So the racters, to bring back the thoughts which crowded my mind to the scene I awaited, so these racters might be the largest political party of Vallia with most of the big guns; they were not, in my view, by any means the best. Not by a chalk.

Presently in came Nath Ulverswan, Nov of the Singing Forests, just the same, tall and lean and with his scarred face vivid in the fireglow. He wore a lounging robe all of deep dark purple, and the black and white favor was pinned to his shoulder. For all the informality of his attire, the rings and the jewels about him, he carried a rapier and main gauche belted up around his narrow waist.

I said, "We have had no real addition to our parties to talk, kovneva."

The old biddy cackled at this, sticking up her lower lip. Nath Ulverswan was notorious for saying so little as to be practically mute. He gave us a surly "Lahal" and sat down and the slave girls brought wine.

The third attendee—one tended to discount the Kovneva's son in these affairs, rather cavalierly, true—turned out to be Nalgre Sultant, Vad of Kavinstok. I was hardly overjoyed to see him, for we had pointedly ignored each other during the times when official business threw us together. He did not forget my harsh treatment of him when the galleon *Ovvend Barynth* had been attacked by shanks. He was not only a dedicated racter; he hated my guts.

Now he stalked in, and I saw the way he postured, using those thin lips and arrogant eyes to put me in my place as a loutish clansman who had had the temerity to burst into civilized Vallia and marry the emperor's daughter. He gave me a nasty look and sat down on the other side of the Kovneva with a mumbled "Lahal."

I cocked an eye at Natyzha Famphreon. "Any more?"

"One only, for this night's work."

The trouble with these Opaz-forsaken racters was that they were evil in ways they could not understand themselves to be evil. They were not committing any consciously criminal acts. If I died, they would joy, but they would not send stikitches after me to assassinate me in a dark alley—at least I did not think so. My death would have to come as a result of an open quarrel, the legality of my demise beyond dispute.

They made their money through the possession of land and all the wealth that brought. They also operated the Companies of Friends, the trading ventures of Vallia. A great deal of their wealth came from slaving and investment in slaving. With the ruthlessness of those in possession, they ensured the continuation of their wealth and with it all their fancy titles and the very real powers they had taken into their hands.

Under torture, each one, I have no doubt, would swear she or he did what they did for the ultimate good of Vallia. They believed this. This kind of conviction made it hard for anyone with differing views to make any kind of coherent sense in their eyes.

Each of these people with me now, discounting the young kov, was a personality: Natyzha Famphreon, Nath Ulverswan, Nalgre Sultant. Each was a strong personality, a real live person with passions and desires and secret hungers and fears they overcame. Of their family lives I knew little. But to them I was a mere wild clansman from the wide Plains of Segesthes, the Lord of Strombor, a man from outside who had dared to wed the Princess Majestrix and to make himself the Prince Majister. That I had won the title before the wedding would no doubt conveniently slip their memories.

The last racter who wished to speak with me arrived. By the tardiness of arrival and by the sweat stains on Trylon Ered Imlien's buff riding clothes I judged my apprehension had come with speed, and these conspirators had been summoned with great urgency. This Ered Imlien, Trylon of Thengelsax, I had seen from time to time and, knowing him to be a racter, had treated him with my usual courtesy tempered with viciousness. I supposed he detested me like all the rest, and I returned the destination with what I hoped was greater measure.

A short, squat man with a square red face and deeply set eyes of Vallian brown, he moved with a rolling gait and boomed every word and liked to use a riding crop on his slaves just to tone 'em up, as he would say, bellowing.

"So he's here, is he!" he bawled, bashing his riding crop against his booted leg. "Well, put it to him, kovneva. Tell the rast what we want."

This vastly amused me.

It did not amuse Natyzha Famphreon, and her lower lip thrust upward like a swifter's beak rising over the apostis of a beamed foe. "We waited for you, Ered. Have the courtesy to bear with us." Cutting irony was lost on Ered Imlien.

"Why wait? Time presses. The bitch queen is gloating this very minute."

"Just so. Now, Prince Majister." And Natyzha Famphreon gestured so that we listened and marked her words. Indeed, she was an old biddy, but she had power and was accustomed to its use. "We know you have been banished from Vondium. How does not matter."

"Oh," says I, very easy, interrupting. "Spies only cost gold."

"Just so." That was a fact of life to her, if not to me, as you know. "The emperor is no longer fit to rule. We run the empire. There is no shilly-shallying about that."

I wanted to argue the point, but reality forbade. The emperor had the final say in many things, and he balanced party against party, but the power of the Racter party so often bent dividends and results in the directions they desired.

So I said, "I may have my disagreements with the old devil; he is sometimes impossible to live with. He hates me." This was not exactly true. "But he does rule the empire. He keeps you racters toeing the line, for one."

They didn't like this. Again, it was only a half-truth.

"He hates you," spat out Nalgre Sultant. "He is not alone in that."

I ignored the man.

"There is no profit in supporting the emperor any longer," said the kovneva.

"He is doomed!" bellowed out Ered Imlien, red of face, grasping his wineglass as though to splinter the delicate globe.

Movement and shadows beyond a glass screen attracted my attention. This place would be like most of the villas and palaces of Kregen, a rabbit warren of secret ways. But I fancied I could find my way out. Now I saw past the end of the glass screen the unmistakable outline of a Chulik's head. Chuliks, powerful warriors trained from birth to the use of weapons, have oily yellow skins and shave their heads to leave a long pigtail. But the characteristic that betrayed this Chulik to me was the upthrusting tusk at the corner of his mouth. I saw this plainly. Chuliks generally command higher hiring fees than other races, Pachaks apart, and are finicky in their choice of employer. Their delicateness does not come, as it does with Pachaks, from honor or sentiment; their choice of employer rests solely on his or her ability to pay.

Now this Chulik lifted his head, talking to a comrade, and the profile showed me the hard tusk lifting from his curled lip.

Two savage tusks, a Chulik has, and he uses them when he fights, as I can testify.

If I had to fight an army of Chuliks here—well, wasn't that half my reason for going with Strom Luthien in the first place?

So I dissembled a trifle and made the conversation more general, and hinted obliquely that, well, perhaps the time had come for me to give up my allegiance to the emperor. I did say at one point, rather sharply, "But if the emperor dies, his daughter and her husband will take the throne and the crown. You have thought of that?"

"If the emperor dies you are out of it, Prescot. If he dies before things are settled the land will run red with blood, for it will mean civil war, without doubt."

"And you would run that risk?"

"It would be no risk for us," said the kovneva, and she chuckled in her crone-like way, her gorgeous body incongruous in the soft swathes of silk. "For we will win whatever the intervening chaos may be."

They believe that, these high and mighty of the world.

Of course, by Makki-Grodno's disgusting diseased left kidney, it is often true.

"Do you expect me to connive at the murder of my father-in-law?"

"If you were a man with blood of Vallia in him, if you had the breeding, then it would be nothing to you."

I did not say, "If that is breeding a fellow is better off without it." But it was a near thing.

The swathing buff cloak could be ripped off in a twinkling. Depending on the danger, it would be the longbow or the longsword. Either would suit me in my frame of mind.

Eventually they offered a deal in which I would have no part of the death of the emperor and in which I would keep all the lands and titles I now held in Vallia with the exception of Prince Majister. They could not know how little I valued that. In return I was not to oppose them, and was to make sure my people did not interfere during the coup. I asked about this, but they were too cagey to give me any details.

Without attempting to imply any false modesty, it seemed to me they were anxious to get me out of the coming conflict because they feared my influence. They must have some apprehension of what I could do. Otherwise the terms would not have been so generous. Whether or not they'd keep their side of the bargain would be in the laps of the gods.

Had I been acting only for myself, for the old impetuous Dray Prescot who thumped before he thought, I'd have roared out some obscene suggestion at them and then gone swinging into action. I felt a keen regret that I could not do this. I needed the exercise. But more than mere gratification of my injured ego hung on this. The fate of

Vallia depended to a very great deal on what was decided here in this conservatory. It was in my interest to appear to go along with them, giving them rope, so that I might more surely bring them down into ruin.

So I said, "Let me think about this. There is the Princess Majestrix to be considered."

Ered Imlien burst out with: "Do not worry your head over her, you onker. The Princess Dayra occupies her mind."

Furious, Natyzha Famphreon rose from her wicker chair. "Speak not of things of which you know nothing, you fambly!" She would have gone on. But I took a few steps toward this Ered Imlien and clutched up his buff tunic in my fist and shook his head a little and I glared into his eyes.

"But you had best speak to me, rast! And quickly!"

Chapter Fifteen

Of Natyzha Famphreon's chavonths, and her son

"Speak up, cramph!" I loosed my grip a little and some air flowed down with a great whooping gasp into his lungs. His face was a bright purple, like a rotten gregarian. He wheezed. I thought his eyes might roll out of his head. So I shook him again, just to keep him in the right frame of mind.

He choked out: "The Princess Dayra, she is nothing more than a—"

I hit him before he could say whatever he was going to say.

I suppose I was oversensitive about my daughters because I had held my Velia in my arms as she died. I could never forget that—what father could? So I hit him again and said, "Speak carefully, Imlien, speak very carefully."

"I do not know!" he blubbered out, his face already beginning to swell, a trickle of blood down his chin from a split lip. "I hear only that she—"

"Careful!"

"She runs wild! I cannot tell more for I do not know!"

I became aware of the conservatory again, and of the others frozen in postures of horror. The Chuliks had trotted out from behind their glass screen, their weapons ready, and the kovneva waved them down. If they wanted a fight, by Vox! I was in the mood now, right enough, to my shame.

"He speaks the truth, Dray Prescot! No one knows what your daughter Dayra is up to. That is where the Princess Majestrix has gone. More than that no woman knows."

I let Ered Imlien fall to the floor. I glared at the kovneva. "You are not of the Sisters of the Rose?"

She drew that gorgeous body up and her lean crone-like face sharpened. "No."

She made no offer to tell me which order owned her allegiance. I did not ask. She would not have said if she did not wish to.

"It seems," I said, "that if we make a deal I shall have to watch this lump of offal."

"I will answer for him. He is a trylon. Thengelsax is too close to the northeast for his comfort. His estates are raided. He is foolish only in his concern for his estates."

"And his people?"

"They fight for him as is their duty."

The idea that Dayra had something to do with the raids from those hard folk of the northeast crossed my mind. But it seemed too preposterous. And, anyway, was not all the island one? Was not Vallia Vallia? Perhaps there were no raids at all, and this was an invention of this miserable Ered Imlien to his own dark ends. I looked at him. He was drawing himself up and quite automatically reaching out for his riding crop. If he'd attempted to hit me with it I hadn't noticed. But it was broken in half. Had I done that?

"You have shamed me, Prince," he said, and the words gritted out through his teeth.

"Not so, Imlien. Not so. You have shamed yourself."

"One day—"

"Ered! Keep silence!" Natyzha Famphreon glowered on the miserable trylon and Ered Implien turned away, muttering, but he kept silence as far as I was concerned.

To the kovneva I spoke and I admit with some trepidation I was astounded at the quality of my voice. It hardly sounded like the bull-headed, vicious, intemperate Dray Prescot I knew.

"And can you tell me nothing more about my daughter?"

She shook her head. I thought, but could not be sure, that a dark gleam of triumph crossed those arrogant features.

"Nothing more is known."

There was nothing more I could find out. Whatever it was that Delia had gone to sort out, I could only hope that she and Melow would be successful and return swiftly to me.

They had to be successful! We had lost one daughter. We could not bear to face the anguish of the loss of another.

I forced myself to calm down. I could trust my Delia. She was supremely completent in these matters. I had a job to do here and that I must do. There was one other matter I wished to discuss before I left here, either walking out with all due civility, battling my way out with the Krozair brand in my fists or carried out feetfirst.

So I smashed myself out of that fearful frame of mind. One must, as they say on Kregen, accept the needle.

"We have ranked our deldars in this matter of the emperor," I said. "And we agree I shall think on. Tell me, Natyzha Famphreon, what know you of the Black Feathers?"

Her arrogant old head went up at this. She started to walk between lines of potted plants, twirling the green fronds. We all walked with her, although Ered Imlien kept well clear of me. The onker was swishing his broken half of the riding crop about and trying to bash his boot and hitting his knee, whereat I was minded to laugh.

"The Black Feathers? Ah, you have heard of them?"

I said in a nasty voice, "If I had not heard of them I would scarcely be able to ask you."

She had the self-consciousness to flush up at this, at my suggestion, at my tone. She snapped a twig from a sweet little loomin, and twitched the flower about, not gently.

"The provinces are full of rumors. Nothing certain is known, as nothing is certain about anything in this life."

"The provinces, but Vondium?"

"I gave orders to my crebents of my estates to root out the priests. They did not catch one. Here in Vondium I have heard nothing." Then the sly old bezom glanced at me and drew the mauve and white flowers down her cheek. "Perhaps you, Prince Majister, are of the Chyyanists?"

"I have no time for slallyfanting in this, kovneva. I too have attempted to root out the evil and now, I think, it is time for stronger measures. You are aware of the creed preached by the priests of the Great Chyyan?"

She flicked the flower. "I care not. They are not of Opaz and therefore are damned beyond redemption."

Had this old biddy been a commoner she would undoubtedly have formed one of the people in the long chanting processions that wound through Vondium. "Oolie Opaz! Oolie Opaz!" they chanted, up and down, singsong after singsong cadence. "*Oo*-lie *O*-paz! *Oo*-lie *O*-paz!" On and on and on.

"I know they wish to break our heads and take all that is ours," said Nalgre Sultant. He looked vicious and mean, a very natural expression for him. "Red revolution! Aye! That is what these Chyyanists want."

I did not think these nobles had penetrated as far as we had in discovering details of the Chyyanists. I pondered. It might be advisable to tell them more than they already knew. I detested the racters. They had the power and the money. The Chyyanists wanted to take that money and with it the power, in the here and now. Those ends were admirable, in one sense, if they could be achieved reasonably. But red revolution is not reasonable and I have had a hand in more than one red revolution. Once you start to sweep away the old the process can get out of hand. If Vallia ran red with blood from any cause I would sorrow. And I did not believe the designs of Makfaril were simple honest revolution. How, once a little power is put into your hands, the evil and corruption grow!

So I told them what we had discovered. They took these revelations seriously. They would. They were experienced people with much at stake.

"Then the Chyyanists present a present threat." The kovneva had stopped twiddling with her flower. "Once the temple is brought to Vondium and the priests begin to suborn the masses . . . Slaves too, I hear, are sometimes present in the congregations."

"They aim to enslave the racters," I said with some satisfaction.

"That has been tried before and was ruthlessly put down. Once the temple is erected in Vondium the evil will gain a greater hold. We must watch every entrance and stop these priests. The idol you describe is not an easy thing to move."

"I'll get my men down at the docks," said the kov, the kovneva's son, and we all turned to look at him, shocked, as though a ghost had spoken.

"Yes, my son." The kovneva spoke in a soothing tone. "You do that."

No real surprise could be felt by me that these highly placed nobles should know of the Chyyanists. This kind of information would flow into their bureaus all the time. Now they would take more concern over the Black Feathers. This all added up. It all made sense. But I was banished from Vondium. I said, "I am banished from Vondium. I shall leave now, unless you have any other ideas, and see what I can do in the provinces. I am concerned over the Great Chyyan." I had told them that Hamal could be the basis of the new creed, but they indicated that did not signify. They'd smash Hamal when the time came. Even Nath Ulverswan was almost reconciled to that view. The main threat, as they saw it, was against themselves.

There was no point in my telling them that my chief concern, a concern almost approaching a guilty anguish, was for the poor deluded people who believed this evil creed and imagined they might indulge in all the goodness of Kregen, at once, in the here and now. These noble racters would never comprehend that point of view.

Further talk and a little more bargaining more or less sealed the compact in the view of the racters. If they suspected I merely toyed with them, for I was scrupulous in not giving my word, they did not reveal it. If I was going to have to fight my way out, that, too, did not appear on the surface. The Chuliks had gone, dismissed by a wave of the kovneva's hand. We walked through the farther recesses of the conservatory. It was a remarkable place. Cages had been positioned about in which were kept examples of many kinds of wild animals, so the place was also a miniature zoo.

I said, "We are now talking in circles. I will leave." I gave a hitch to the cloak and brought the hat up ready to clap it on my head. I was ready, also, to whip out longbow or longsword and swirl the cloak back out of the way for action.

On the way in here I'd observed the fantamyrrh as was proper. It occurred to me I might not be in the mood to observe it on the way out.

Intrigue and dark secrets flourished here as the exotic plants flourished in their heated glass houses. The passions and the feral viciousness here were scarcely matched by the savage beasts penned in their cages.

A number of the kovneva's Chail Sheom, her pretty

little slave girls in their silks and bangles and silver chains, trailed after her carrying her fan and her perfumes and the gewgaws inseparable from a great lady of high rank. Two hulking fellows carried her chair. I had given these slaves a casual glance and saw their hangdog expressions. They brightened up with smiles and laughs when the kovneva looked at them, which is the way of slaves. It sickened me.

Now, as we stood there with the intrigues between us and the secret passions held down, as we made our plans and no doubt made alternative plans to deal more effectively each with the other, so the realization struck through to me that I, that same Dray Prescot who had so ruthlessly driven the slavers from Valka and had fought them over the fair surface of Kregen, was in reality standing here and plotting with Zair-forsaken slave masters and slave profiteers.

I moved away, gripping the hat, stood by a cage in which a graint shambled upright to grip the bars. The others moved with me and I didn't give a damn if they saw my face and guessed my thoughts. At that moment I'd have cheerfully seen them all consigned to the Ice Floes of Sicce.

A shattering screech and a ripping, tearing, chopped-off scream from the cages we had just passed brought us all around to stare upon a scene of horror.

Two feral beasts leaped from the blood-streaming wreckage of a half-naked slave girl to smash a second away with a splintered skull and to spring on two more. The beasts were chavonths. Past them I saw the two chair men running. Someone had deliberately opened the cage. Someone who hated the Dowager Kovneva Natyzha Famphreon had released these savage killer beasts upon us.

The scene etched itself on my brain. The parallel lines of cages with their heavy iron bars. The maddened beasts within, scenting freshly spilled blood, joined in the savage chorus. The slave girls huddled, naked arms upraised, silks splashed with blood, feathers and fans and jewels spilling across the floor. The chavonths chewed up their victims and turned, their muzzles smeared, to glare with venomous fury upon us.

And the nobles, these racters, screamed and clawed and ran past me screeching their fear, to find their way blocked by a stout iron grille at the end of the row of cages. Whoever had planned this had schemed well. I fancied the chairmen were the culprits. They had run free, arguing a preknowledge. But they had so arranged affairs that the chavonths penned us in against iron bars. We were the caged, the chavonths the masters now!

Chavonths are known as treacherous beasts. They are six-legged hunting cats, powerful, and their fur is patterned in hexagons of blue, gray and black. Their fangs may not match those of a leem, their speed not equal that of a strigicaw, but they can smash a man's head in, their claws can disembowel a poor naked slave girl.

Nalgre Sultant pushed past me and ran for the end of the alleyway and stood, shaking the iron bars that blocked him off, screaming, screaming. Ered Imlien swung away, his red bloated face green. Nath Ulverswan gripped the arm of Natyzha Famphreon and they stood, crouched with their backs to the bars, glaring with awful horror upon the death that snarled at them.

The chinless nincompoop, Natyzha's son, Kov of Falkerdin, stepped forward. He drew his rapier and main gauche. I could see the side of his face, see the sweat dripping there, the way his teeth caught his upper lip. His body trembled. But he stepped out before his mother and the twin blades he held caught the fireglass glow and gleamed.

The dowager kovneva husked out a word. "Jikai!" she said.

This would not be a jikai—well, perhaps a little one—but it would prove to be highly instructive, that was for sure.

I said, "This is not work for a rapier, kov."

His voice panted. "That I know. But it is all the weapon I have, that and my dagger."

I threw off the swathing buff cloak and unfastened the golden zhantil heads and tossed down the gold-laced crimson cape-cloak. Then I drew the Krozair longsword, for the time for bowmanship had passed. Seg might not have agreed, but I knew what I knew about the Krozair brand.

"When they leap, Prince," said this young kov, "do you take the left hand one and I—"

"Give them no time to spring," I said, and took the Krozair longsword's hilt into both my spread fists and so

"I charged forward, swinging the blade up."

charged forward, swinging the brand up in a deadly arc of steel.

Through all the hubbub I heard the gasps of horror at my back. What I looked like Zair alone knows. I hurtled forward. The chavonths had given me no time to smash forward to save the slaves; all were dead or fled. Everything had happened with shocked speed, a few heartbeats separating the first scream and the instant I sprang.

This was what living on Kregen was all about, this horrific transformation, in an instant, from peaceful living to berserk fury, from graciousness to terror.

This must be done right the first time, and quick, damned quick. . . .

The two chavonths did not leap exactly together and so I was able to position and slash at the first. The gleaming blade of the longsword swept in that vicious chopping circle as my hands and wrists and forearms rolled over, and the muscles of my back ridged and extended and I felt all the old pull and power. The steel sliced through the chavonth's furred hide just above his left forequarter—his left foresixth—and I went with the blow and rolled away and the slashing claws razored past. A single roll brought me up and a single twist turned me and a single leap brought me from the side against the second chavonth. The Krozair brand licked out like a bar of blood. I drove it point first into the lean furry flank. A blue hexagon imploded. The onward rush of the great beast almost snatched the sword from me, but a Krozair knows how to hold onto a sword hilt. I gave a vicious twist and then withdrew, swirling the blade instantly into an overhand chop that crunched down on the chavonth's backbone just abaft his center pair of legs.

The yelling shrieking of the wounded chavonths erupted in the iron-barred area, the stink of freshly spilled blood poured out in a warm effluvium. There was no time to stop. This beast was done for, although he spat and clawed futilely at the air and at his ruined back.

The chinless kov was trying to get in at the first chavonth, trying to dart his slender rapier in past the wicked claws of its remaining legs. I hurled myself forward in a desparate rush and almost, almost I saved him completely.

But a wickedly tipped claw swept in from the side and

gashed all down his ribs and he shrieked and fell back and then I was on the chavonth and the terrible Krozair longsword rose and fell, rose and fell, and three blows took the poor chavonth's head clean off.

Natyzha Famphreon had not fainted. Nalgre Sultant, seeing the dead and dying cats, dragged out his rapier and made a great show of coming forward, twirling the blade, ready to face all comers. Nath Ulverswan kept his grip upon the kovneva. Ered Imlien reluctantly walked forward. He was not afraid, that I knew, but he had not considered what had happened as being possible.

I bent to the kov. His chinless face, so unlike the chinless, pop-eyed face of Chid, glared up at me and a grin ricked his lips. His side was badly torn, but he would live. He was in some pain.

"I tried . . ." He spoke with an effort. "My mother . . . it was my duty . . . but . . . but a rapier . . ."

"Lie still, kov." His name was Nath, but I could not call him Nath. There are many Naths on Kregen. "Lie still." I looked up at the others, all recovering from the fright, all sorting out the story they would tell. "You zigging cramphs!" I bellowed. "Run and send for a doctor! Run, you nurdling onkers!"

Ered Imlien ran past the corpses of slaves, the dead and dying chavonths, swirling his rapier, ran to fetch a doctor.

I held this Kov Nath of Falkerdrin, easing him, feeling only a vast pity, a contempt that embraced all his stupid family and the pride that sustained them. I glared at Nalgre Sultant.

"Fetch cloths from the dead slaves, Sultant. We must staunch the wounds. Jump to it, you rast!"

He jumped.

So we waited for the doctor, for I would not allow Kov Nath to be moved. He lapsed into unconsciousness as the doctor arrived, so the acupuncture needles to ease his pain were not necessary and the doctor, a client of the house, could get to work to stop the bleeding and to draw the ragged wounds together and apply his healing paste. Some doctors of Kregen are useless, many are expert; one chooses where one can.

I stood up.

"I am leaving." I picked up my cloak and the cape-cloak. "I will wash elsewhere, wash this place from me. Until I see you again, Natyzha Famphreon, take good care of that son of yours. Maybe we have all misjudged him. Perhaps all Vallia is wrong about him." Then I went out and no one offered to stop me and I did not observe the fantamyrrh.

Chapter Sixteen

Kadar the Hammer rides north to Seg Segutorio

Now began a period of my life on Kregen that, even now, looking back, I cannot decide if I should curse horribly over it or simply stand with my fists on my hips and roar with laughter. It was all a great foolishness. I made my way by the dusty roads northwestward. When it rained in a lashing gale of Kregen that drenched everything and everyone the roads turned to a quagmire and it was useless to attempt to flounder on. Then I sought sanctuary. After leaving Natyzha Famphreon's house where we had hatched intrigues against the emperor I had called again at our villa in Vondium—the Valkan villa owned by Delia and myself—and besides having a long and glorious bath, taking the full Baths of the Nine, I equipped myself a little more lavishly for the journey.

The villa did not see us all that often, for we stayed at the emperor's command in the wing of the palace given over to our use. But everything was ready, as it was bound to be. So I took a strong preysany loaded with supplies, with a harness or two of armor, spare weapons, provisions. Also I packed the old brown blanket cloak and the bamboo stick with the cancealed blade. That had served before; it might serve again.

During the ride north to Seg's estates of Falinur I was embroiled only in four small skirmishes and rode for my life only once, preferring that to fighting the stinking pack of drikingers who howled hairily at me from the roadside and hurled stones and spears and would have skewered me through had I not ducked and clapped in spurs.

This kind of flight was a different matter from running

from one's foes. These poor devils might be evil in the eyes of honest folk, but all in good time my plans called for the alleviation of the conditions that created bandits, if it could be contrived, rather than for the removal of the drikingers themselves.

The zorca-ride jolted up the old liver, as I had said. I am fond of the canals and the canalfolk of Vallia, but somehow this canter through the heart of Vallia seemed more in keeping. The canal folk are a staunchly independent lot, and the men and women of the cuts do not call themselves koters and koteras as do the gentry of Vallia; they are vens and venas. But as I passed through the green countryside I would stop at bridges over the canals and talk and spend some time, for I was maturing plans and had no wish to rush. After all, I was not hurrying to a rendezvous with Delia.

A strong eastward swing was advisable toward the north of Vindelka for the Ocher Limits thrust a tongue-like protrusion between that province and Seg's Falinur to the north. I made no attempt to revisit either of the Delkas, and decided firmly against a sentimental side trip to the Dragon's Bones.

All through this central portion of the island large lakes are to be found, with the Great River twining through, and the canals boring on with man's ingenuity at work to maintain the levels by lock and lift. So I trotted on and entered the Kovnate of Falinur and at once I saw what Seg meant about the demeanor of his people.

They did not offer hostility, although they did not know who I was, and when I put up at an inn and told them my name was Kadar the Hammer they merely sniffed and took no more than the usual notice of a stranger one expects. But the undercurrents were strong. As a simple smith, for that is what they took me to be, out seeking some gainful employment, I posed only the threat of any itinerant labor to the homegrown product. But a laughing group of koters passed, tys and kyrs and even a strom, and these gentry aroused dark hidden looks of anger and envy. Falinur, as Seg had said, was like to erupt in violence at any moment.

These people had backed their late kov against the emperor with the third party and had lost. So why should that still rankle? Perhaps, for I did not bring the precise subject up, perhaps it was not that which was causing their hostility to Seg. Whatever it was, we had to put it aright by fair means. Any other way would be as abhorrent to Seg as to myself. Anyway, with tough independent people as are most Vallians, brutal repression would repercuss with a vengeance.

A shrunken little fellow with one eye and swathed in furs against an imagined cold gave me a portion of the answer. He rode a hirvel and led a long string of calsanys, all loaded down with trinkets that this ob-Eye Enil hawked from village to village. We rode together for a space, and I listened.

"Aye, Kadar the Hammer! You may well ask. We ride through Vinnur's Garden here and the land is rich." His one eye swiveled alarmingly to regard me with cunning. "And where the land is rich, there, by Beng Drangil, men will fight and kill for it."

The Great River which bordered Falinur's eastern flank made a kinked loop to the east here on the border between Falinur and Vindelka. The Ocher Limits ended to the west. In the fertile area of Vinnur's Garden riches could be won by agriculture on the fertile eastern sections by mining on the more barren western. The border between the two kovnates ran to the north of Vinnur's Garden. The people living there had been under the rule of both Vindelka and Falinur at differing times. Now Vindelka demanded their loyalty, and their taxes. But many folk north and south of the border wished that dividing line to be redrawn much farther to the south, cutting off Vinnur's Garden from Vindelka and giving it to Falinur.

It was scarcely necessary for Ob-Eye to say, "But the new kov of Falinur, this Seg Segutorio whose past is a mystery, refuses to countenance any move against Vindelka."

Ob-Eye wandered the central portions of Vallia, and although he confided that he had been born in Ovvend, he could look upon these squabbles with the single eye of the interested observer.

I knew why Seg would not allow his people to go raiding down into Vinnur's Garden, why he made no move to annex the place from the Kov of Vindelka. For this Kov of Vindelka was Vomanus, a good comrade to Seg and me, and we had fought at that immortal battle at the Dragon's Bones.

But I sensed this did not explain all the hostility to Seg

and Thelda. As we rode north and left the parochial problem of Vunnur's Garden to the rear, still the impression I received was one of implacable hatred to the Kov of Falinur. I own I was put out by this, upset, angry and baffled.

There were slaves still in Falinur, though there were not many. And I gained some more insight. Acting not just because it was my way but from honest conviction, Seg had given orders that from henceforth no slaves would be allowed in his kovnate. He was obeyed surlily and his edict was broken more and more often, for all that his guards rode to stamp out the evil. One consequence of the abolition of slavery, in intention if not yet in fact, was the resurgence of the slavers who preyed where pickings were ripest. This added another strand; it still did not explain it all. So, taking the chunkrah by the horns, I began direct questions about the Black Feathers.

The answers Ob-Eye gave me filled in about another fifty percent of the problem.

Yes, there were temples and priests and traveling churches spreading the great word and, by Beng Drangil, the great day is coming, the Black Day, and in that day will the Great Chyyan reward all his loyal followers! Thus spake Ob-Eye Enil, swearing by Beng Drangil, the patron saint of hawkers.

This was no fantasy. This was stark reality. As I jogged along toward Seg's kovnate capital city of Falanriel, a place which, despite its architecture, I always looked forward to visiting, I realized more and more the hold the Chyyanists had on these people.

On a day when the suns broke through scattered clouds and the joy of living should have burst all worries—and, sadly, did not—we trotted through a ferny dell. With horrid shrieks designed to chill us, the drikingers leaped from the ferns, waving their clanxers and rapiers and spears, roaring at us to surrender or be chopped.

With a curse I ripped out the clanxer scabbarded to Twitchnose. A smith may carry samples of his wares. If it came to it I'd use the longsword on them.

Then I checked. The bandits closed up around us, fierce, hairy men with thickly bearded faces and bright merry eyes, darting the points of their weapons at us. But Ob-Eye pulled out a leather wallet from his loose tunic, opened it, waved a scrap of black feather in the air.

"Peace, brothers!" he squeaked. He was only a little frightened, I saw, and marveled. "We are all Chyyanists together, you and I. Listen to what Makfaril has said through his priests, listen and rejoice, for the day is coming."

And then these fearsome bandits set up a yelling and a hullabaloo and crowded around, laughing, slapping their thighs and bellowing greetings, and every other sentence had to do with the Black Feathers. In no time a fire had been lit and we were sitting around listening and smelling roasting vosk haunch. The wine went around. It was good too, plunder from a vintner's caravan. Good humor prevailed, although the leader, a ferocious villain with a spade beard he had threaded with gold wire and with golden earrings that caught the lights of the fire and of the suns, did bellow out, "By Varkwa the Open-Handed! If many more travelers are Chyyanists the pickings will be small!"

"But soon all Vallia will be ours for the looting!" bellowed his lieutenant, and the gang set up a racket of laughter and promises of what they would do on the Black Day. Chief among these was the heartfelt desire to go into Falanriel and sack the place and take all. And what they would do to the kovneva, the high and mighty, stuck-up, prideful and ignorant Kovneva Thelda, would have set the Ice Floes of Sicce alight.

I chewed on succulent vosk and kept my face down. Listening would help more than a stupid sword-swinging affray. Was this another piece of the puzzle? Was poor Thelda, who always meant well, overdoing her part as a kovneva? She loved the title and took immense pride in her status. Yet once in the long ago she had been forced to spy and scheme for the racters. Now my good comrade Seg had her in his keeping. I made a little vow that not only would I speak to Thelda as a friend, I'd stick a length of steel blade into any of these drikinger cramphs who tried to harm a hair of her head. But, all the same, she could be a terribly tiresome woman, and goodheartedly never be aware of it.

There could now be no doubt that the Chyyanist creed had caught on like a prairie fire here in Falinur. An attempt had been made to spread the word in Veliadrin. Delphond had been under attack—I was sure Delia was right and there was the black feather to prove it—even though we did not know how far the Chyyanists had reached there. I fancied that Inch in the Black Mountains and Korf Aighas in the Blue Mountains would be facing the same challenge.

If I allowed myself to be swayed by the megalomania I have been accused of, I could see a clear pattern. But Natyzha Famphreon and the other racters knew of the Black Feathers, and their provinces had been infiltrated also. Makfaril, whoever he was, surely intended to sound the call for the Black Day at the same time all over Vallia. With a little knowledge I have of human nature, with a little knowledge of running affairs of state, and with the knowledge borne in on me by the demeanor of bandits around the campfire, I knew with a dark foreboding that Makfaril might not be able to hold his followers to his timetable. The explosion might erupt at any moment, triggered by any silly stupid event. The day of the Black Feathers could strike tomorrow. . . .

That ride up through the heart of Valka was all a great foolishness. Bits of it recur to me now. I had hoped the long ride would soothe me and calm me down, but the more I saw and heard the more fraught and tense I became. And the burden of my fear, a true and deeply abiding fear, must be shown by the first words I spoke to Seg after the joyful Lahals.

"And the news from Delia, Seg? Where is her letter?"

He shook his head. "No letter from Delia has arrived here, Dray. There are packages for you forwarded on, flown in from Vondium and Valka, and coming from—well, you know the names."

I did. There would be estate information from Strombor and chunkrah counts from Hap Loder and the Clansmen. There would be news from Kytun and Ortyg in Djanduin. But I hungered to hear from Delia, for now I knew she struggled against some unknown evil that threatened our daughter Dayra.

I asked after Thelda, and Seg spread his hands and said she had been visiting in Vondium and was momentarily expected.

The impression Seg gave was that he wanted to take up his great longbow and go ask the emperor to repeat the words that had banished me. I fancied the emperor would find life exceedingly uncomfortable thereafter if he did repeat them.

Well, by Vox! how long does he think to keep you banished, the old onker?"

"Only from Vondium. And the Black Feathers have not sprouted there as yet."

"Come and wet that dusty throat of yours and let us see what we may contrive."

We went down from the battlemented gateway and so across the outer yard and through the inner walls and up through narrow winding stairways of stone into Seg's private chambers in the Fletcher's Tower. Once it had been the Jade Tower, but Seg had changed all that. This castle fortress of his, frowning down over the city of Falanriel, had been built to withstand a protracted siege. Seg kept the place amply stocked. He had a small guard of Bowmen of Loh, backed up by a regiment of Pachaks with a few other diffs in their different specialities. He was no fool, was Seg Segutorio over these matters, with the wild fey ways and shrewd practicality of his mountain people.

All the same, as we sat and drank in the quiet ease of his rooms, I had to say, "It does look as though we are the high and mighty of the land now, and grind down the poor."

"To the Ice Floes with that, my old dom!" Seg looked annoyed. "I was a miserable starveling, a mercenary, a slave. I know. If a man works in my province of Falinur he is assured of a living and of comfort."

"Slaves?"

Seg made a face and drank his wine. "These devils are sly and secret and run slaves no matter what I do to stop 'em."

"Vinnur's Garden—"

He did not let me go on. "My nobility here, all owing their fine estates to me, all prate on and on about marching into Vinnur's Garden and taking it for Falinur. But Vomanus—"

"He is seldom at home. He is almost as much of an absentee landlord as I am."

"Well, I have put in my stint here. And it looks as though I'd have done better to have stayed in Vondium, or visited Erthyrdrin again, for all the good I have done here."

When I told him, during the course of our long talk through the evening and most of the night, about Natyzha Famphreon and the chavonths, he grimaced and said, "I'd rather not hear what she did to her slaves. They'd all be punished to make sure the guilty got it in the neck, to the devil with the innocent."

"Aye."

"And they actually expected you to fight your father-in-law?"

"Not exactly fight him. But certainly not assist him."

"Remember the Dragon's Bones?"

"Now there was a bonny little fracas."

"Bonny little fracas! Dray, Dray! That was High Jikai!"

"I wouldn't have said so, but it was squeaky, all the same."

"Those days when you and Delia and Thelda and I marched across the hostile territories! Ah, but they'll never come again."

I was not at all sure of that. Kregen is a world of ups and downs. So we talked on through the night, amicably drinking, and our thoughts were as often of the stirring past adventures as of the terrors of the future and the problems we faced.

Two days later Thelda arrived back in Falanriel, flushed, bright-eyed, bouncing, filled with glowing stories of her time in Vondium. She had been desolated that her great friend Delia had not been there. Of all her sprightly babble we took the due meed of attention. "And the dear queen! Queen Lushfymi! What a charming woman she is, and so regal. I own she has quite won me over. And yet the ignorant fools call her Queen Lush. It really is a disgrace."

Seg asked a casual question about the Queen of Lome and Thelda fired up instantly. "Beautiful, oh, yes! She is radiant. And so cultured. She is rich too. Lome is not the largest country in Pandahem, but her wealth is dazzling. The presents she brought, the length of the procession—the animals and the people and the displays—you should have seen it all, my dear. You would have enjoyed it."

"I'm sure," said Seg, looking at me with a straight face.

Seg and Thelda loved each other; that was true, and gave me great joy. When couples split apart friends are hurt also. I felt as confident as of anything that Seg and Thelda knew each other well enough by now. As for their children, the eldest son, named Dray for some odd quirk of desire on Seg's part, was off adventuring. The twins were at school No—here Thelda pursed her lips up most comically—Silda, the girl, was with the Sisters of the Rose.

I sat up.

"But you are a Sister of Patience, Thelda."

"It's none of your business, my dearest Dray, for you are a man. But, yes, I am. And Silda hankered so after the SoR I had to let her go. I own it mystifies me."

In his droll way, Seg said, "Delia was mystified too."

So, of course, that explained it. It also made me think again about what I both might and ought to do.

A very great deal of our conversations concerned Queen Lushfymi, the Queen of Lome. Lome is the country situated in the northwest of Pandahem where the long east-west central chain of mountains sweeps up northwestward and, extending out to sea, forms the straggling line of the Hoboling Islands. Lome is rich although not overlarge, occupying the space east of the mountains to the border with Iyam. East of Iyam lies Menaham, occupied by the Bloody Menahem. Then comes Tomboram where I harbored most guilty memories of Tilda and Pando. And, in the jutting northeast corner of Pandahem is situated Jholaix. One smacks ones lips at the thought of Jholaix.

So after the Vallians had kicked the Hamalese out of Pandahem after the Battle of Jholaix, it seemed the emperor was attempting to make friends with at least one nation of Pandahem, for that whole island had been in a state of near-conflict with Vallia for many seasons. I welcomed this move. It was statesmanship at the level I sought. I devoutly wished Vallia and Pandahem to come together in comradeship, at first against Hamal and then, and much more importantly, to stand together with other countries of Paz against the raids of the shanks from the other continental grouping on the otler side of Kregen.

What with talking about Queen Lushfymi and arranging a party for the castellan's eldest son who was about to go off to be a mercenary, disdaining service under his father, Thelda was kept busy. Seg and I rode and hunted and talked and drank. But for his generally subdued air, Seg was in good spirits, considering the circumstances. He got through a prodigious amount of work. But for the malignant animosity in which these confounded idiots of Falinur held him, he would have been a perfect kov. As for Thelda, she was quite wrapped up in her own doings and seemed unaware of the atmosphere. Seg had even refused to go up to Vondium to greet the emperor on his return, as Inch had likewise not gone, because of his concern.

How I felt the old guilty stab that, when I asked him, he would always manage to get away to aid me!

And more importantly, how he would race across half a world to rescue me from a sticky corner, as you will know.

Only two sword-swinging occasions of note occurred during that stay in Seg's castle of Falanriel, the castle some men called the Falnagur. I will speak of one only, seeing that the other bore on threads of intrigue outside my present concerns, but intrigues that were to plague me woefully in later days, as you shall hear.

The messenger staggered through the main gate, his zorca dead a dwabur down the track, his blood bedabbling his hacked armor. The story was soon told, and familiar. As we mounted up and set spurs to our mounts and galloped headlong out through the frowning gateway of the Falnagur, I found I harbored deep agonies of indecision. Could I cut down some poor wight of a ponsho farmer, a chunkrah herder, a vosk breeder, because they had been willfully misled by the devil Makfaril and his creed of Chyyanism? We rode through the night with the moons casting down their fuzzy pink and golden lights, our shadows blobs of purple darkness, the sound of the hooves and the clattering of armor clear warning to all who would listen.

Seg had placed a number of people he thought loyal and hardworking in positions of trust, trying wherever possible to choose native Falinurese. But as a result these folk were regarded as the minor nobility, which they were and hated accordingly by the rest. In a steading a mere three and a half dwaburs off along a tributary of the Great River, Tarek Nalgre Lithisfer was beseiged and near to exhaustion. We rode. A tarek is of the minor baronage, a gift within the giving of a kov. Seg had told me of Tarek Nalgre, saying he valued him. Now the Black Feathers had risen openly against him, burning barns and dreadfully killing women and children, and I knew that a bamboo stick might not be enough, that the edge of steel might horrendously have to be employed.

In any event, we were able to ride and scatter the beseiging people. Mixed with my remorse I found a little comfort in the fact that the hard core of the beseigers was formed of a body of drikingers, three or four bards joined together to effect the mischief. We fought them. Seg's Bowmen shot their terrible shafts. His Pachaks twirled their tailhands and the blades glittered under the moons. Yes, we fought these bandits, for the country folk mostly ran when we galloped up.

But I did not enjoy the work. I mention it to illustrate just how far the malcontents had aroused the countryside and in allying themselves with the Black Feathers acquired a kind of respectability in the eyes of the ordinary folk. It is often thus. Bandits, knaves, villains, all take on the jargon of a new and zealous creed, an idealistic revolutionary appeal, and use what is honest and subvert it to their own dark ends.

Had Chyyanism been an honest religion, had Seg and his baronage been ruthless tyrants, then the situation would have been entirely different. Although it seemed I fought for the haves against the have-nots, the truth was far from that.

We trailed home with one or two wounded, having made sure Tarek Nalgre was safe. The steading had not burned. Seg left a guard there. But our resentment against the Chyyanists had been inflamed. The immediate cause of this outbreak had been Tarek Nalgre's order that a certain slave girl was to be released immediately. The girl's owner, malignant, had appealed to the local leaders of the Chyyanists, and the burnings and killings had followed. No, I was in an ugly mood as we rode back to Seg's castle, the Falnagur, and doffed our armor and rubbed our bruises and counted the cost.

"This Tarek," I said to Seg later, as we tried to relax after a capital meal, quashing all guilt thoughts. "He seems a quality fighter and man."

"Aye. He is a bonny fighting man, and honest and loyal."

"The very man for the order."

Seg looked pleased at this, for he took his position within the order with great seriousness. I spoke to match his mood.

"We must begin with seasoned men. Once we are established and have a base and the beginnings of a tradition—how the Krozairs are fortunate in that!—we can enroll likely young lads and give them the full benefit of proper training."

"And will you find one of your Krozair brothers willing to travel all this way, to teach what he may regard as breaking his vows?"

I had thought of that. "There is no betrayal in teaching young men to be upright and honest and to respect their own strength. There is altogether too much banging and bashing around on Kregen by the strong against the weak. I speak in general terms. I think we are both too cynical ard beyond the naive area of simple chivalry. Sometimes a man must be a bit of a villain to survive. But if more people thought more and struck less, then the demands of villainy would die out."

Looking back and seeing myself as I was then, I can smile a little indulgently at my foolish self. Even then I was dreadfully young in the ways of Kregen, for all my vaunted experience—at least, vaunted by others, not by me, who knows far too much about Dray Prescot for comfort.

Came the day when I told Seg and Thelda I must wish them Remberee. I shook my head when they asked if I would visit Inch.

"I think not. His letters say that his Black Mountain Men have little sympathy with the Chyyanists. And as for the Blue Mountain Boys, there was a most distressing occurence with a Chyyanist priest. Something to do with burned tail feathers, I believe. Most injurious to pride and stern ends."

Seg managed a smile at this. He did not burst out with a complaint that he only wished his Falinurese were of the same caliber as Inch's Black Mountain Men. For that I respected him. He was entitled to the complaint; fate alone had decided this.

"Well, Dray my dear," said Thelda in her managing way, "then it will be Delphond, I suppose. Or," and here she cocked her head on one side in a calculating way, organizing things for me, "or you could go to Strombor. I need some of their beautiful—"

"Thelda!" said Seg, half laughing. So whatever it was Thelda wanted from Strombor we did not find out.

"I shall," I said, "go to Vondium."

"But!" said Seg.

"But," said Thelda, "you are banished! The emperor has published an edict of proscription. The dear queen told me so herself. You will be taken up if you go back to Vondium."

"Maybe. And again, maybe not. But I am not prepared to let the emperor stand any longer between what I must do and my own frail desires. By Vox! I am tired of shilly-shallying around."

"So it is Vondium then, my old dom."

"Aye! And if the emperor or any of his men try to stand in my way it will not be me who will be sorry!"

Chapter Seventeen

What chanced during the bath of Katrin Rashumin

Well. From those stupid boastful words you will see exactly how I had been rattled. If only I knew what Delia was up to! If only I was sure that Dayra was safe! To Vondium I would go and try to sort matters out.

And if any chanting, hypocritical, venomous Chyyanist priest got in my way with his damned Black Feathers he had better look out sharpish.

And so, with yet another vainglorious boast in a most un-Dray Prescot-like fashion, I took one of Seg's fliers back to Vondium.

I'd be either Nath the Gnat or Kadar the Hammer as opportunity offered. On Kregen one has to handle names carefully, for names are vital. I own to a delight in handling names, and yet I do not forget that however important names are, and however much it behooves a man who wishes to keep his head on his shoulders to remember names and get them right, it is the reality behind the names that matters, the personality and inner being that counts.

The twinkle and shimmer of Vondium rose before us and the flier swooped down. Seg's pilot helped me unload my zorca and the pack preysany, and I stood to wish him Remberee. Then I mounted up and, wearing my old brown blanket cloak and with the bamboo stick across the saddle, started to jog gently along the dusty road toward the city whose topmost towers were just in sight.

If I had been put out of countenance by the changes in Vallia after my absence of twenty-one years on Earth followed by the seasons at the Eye of the World, I could only be dismayed by the changes in Vondium during this my latest absence.

The first thing I saw was a wayside shrine to one of the old minor religions of Vallia, tolerated and even given some small affection by the masses who hewed to Opaz. The shrine's old statue had been removed and the niche with its symbols and little flickering lamp was bedecked with black feathers, and the crude statue of black chyyan replaced the old. I reined up, staring.

An old toothless crone at the roadside cackled.

"Come the day, good sir, come the day."

I said nothing, but shook Twitchnose's reins and cantered on.

By Zair! Did the emperor—did the nobles—do nothing about this?

There was no difficulty in getting into Vondium. The place bustled with life. People scurried everywhere. The guards at the gate barely gave me a glance. They were Rapas, and usually relished a little idle amusement in hazing travelers they considered suitable game for sport. Now I rode through and found myself in a beehive of rumor and speculation and gossip. The brilliant colors, the jostling lines of calsanys, the palanquins, the tall flickering wheels of the zorca chariots racing fleetly along the wider boulevards, the long steady streaming of narrow boats along the Cuts, the shouts and yells of vendors, all the heady brilliant hurly-burly of a great city broke about me as I guided Twitchnose and the led preysany toward the smith's quarter and the tavern called the Iron Anvil. The area was known to me only vaguely—this was not Ruathytu—but after a few directions I arrived and, by showing the edge of a golden talen, secured a room in the hostelry above the tavern. From here I would have to work.

It would not be proper for me to reveal all the steps that led in the end to a plain lenken door, brass-studded, in a flat gray stone wall on the Hill of Tred'efir. The hunt began at a hospital for slaves, led by way of a school for the children of poor mothers, through a number of other establishments, to this calm white-stuccoed house in its bower of greenery. The guards would only let me through into an outer courtyard, and there I had to kick my heels. The guards were all girls, young and limber and rosy in their health and strength. They were clad as the messenger from Delia, Sosieti Drakanium, had been clad, and they handled their rapiers with the professional ease of those who understand pointed and edged weapons. There were also girls wearing cool floating robes of many colors, who came to a pierced stone screen to peer at me and laugh quietly amongst themselves.

Presently a lady whom I can only call the Mother Superior came out, although that is nowise her rank or calling.

"Kadar the Smith?"

"Kadar the Hammer, and it please you, lady."

She nodded, studying me. Her smooth face within the framing crimson cap and veil reposed in calm confidence. In her I could trust, as far as a man may trust a woman. I told her what I wanted. She did not laugh, but the corners of her eyes betrayed extra wrinkles and her soft mouth turned up, just a little.

"You must know that is impossible."

"I wish only to speak with the chief of the Sisters. That is all. If you wish I can be blindfolded, in a darkened room. But I must speak with her." I had no need to put any false emotion into my words. "This is very important to me."

"Is it important to the SoR?"

"I do not know. I think so."

"You are honest. But the thing is impossible. Now go, and go in peace, Kadar the Smith."

"Kadar the Hammer. Very well, I will go. But I will not give up."

But she turned away and made a sign and lo! four sharply curved reflex bows held in young supple hands—and four exceedingly sharp steel arrow heads—pointed at my midriff. I took the hint. After all, had some wandering gypsy-like woman approached me and asked to see the Grand Archbold of the Krozairs of Zy I might have reacted in the same way. So I went.

Now I would have to play my penultimate card. I had not wished to do so, for although Katrin Rashumin had been a good friend to Delia and had benefited from our advice over her island kovnate of Rahartdrin, I had not seen her lately, for obvious reasons, and had no way of knowing her present feelings. But, as they say in Hamal, one must come to the fluttrell's vane.

A single inquiry elicited the information that the Kovneva of Rahartdrin was in Vondium.

I took myself off to her villa, a most gorgeous place and splendidly eloquent of her position, for her fortunes had vastly improved after Delia and I had sorted out her island estates for her. We had had to discharge a crooked crebent and put a stop to certain nefarious practices. Katrin had been grateful then. I think she always remembered a certain flight in an airboat with me, and remembered it with regret. But she had remained loyal to Delia, or so I hoped.

The porter regarded me with disfavor.

"Go away, rast! We have our own smith, young Bargom the Anvil! He will make mincemeat of you!"

The porter was a Fristle, and his cat-face bristled up with his whiskers bright and stiff. I sighed.

At this time I had noticed that the Vallians, as a general rule, did not favor diffs. There were very fed diffs among the wealthy and the nobility. They employed diffs as servants and guards and had no scruple about enslaving them.

The villa's wall ran alongside the road for a space and then shot off at a right angle through woods. Further upslope lay the abandoned villa of Kov Mangar the Apostate. I slipped along between the trees and soon found a place where I might climb over. The way was not difficult and I saw no one, walking rapidly but without obvious signs of haste through a large market garden filled with lettuce and gregarians and squishes. I even picked a handful of palines as I went.

The kitchen gateway showed ahead and just as I was casually about to enter, a Brokelsh guard and a girl, a young Brokelsh slave girl from the kitchens, came out, laughing and talking together. The guard, a big fellow, all bristly hair and bully-boy manner, swelled his chest under the armor. His hand fell to the clanxer at his waist. He wanted to show off for the girl.

"What are you doing here, onker?"

I, Dray Prescot, took a chance. It was a risk. I said, "By the Black Feathers, dom! I am glad to see you. Where away are the confounded stables?"

At this he relaxed at once. I felt my relief at the easy outcome of the confrontation more than tempered by the vast feeling of unease. Chyyanism was here, in a great noble's villa. Well and truly had the Temple of the Great Chyyan reached Vondium. So much for the protestations of vigilance given me by the racters!

So with a direction to the stables I wandered off, saying my thanks and moaning over the hardness of life. Presently, by taking a smart right turn, I managed to find a smaller doorway near the stables. Actual ingress to the Villa's interior could only be achieved by my sending a Fristle guard to sleep standing up, but I did lower him gently to the ground. Then I walked swiftly inside, not looking around, and began to nose my way toward Katrin's apartments. I did not wish to cause too much mayhem, but a little was inevitable.

Had she been anywhere else but Vondium there would have been no problem. The trouble with secret societies is that they are secret. At the least I knew Katrin Rashumin to belong to the Sisters of the Rose. Or so I had gathered from the way Delia had spoken on occasion.

A big burly Womox, his fierce upthrusting horns wound with golden wire, bellowed at me, and I had to skip and jump and put him to sleep horizontally. His harness fitted me, more or less. It hung about my waist, but the shoulders snugged well enough.

So it was as a guard in the employ of Kovenva Katrin I went avisiting. The colors of Rahartdrin are yellow and green with a double red stripe slashed diagonally across them. Katrin also had a fondness for the lotus flower, so this was emblazoned on the breast and back of the brown shifts of her servitors and was picked out in embroidery on the guard's tunics. So I marched along and took no notice of anyone and no one took any notice of me, which is perfectly normal in these gigantic households of many slaves and many guards, not all of whom are apim.

I was stopped by two Pachaks at an inner door. You know about Pachaks. There was no talking my way past these two fine fellows and I would not slay them, for Pachaks are dear to me, so I had to feint with one, knock the second down and deal instantly with his comrade. This I did. Then I pushed through, taking the ivory wand one of the Pachaks had gripped in his upper left hand as his sign of office and tour of duty at the kovneva's private apartments.

I was allowed past a number of girl slaves and somewhat effeminate man slaves until, at the last, I reached places that, by the perfume, the sounds of running water and the warmth and languorous feel in the air, told me plainly enough that no man, and certainly not some hired mercenary, not even a paktun, more likely a thieving masichier, would ever be allowed.

So, saying simply, "If you do not let me in to see the kovneva she will have you girls flogged jikaider," I walked past the befuddled maids. They shrieked out as I dragged the purple curtains apart. Scents of steam and soap and unguents arose. Katrin was taking a small and private bath, not one of the Baths of the Nine, and a gorgeous black girl from Xuntal dropped the sponge in her terror as I barged in.

I knew I had perhaps ten or so murs before the guards came arunning, and they would seek to kill, I made no mistake about that, no mistake at all.

Katrin turned lazily, the soapy water running over one gleaming shoulder, and she looked at my legs and the bottom half of the uniform and the war harness and she said in her caressing voice: "You realize you are a dead man?"

And I answered, "Only if you give the word, Katrin."

And she looked up, shocked, the blood rushing into her face, the water swirling in soapy whirls about her boyd.

"Dray!"

"Aye! And don't shout all over the villa or—"

"Yes, I know!" She stood up, completely uncaring of her shining soapy nakedness and said in her sharp woman-managing voice to the Xuntalese maiden, "Xiri! My wrap!"

With the lotus-flowered wrap about her she walked swiftly to the door and said to someone outside, "No one enters on pain of death! Tell the Pachak jiktar! Hurry! No one, mind!"

Then she kicked Xiri out and slammed the door herself, drawing the heavy purple drapes.

She turned to me, and the lotus-flowered wrap half dropped from a shoulder. It was not coquetry. I know she had tried once, and she knew what Delia meant.

"Thank you, Katrin. I have no time. The emperor—"

"I do not know if he will kill you if he finds you in Vondium, my silly woflo. But I would not take bets on it."

"I must know where Delia is."

"Ah!"

I wasn't sure. Did she know?

Her dark hair gathered into a protecting net broke in a cascade as she ripped the cap off. Her face had softened over the years, but still she could act as haughtily as any fabled Queen of Pain. Her lips, a trifle thin, smiled up as she tossed her hair loose and began to rub her body with a yellow and green towel. The two slashed stripes of scarlet looked like threads of blood.

"I have an appointment with Master Hork in two glasses. He is a master jikaidast and I hope to learn much of the game."

"I'm playing no game."

"You cannot see Delia, has she not told you?"

"Only that she has gone away, and an onker knows that." I eyed this Katrin Rashumin evenly, knowing what I knew about her. "I am in a desperate hurry. I must speak with the chief lady of the Sisters of the Rose. She will help me, I am sure she will."

"The chief lady," Katrin said, laughing, and there was a deal of mockery in that laughter. "I do not think there is a single man who knows her name or title."

"Well? Blindfold me, then, a darkened room. Katrin!"

"You remind me, my dear Dray, of Tyr Korgan and the mermaid. You Valkans are famous for your songs."

"In the end you know what the song says occurred between Tyr Korgan and the mermaid. I must meet the Lady Superior—I do not know her rank or name or title. Katrin! Listen, my daughter Dayra, there is some trouble and—"

"Trouble!" About to go on with a quick and passionate outburst, Katrin held her tongue. The effort brought a flush again to stain her cheeks, made her grip the green and yellow towel. When she had recovered, she said, "Let me do what I can, Dray, out of our friendship. But I will promise nothing."

"A message for Kadar the Hammer at the Iron Anvil will reach me. But for the sweet sake of Zair, hurry!"

"It would be more appropriate to swear by a goddess, do you not think?"

Katrin had probably never left Vallia. Certainly she had never visited the inner sea where the power of Zair was very real. So I said, "In the blessed name of the Invisible Twins made manifest in Opaz, neither man nor woman. Katrin, hurry!"

"And my jikaida?"

So I knew she had learned from Delia. Her jikaida, I knew, along with the jikaidast, this Master Hork who was famous in Vondium for his command of the chuktar's right-flank attack, could be forgotten. We had been old allies, against her will; now I thought with sincerity she would do what she could.

"I will have you smuggled out of the villa. Talk does no one any good, these days in Vondium. The queen . . ." And here Katrin revealed the differences between herself and Thelda. "The queen is a dear creature and has her damned spies everywhere."

My own calmness amazed me. This calm was like those brazen flat calms which often precede a violent rashoon of the Eye of the World. But I managed to say, "This Queen Lushfymi. Is the alliance progressing? Does the emperor find her congenial?"

"Oh, most, most congenial. Queen Lush is all woman, and I know." She lifted and redraped the wrap. "I will see you safely out. Xiri can be trusted, as can the jiktar of my guard."

"I can only thank you, Katrin, and ask you to make all haste."

"The SoR are not inexperienced in intrigues!" She spoke as sharply as she had during the entire interview. Then: "*Xiri!*"

So I was seen out. Just how I was going to make myself wait for Katrin's message eluded me. I have waited for happenings in my life. On every occasion the wait has been unpleasant, it seems to me. Secret are the ways of Kregen under the Suns of Scorpio, secret and deadly. Plots and intrigues flourished in Vondium. So much of the world is open and bright, filled with the clamor of sword and spear, the bright blaring of the war trumpets, the quick onward rush of mailed chivalry and the high conflict of flyers in the air, and so much is dark and hidden in sorcerous ways, phantasms conjured from the hideous vaults of time, wizardly powers breathing a miasma of fear across the bright suns-light: there are also the darkly secret machinations of ambitious men and women to topple thrones and seize powers and take all unto themselves. Well may Kregen be called Secret Kregen.

Outside I walked almost blindly. I had just passed over a cut on a little brick bridge with pretty little caryatids entwined with loomins enhancing the loveliness of the setting—in my stupor I noticed this by reason of the abrupt chaos that broke beyond. One of the long chanting processions passed down the parallel Boulevard of Gregarians. They were clad in bright clothes, garlanded with flowers, carrying the images and the flags, with flowers and music everywhere and the chant, the omipresent chant, going on and on and on. "Oolie Opaz, Oolie Opaz, Oolie Opaz." Over and over again.

The people near the center of the procession abruptly scattered. People were falling and struggling on the road. The chanting wavered and died and then picked up again only to falter and fade away. I saw clubs upraised. I saw the distorted faces of men and women who, bare-armed, brandishing bamboo sticks and balass rods, were smiting the worshipers of Opaz, driving the procession into a shrieking, formless mob.

And more I saw. I saw the black-feathered hats. I saw the lifted staffs entwined with black feathers. I saw the hateful symbols of an evil creed flaunted openly, chastising the worshipers of Opaz, the manifestation of the Invisible Twins.

All roiled into a screaming confusion. The bamboo stick in my hand might be put to some use here. So I ran off the little brick bridge and across the Boulevard of Gregarians and plunged into the shouting ranks of the Black Feathers.

Most of the worshipers of Opaz were fleeing, or scrabbling about on the ground with bleeding heads and broken limbs. I delivered a few tasty thwacks with the bamboo, letting all my frustrations boil over, dealing out buffets that stretched the followers of the Great Chyyan senseless alongside their victims.

Someone set up a yelling about the guards, and the mobiles galloped up on their totrixes. Everyone was running, and the long official staves were beating down on heads and shoulders. People scattered. Screams shattered the bright air. I ran. I had no wish to be hauled up before a supercilious magistrate or some petty noble and my identity revealed. I ran and as I ran so I struck three shrew blows that crunched in on black-feathered hats.

The blue coolness of an alley served to conceal me, but I ran on and took no notice of any who sought to stop me. At last I reached the Tunnel of Delight and passed through onto the brilliant Kyro of Jaidur Omnipotent with the hard-edged double shadows of the Forlaini Hills Aqueduct lying across the broad smooth paving stones. I slowed down and walked. People paid me no heed. Everyone was about private business. Riots were more common now than anyone could remember since the third party sought to topple the emperor. I forced myself not to tremble. What could the emperor be about? What was the old fool doing? Didn't he know how this evil creed of Chyyanism had taken so strong a grip upon his citizens of Vondium that a religious procession, one of the most sacred rites of Opaz, could be set upon, attacked, beaten and scattered? Were the racters all blind or fools?

Why was the canker of Chyyanism being allowed to eat out the heart of Vondium the Proud?

Chapter Eighteen

The Sisters of the Rose are kind to me

The chief lady of the Sisters of the Rose, whose rank and title and name would never be revealed to me if the Sisters had their way, condescended to see me. The message reached the Iron Anvil as I sat, not drinking, sharpening up my old knife, sitting alone in a dark corner of the inn. The smiths talked about their trade and of bad times for business and of the latest consignment of copper to arrive down the Great River and of the price of tin. The serving girl, a little Fristle fifi, whispered that strangers wished to speak with me, so I rose and went outside, the bamboo held ready. Cloaked figures riding zorcas awaited me. I mounted the animal they provided and with only the single word "Rose!" uttered between us, followed where they led.

While it would not be proper for me to reveal all the circumstances of the meeting, I can say that through it all I had no sense of being ridiculous, of acting the fool. Here was I, a fearsome fighting warrior, renowned swordsman, savage clansman, told to strip off, to wrap a piece of white cloth about my loins, to stand meekly in a room with two samphron-oil lamps shining up, leaving the end of the room partitioned by a pierced ivory screen in absolute darkness.

From the screen the soft rustle of feminine garments told me that the chief lady did not wear hunting leathers or the grim panoply of war, as many of the Sisters did. And this was fit and proper. The Sisters of the Rose, after all, is a female order, and girls do not have to ape the ways of men. Although when they do, by Zair, they often are very good indeed.

"You wished to speak with me, Kadar the Hammer. Your request was put most forcefully; a very strong case was made out for you. Why do you plead to see me?

I said, "I think, lady, you know my name."

"Kadar the Hammer." A light tinkle of laughter. "Is that your question? You had forgotten your name?"

"I can never forget. I do not know yours. In that, you have the advantage, lady."

The laughter stilled. Then: "I know you. I can tell you nothing."

I flared up. "This is not good enough! I must know where my Delia is. Is she safe? Is Dayra safe? Just that, just that to put my heart at rest."

If this powerful and secret woman decided to obey the emperor's orders and handed me over to him, there would be a few broken skulls. That I knew. But that was a trifle.

"A man's heart, aye! Now there is a wonderfully elastic object."

"I did not come to bandy words. Tell me, for the sweet sake of Opaz."

"Your Dayra has been . . . is causing . . ." A hesitation and then, in a sharper tone: "Your Dayra is proving a true daughter of a wayward father."

"And if I am wayward that I do not quarrel with. But you have educated Dyra! I have been away and I own my fault in that. But Dyra—"

"Do not blame the SoR for all! We teach chastity and humility and pride. We teach a girl that she is a girl, and in this world a girl must be as good as a man. Not better. As good. We are all people in the sight of Opaz, the manifestation of the Invisible Twins. Dayra could not exist without a man and a woman."

"And I am that man!" I bellowed, despite my promise to myself to behave. "And I ask about the woman!"

An indrawn breath. Would I be hurled out? Would a steel-tipped shaft drive through? Would—exotic thought—a bevy of half-naked damsels seek to destroy me by women's wiles?

Then: "I shall tell you, Kadar the Hammer, that the woman of whom you speak is alive and well and reasonably happy. She goes with her eldest daughter in search of her wayward daughter. When they are successful they will return."

So that explained why Lela, as well as Dayra, had not visited their father in Vondium. "Suppose they are not successful?"

"That may well be. The task is difficult. But Opaz is all wise. If that should be her will then so be it." Naturally Opaz, being the twinned life-force, could be either male or female. "If so, your lady and her elder daughter will return."

"And is that all you will tell me?"

"There is nothing more to tell. You are supremely fortunate even to have spoken with me, Kadar the Hammer. The emperor is looking for a smith to sharpen up the edge of his headsman's ax."

That was as clear a warning as you could desire, or not, considering.

The rustle of clothes told me she was leaving. There were a thousand questions buzzing in my stupid head, but I could speak none of them. I was led out by competent girls who carried their bows nocked and their rapiers naked in their hands. Of what use or value my knowledge that I could have fought and beaten them all? Would that bring my Delia any closer? Of course not.

Only half reconciled to what I considered a fobbing off I dressed and, once more clad in the old brown blanket cloak and with my bamboo stick in my horny fist, I was seen off into the moons-shot darkness.

I have said nothing of the rites surrounding this interview or of the room itself. Or of what I observed. Quite so.

One thing I believed with all my heart: my Delia was safe. And Lela and Dayra—whatever that little minx had been up to—were safe, also.

So, and not as easily as I may make it sound, I could go back to the more congenial task of mayhem and murder and smashing up these Opaz-forsaken rasts of the Great Chyyan.

The last thought I allowed myself about the Sisters of the Rose was the reflection that a fellow had to brace himself up and keep a brave face on it when these scheming women put on that kind of show. Many a man would have been half dead with fright at all the mumbo jumbo, and his knees would have knocked together when he stood in the dread presence of the chief lady of the SoR.

Before I went back to see Natyzha Famphreon and try to shake some sense out of the dealings—or apparent lack of them—of the racters, I'd have to nip back to the Iron Anvil. I had no real desire to investigate her warren of a villa with only a bamboo stick, despite the concealed sword, although if it came to the fluttrell's vane I would do so.

"By Odifor!" spat a Fristle who balanced an enourmous load on his head. He staggered against the doorway of a house whose overhanging balcony dripped vines and moonblooms. I was scarcely aware of bumping him. "Look where you're going, you apim rast!"

I turned my head away and walked on. There were far more important demands at work this night in Vondium than a stupid affray with a Fristle. His cat-face looked fierce and his whiskers shone in the light of torches. I supposed then that I might some day learn to rub along with Fristles.

Walking thus in a heightened frame of mind, to put my frame of mind in a certain light, I realized that all Vallia could go hang to the Black Feathers just as long as Delia and the girls were safe. But then I reconsidered. That was only a half-truth. It is often easy for the outcast—and I had been chucked out of Vondium—to look at himself in the role of poor Pakkad. No one of Kregen could say with certainty if Pakkad had been a real person of if he was a figure from myth. He had been cruelly treated by the arch devil, Mitronoton, the Destroyer of Cities, the Leveler of Ways, and nowadays, although seldom referred to, Pakkad stood for the image of the pariah and the unwanted. As for Mitronoton, the Bane of the ib, the Reducer of Towers, he was a devil of horror that no sane man would approach.

The Fristle snarled some obscenity or other and hitched his bundle straight; a string snapped and the bundle burst, and a glittering shower of trinkets and trashy bangles and rings cascaded to the cobbles. An uproar began at once as, from nowhere and at this time of night with the moons shining above, a torrent of children burst out and fell upon the gewgaws.

Young girls and boys were scrabbling along the cobbles, snatching up the rolling bangles and rings, stuffing little ornamental figures into their breechclouts. I realized in my half-blind wanderings I had blundered into a net of poor alleys off one of the jewelry souks. The hullabaloo was rather splendid. The Fristle was frantically attempting to preserve his wares, yelling threats and trying to bash kids away and being tripped up and—it was all over in a twinkling—standing up and shrieking his anger and casting about upon the empty cobbles.

He found one trashy little figure of Kyr Nath made from cast brass and he flung it down so hard it bounced and hit a laughing fellow in the eye. That started more trouble. I ambled off, deliberately not going fast.

Of such trifles are the destiny of empires made.

The last I heard of that incident—as I thought, as I thought—was a fat apim with an apron yelling: "The Fristle stole this stuff! Thief! Thief!"

The Fristle let out a yell and raced off. The apims followed all ayelling and ascreeching and the whole pack vanished into a side alley, even more odiferous than this one. So, going on, I came out at last into the silversmiths' wharf running alongside a canal that gleamed limpid and pinkly golden in the night. I saw the Fristle running across an arcaded bridge. He saw me too, for the moons-light picked me out brightly. Only a handful of other people were walking near. He knew me. He vanished into the shadows. I dismissed him—thieves would have to be treated as rulers usually treated the devotees of Diproo the Nimble-Fingered—and walked on to the Iron Anvil in the smiths' quarter.

My surprise was complete when I found the Wizard of Loh Khe-Hi-Bjanching waiting for me in my room. As I came in he started up the steel in my fist winked at his throat and then I recognized him. I drew back.

"Dangerous to do that, San."

He laughed a nervous laugh and felt his throat.

"All right, Turk." As he spoke the curtains over the window shook and Turko the Shield climbed in. He was followed by Balass the Hawk. Then Oby wriggled in, most fierce, slapping his long-knife into his sheath.

Well!

It turned out that Khe-Hi wished to obtain a piece of my skin, a hair and a piece of toenail. I do not give these things lightly, for although it is all stupid superstition, there is no doubting the power of the Wizards of Loh.

"Phu-Si-Yantong has been searching for you, Prince," said this wizard who had followed me. "I need to create a new and somewhat different . . . ah . . . arrangement to hold him off. He has let you slip out of his range of observation. But he has been in lupu and spying a very great deal lately. I think"—and here Khe-Hi chuckled in a very down-to-earth and unwizardly way—"I really think the old devil is worried."

"Amen to that."

I had noticed that Khe-Hi did not mention that he was creating a spell or an enchantment. They were for the lesser sorcerers.

So needing the simple artifices of that trade, he had come to find me. And the others would not let him go alone. I asked, "And how did you know where I was and my name?"

"We had a flier letter from Seg, from Falinur, and—"

"And from now on I'm staying where I belong," said Turko the Shield truculently. "By Morro the Muscle! At your side with my shield lifted."

"That will not be very practical in Vondium."

"Well, my long-knife will arouse no comment," said Oby.

We all told him coarsely that his long-knife would not arouse comment anywhere—except Khe-Hi, who was above that kind of nonsense, of course—whereat he grew most enraged and lively and started swinging his arms about.

Balass the Hawk butted in with: "I know most about the Black Feathers so I am the one to go with the Prince."

While they wouldn't have started in on each other with the weapons each knew so well how to use, they waxed exceedingly warm. I said, "No one goes with me. This is a lone task. Balass, what of the Black Feathers?"

His story confirmed what I had seen. Someone had brought a temple into Vondium. Wandering priests had gathered. The city was like an overripe shonage, ready to burst and spray every which way.

"By the brass sword and glass eye of Beng Thrax!" I used the old arena oath talking to Balass, the hyr-kaidur. "When will your spies find this Opaz-forsaken temple! By Kaidun! Time grows perilously short."

"We have men out everywhere. The racters also search."

A thought occurred to me and I turned to Khe-Hi. "If Phu-Si-Yantong has missed me and is searching, will not your visit here put him on my trail once again?"

"No, my Prince. I can cover myself and those with me. He cannot find you through us."

"That is some comfort. But if he really is this Makfaril, and there is no proof, what chance is there he will come to Vondium himself?"

Khe-Hi pursed up his lips. "Very little. He can work his mischief through his agents."

"Quite so. Well, be off with you then, the pack of you."

They wanted to contest this, but I would have none of it. So they climbed out through the window, agile as monkeys, even Khe-Hi, who had done a little climbing with me on Ogragemush.

Working swiftly, I donned my familiar scarlet breechclout and strapped and buckled my weapons about me. This time, to be on the safe side, I shrugged on a close-fitting coat of mail, a mail shirt presented to me by Delia, one of those superb harnesses of mesh mail manufactured in the Dawn Lands around the Shrouded Sea in Havilfar. The value of that single piece of armor would leave a rich man breathless. I swirled the big buff cloak over all as usual, but this time hung the Krozair longsword scabbarded at my left side. I picked up the faithful old bamboo and went to place it safely in a cupboard when those confounded Fristles arrived to ruin that particular scheme.

The Fristle thief, no doubt calling on Diproo the Nimble-Fingered, had rustled up some of his friends. The door burst in with a smash and they catapulted into the room. For the tiniest fraction of time I thought they were my comrades, come back this time to insist on going with me. Then I saw the fierce snarling cat-faces, the up-pricked ears, the lean jaws and the furry hides. Spitting their fury, they charged straight for me.

They carried long-knives and wharf-rat knives, and two had stout staves tipped with bronze. The bamboo switched up and deflected the first stave, bounced off the skull of its owner lined up and prodded deeply into a furry midriff. Two Fristles staggered out of the fight. But the others, three or four, bored in. A flung knife whistled past my head as I moved and smashed into the horn window. A stave swirled down at me and I ducked and stepped back, making no attempt to strike with the bamboo. I was annoyed. I was quite unsure whether to bash them over the head with the bamboo or to whip out rapier or djangir and settle their hash.

So stepping back, I trod on a forgotten gregarian and skidded. I skidded across the floor, flailing my arms to remain upright. I lost my balance and staggered back.

With shrieks of feline glee and the Fristles flung themselves on me. They had no compunction. The thief had lost his night's swag and he wanted to take his revenge out on my hide.

I rolled, ready to spring up and bash them all properly, when a great booming numin voice roared joyfully: "Now, by Vox! What a pretty pickle!"

And in rage Rafik Avandil, his clanxer deftly cleaving down a Fristle skull and slicing back to chop another. The other Fristles screamed now, screams far different from those shrieks of savage fury of a moment ago.

"If I make a habit of this, Nath the Gnat, blame only yourself!"

And the golden numin, Rafik Avandil, joyfully despatched the next Fristle and kicked the last headlong out the door and down the blackwood stairs.

Chapter Nineteen

In the Cavern of Abominations

The way I extricated myself from the possible little embarrassment of this golden numim's discovering all my arsenal of weaponry buckled up about me, when I was a mere wandering laborer, amused me at the time. Afterward, well, as they say, no man or woman born of Opaz knows all the secrets of Imrien. I gave an almighty yawn and covered my mouth, palm out, and said, "I crave your pardon, Koter Avandil. I am for bed. I have had a plaguey day. How did you find me here?"

If he thought I shot the last question out a little sharply, he gave no sign.

"I heard the commotion and ran up, hoping for a little exercise. It seems I was in time, once again."

"And much am I beholden to you, Koter Avandil. What are you going to do with the Fristles?"

"The landlord will take care of them. Come with me. You cannot stay here now."

This was an eventuality I did not relish. I reached up and touched the bowstave. He nodded, half smiling, his whiskers fierce.

"Yes. I see you have bought yourself a bow with the money you acquired, to go along with your zorca. You should be careful how you spend your cash. Buying things you cannot use is a dangerous pastime."

"Yes," I said with a fine free meekness, adding, "koter."

He laughed again, that great booming numim laugh. "I warrant the fellow whose throat you slit for the money wishes he was here to spend it instead of rotting in a ditch."

"If you think that, why bother your head over me?"

"You ask questions, Nath the Gnat, more than is seemly."

"I crave your pardon. But the landlord will throw these cramphs out and I can sleep." I kept forgetting, the more he pestered me, to add the required *koter* into the conversation.

He saw I meant it when I again refused his invitation, so at last he left. I pondered. One more day, would that make so much difference? I could go up and see Natyzha Famphreon later, after sleep. Yes, that would be the answer. I somehow or other did not relish the thought of slipping out the window and finding Rafik Avandil smiling and waiting below for me.

Had I not sent my comrades away they would have created a diversion. Those Opaz-forsaken Fristles. But for them I'd have been halfway to Natyzha Famphreon's villa by now. So, cussing away in my stupid fashion, I stripped off the gear and slept.

The sleep was needed and I awoke refreshed before dawn with that old sailor's knack of setting alarm bells ringing in my skull, echoes of Beng Kishi's Bells. I ordered up a huge breakfast which I demolished in short order.

The fate of empires hangs on tiny threads.

But for the Fristles I would have been long gone to the racters; but for the state of the haggard old crone who served the breakfast I would have left at once. Now there is disease on Kregen, as seems to be inseparable from man and his nature and the state of the universe in which we live. The ordinary ailments are treated matter-of-factly, and the needlemen of Kregen are skilled at relieving pain, even during surgery, with their cunning twirling needles. I have not so far mentioned the disease which strikes horror into the heart of a Kregan. It is seldom mentioned in polite conversation, just as once on this Earth cancer was not a subject for decent conversation. Kregans can confidently look forward to two hundred years or so of life. Right up until their very last years they do not change much, do not appear to alter. This disease—I will tell you its name just the once—this chivrel prematurely ages its victims. Oh, the men and women stricken down live on. They tend to die around their two hundredth year or before, rather than living that extra golden autumn, but their appearance and their strengths are those of ancients of days. This, as you will readily perceive, explains the appearance of old crones and decrepit men in my narrative of life on Kregen.

The serving woman was old, suffering from that disgusting disease. How it was caught, how transmitted, no one knew. No cure was known. Whenever I think back to my days on Kregen as I fought for what I believed was worth fighting for and recall the conversations and the oaths spoken, always I change that particular curse into a different English equivalent—leprous is an example. People were not afraid to live with the sufferers. Body contact, breathing the same air, none of these things caused the disease.

So instead of flinging my cloak around me and rushing out, I stayed and helped her stack the tray and lifted it so that she might open the door. I was in the act of closing the door after her, ready to don my equipment, when the ghostly form of Khe-Hi-Bjanching materialized across the chamber. He stared at me, peering, as though his trance state of lupu was not perfect. Then his misty body solidified. It seemed the wizard stood in the chamber with me.

Never had I seen the lupal projection of Phu-Si-Yantong spying on me as clearly as I saw Khe-Hi. He held out a paper. Like an onker I stretched out my hand to take it. My fingers passed through the yellow paper. I cursed. Khe-Hi pointed. So, a fambly to the end, I looked down and read what he had written.

Famphreon's villa is under observation by the emperor's spies.

As I finished reading, the lupal projection of my Wizard of Loh thinned and wisped and vanished. I stepped back. By Krun! Was I to be foiled by a pack of miserable imperial spies?

I debated.

A hot gratitude to my friends for their work made me realize that they, having discovered the information and sending it as fast as they could via wizardly sorcery, would feel poorly rewarded if I simply barged up there anyway. Mind you, they'd half expect that kind of oafish barbarian behavior from Dray Prescot. But intrigue breeds intrigue, plot conjures forth counterplot.

No, by the Black Chunkrah! I said to myself. I'd play this one very coolly indeed, like a warrior prince rather than a naked, hairy, howling barbarian.

And then the door opened and I swirled about ready to

use whatever weapons might be necessary. Rafik Avandil started back.

"Nath! You look—"

"Koter," I said, and I let the barbaric instincts leach from my muscles. Zair knows what he thought then.

A civilized man can display the quickest of reactions when, here on this Earth, he is aware with his civilized sense of an automobile hurtling down on him on swishing rubber tires. Then he will jump. With my Clansmen on the Great Plains of Segesthes and venturing among the southern forests I had learned to jump when a leem attacked. Rafik Avandil slid his half-drawn clanxer back into its sheath. He had not touched his rapier. He carried both swords in a fine raffish way, slung low on his left hip.

He said he had come to see if I was all right.

I said, "You show great concern for a common laboring man."

"I am at a loose end. You appear to bring me opportunities for a little light exercise. Let us go out and find an open-air tavern and sit and drink sazz and watch the girls."

I, Dray Prescot, replied, "With a will, koter."

Mind you, at the first opportunity, crossing a wide avenue where the zorca chariots rolled glittering in the dawnlights and the people were already about their hurrying scurry of another day, I lost him. I skidded down a narrow alley on the far side and watched him go running along the avenue, in a right paddy. Numims, as I knew from my friend Rees, have generous hearts. Well, some of them.

So I spent the day prodding and prying. It became clear that, dressed as I was in an old brown blanket cloak, I could penetrate places closed to anyone not of the laboring classes. In Vallia the social structures were organized differently from the way they operated in Hamal with the guls and clums there. So, all in the fullness of time, I picked up the black feather and rolled it in my fingers, looked at the fat apim with the sweaty jowls and small vosk-like eyes and said, "Tonight, dom. I shall be there, to the greater glory of the Great Chyyan."

That had been in a dopa den. I gulped the fresh air as I went outside, for all it was blowing from the fish wharf nearby. The search had not taken me overlong. I pondered.

If I chanced my arm and visited Natyzha Famphreon and the emperor's spies took me up, that would place the old devil in a pickle. Would he take my head off this time? Or would he think of his daughter? The racters with their schemes would have to wait. The Black Feathers posed the greater threat.

The impression of the great city as a gigantic wen about to suppurate and burst and release all the evil oppressed me. Black feathers were to be seen, worn in the fashion of the colored favors of Vallia. My ugly old face drew down into grim lines. Intemperate and headlong as I am, I forced myself to ignore this tawdry panoply of evil and wait until the night's meeting.

I thought of Delia. In all honor I had rejected the notion of having Khe-Hi go into lupu and seek her out. That would negate the understanding between us, if not question her self-sufficiency as a woman. The chief Lady of the SoR had said Delia was safe. I believed that, and suffered and hungered for her, and so compensated my own evil by my intentions to deal harshly with the priests of the Great Chyyan.

The chanting of "Oolie Opaz" heralded yet another procession, flower-bedecked, carrying the golden images, wending along a boulevard. People moved respectfully out of the way. According to the season the words of the hypnotic chant are slightly varied, and among all the Oolie Opazes are to be heard the Oolie Ravox and the Oolie Radrak. Oolie, Oolie, they sing, gyrating, swaying, flower-bedecked, letting their inmost spirits lift and rise and soar and conjoin with the spirit of Opaz. Well, I walked discreetly along in the rear, gripping the bamboo staff, and ready for—aye, more than ready, longing for!—a dastardly attack from the fanatical adherents of the Black Feathers. Then a few skulls would be tapped and the claret flow.

A crowd of people in ordinary rough clothes burst from a side avenue. They belched out onto the boulevard. The black feathers flew. I started forward and out of that screaming mob a single face jumped. The face of a man leading them on, waving his arms, berserk with rage, screaming, urging his followers to smash and destroy.

Himet the Mak!

"Right, you cramph!" I shouted. "I'll get you!"

Foolish, stupid me, Dray Prescot, Krozair of Zy, Lord

of Strombor, shouting across a street brawl, promising a villain what I would do to him! How low I had sunk!

Before I could bash my way through the struggling, frenzied mob the guards arrived, the mobiles on their lunging clumsy totrixes, laying about them with the long official staves. I ducked a blow. Himet was running. I saw him cast a vicious glance of baffled rage at the guards. He dived into an alley between a tavern and a private house of some wealthy koter. I followed. Men and women ran with me. The black feathers pinned to their clothes incensed me as they riffled as the people ran.

One priest of the Great Chyyan would be a prize worth taking.

The fleeing mass broke across an adjoining square. Fragments of the main body ran into side turnings. I stuck with a gang of men who intrigued me. Although dressed as ordinary laborers they carried themselves with the air of soldiers. They kept together. Some tavern or inn at which they stayed would offer a place to spy on them. These must be masichieri, common mercenaries of low character, employed by the priests of the Great Chyyan. All the masichieri encountered in Autonne had been accounted for and it was highly unlikely any of these would recognize me. A coin does not often bear a true likeness and they would not have been court portraits. Himet was the man to recognize me, and as we passed through barred sunslight and shadow, I kept a wary eye on him.

This was a chance and I would seize it. Soon the outlines of a half-ruined tower appeared ahead, standing alone in an abandoned plot of ground between two canals. Little as I knew of Vondium, I knew of the ruined temple of a minor religion devoted to the worship of Hjemur-Gebir. So the Chyyanists were up to their old game of taking over small or discredited religious shrines. The masichieri passed in a bunch across a wooden bridge over the canal and headed for the tower. Gray stone showed the livid blotches of algae, and vines and creepers hung down, patterned with blazing Kregan flowers. All pursuit had vanished. As an orderly group we entered the fane. No one challenged me. There were many bands of masichieri here, and many were strangers.

A huge stone caked with detritus and bat droppings lifted as powerful muscles hauled the iron-linked chains. Two by two we dropped down into the black hole thus revealed and crept carefully down the slimed steps. Luminescent fungus grew. Water dripped dolorously. Down and down we went, spiraling around a gigantic well in the solid earth. Echoes bounced eerily. The flare of torches lit in ruddy hues the sheen of water below and the slimed path. Along the path we passed, two by two, and no man spoke.

However poor quality these mercenaries might be, they were well drilled. No one spoke a word until we all passed through an ancient doorway with rotting posts decorated by lichens and bulging fungi. A new world opened beyond, for in the deepest recesses of the crypts of this deserted fane had been built a soldier's barracks. The bunks, the arms racks, the cooking and toilet facilities were all of the best. The instant everyone was in, and there were about sixty or seventy men, bedlam broke loose.

Everyone was talking and shouting at once, laughing at what they had done, knocking a poor old woman over, kicking a young worshiper of Opaz in the guts when he was down. They complained bitterly of the untimely arrive of the guard. They had not expected that.

Himet the Mak stood up and they quieted down. He regarded them from the far end of the chamber from a dais of stained stone.

"Rest and eat, my bonny masichieri. Then we will sally forth again and break a few more heads of these Opaz-loving cramphs!"

"Aye!" they roared it back at him. I kept my head down.

Four or five other priests, evidently of the same importance as Himet, harangued the masichieri. Then we all sat down to tables loaded with ample if coarse fare. So I ate. Very few Kregans turn down the offer of a square meal, particularly if it is free.

Among the bunks and along the walls between the arms racks stands held uniforms, black leather and bronze harness, with black leather helmets, all adorned with the black feathers. There were also shields here, as well as parrying-sticks, oval shields with the black representation of a chyyan painted against the thin bronze coverings to the linden boards.

As I ate, my head down and spooning the food up like a wild beast, I kept one hand against my brow. My eyes seldom left the figure of Himet the Mak, dressed now in flowing black robes embroidered with the golden chyyans. He laughed a great deal and was most lively. Yes, I said to myself, by Vox, you cramph, you may laugh now!

The chances were I would have to grab him by the scruff of the neck and drag him out. I'd given no thought to means of egress. So much for the cool calculations of a warrior prince! In this I had acted in my natural barbaric manner, red and wrathful, recking nothing of consequences.

After the food the masichieri spent the time in the usual ways of swods waiting for duty. They drank sparingly, although more than I would have allowed my men in like circumstances. They played Jikalla and gambled with knucklebones and dice and some pulled out Jikaida boards with games in progress. This proved they had been here some time. Presently I was able to lounge off, with a few coarse remarks, and follow where the priests led down a narrow corridor, smoking with cheap mineral oil lamps, to a moldering door at the far end. Here guards waited, men in uniform. I waited also, until an appropriate moment, and then the guards went to sleep standing up. I propped them against the architrave and eased the door open, went through like a leem and shut it silently.

Beyond the door the corridor continued, ominous, quiet, with the flat tang of oil lamps burning from brass hung bowls.

Creeping along, I listened at the closed doors lining the passage.

Not a sound disturbed the silence. The corridor opened out into a vast shadowy area, lit by vagrant shafts of light falling from a ceiling hazy and distant, festooned with creepers and hanging vines. Lamps and torches shone about the walls. A circle of mighty stone columns upheld the cavern roof. Above that roof the people of Vondium went about their business all unkowning of the chasm beneath their feet, or of the squat and hideous idol crouching on its black obsidian plinth at the center.

The image was of a toad-thing, enormous, crouched, malignant. But its eye sockets gaped emptily, the jewels they had once held long since gouged away. The stone was cracked and flaked away and one of the front clawed arms was snapped off and lying in a scatter of detritus. This, then, was the pseudo-god Hjemur. No wonder honest folk had abandoned his worship!

There was no sign of the priests. If this was to be the place of the temple—and I doubted that—a labyrinth of warrens would stretch out ahead. I went forward cautiously, moving from shadow to shadow.

Spiderwebbed niches along the ebon walls held crumbled statues, tentacles and tusks and obscene conjurations cracked and broken and tumbled away. The blight of powerful superstition had gripped an enslaved people and here lay all that remained of that once-mighty devilry. I passed the profane rotting idols and my fists gripped the bamboo and I prowled, I think, as a leem prowls seeking prey among the chunkrah herds.

Shadows ahead, dark forms, moving in the dim lighting from guttering torch and wavering lamp, halted me, motionless, scarcely breathing, ripe for abrupt massacre.

A small party of masichieri in black armor, led by a deldar, passed uneasily. They gripped their weapons and their eyes roved. They spoke in low whispers, oppressed by the evil of this ancient and profane shrine.

"Come the Black Day, dom, and I'll never go down a cellar again!"

"Come the Black Day and I'll be drunk for a sennight."

"Come the Black Day and I'll take my pay and be off to Menaham before Armipand can jump!"

Yes, they were uneasy here, these rough tough sadistic mercenaries. They talked of guard duty, of dopa and women and were gone, walking carefully through the torch-lit shadows.

I let them go. They were masichieri, mercenaries for hire; I needed to get the scrawny throat of their paymaster between my fists.

A sudden outcry ahead made me halt again. The sound of scuffles, blows, the grunted cursing of men in action, left me unmoved. Then a woman's scream rang shockingly through that cavern of abominations. I could hold back no longer. Fool that I was, I ran and hurled myself through the crimson and ocher shadows, whipped out the sword from the bamboo and raced on, and found nothing. No sign of men or women struggling met my gaze as I searched. Had I heard some phantasmal echo of infinite evil from ancient times? Did the foul deeds perpetrated here linger on?

The torchlights near the toad-thing had revealed dark streaks running down the obsidian slab. The marks of dark blood looked recent; there might be a thousand seasons between now and the time the sacrifice screamed and shrieked until the jagged glass knife slashed his or her throat.

Prowling on around this vast cavern I saw hideous things, abominations, things that were never meant to exist in the sweet sunshine of Zim and Genodras. A strange sliding clicking drew my instant attention to a jagged wall where the naked rock gleamed with the green of lichen. Shadows flittered like bats.

Pressed close against a slimy pillar forming one of a rectangle enclosing a small side chapel—and the very word "chapel" brings a blasphemy upon the evil of that place—I saw a rope ladder swinging down from the darkness above. At its foot a man stood, grasping the end, shaking it. The wooden rungs clicked against protrusions in the stone.

He turned slightly and I saw him.

His powerful numim frame was clad in brilliant armor, gilded iron corselet and greaves. His helmet glistened. He held his clanxer in his right hand as his left hand released the ladder. He swung about, big and burly and fighting grim. I felt only the smallest surprise.

About to step forward and say, "And what brings you here, Rafik Avandil?" I saw the slinking shadows at his back, stealing up from the dimness between torches. I saw the black and silver and the quick glitter of weapons, and so I cried, "Your back, Rafik! Beware!"

He swung about like the great lion-man he was, and the first leaping shadow slashed and clanged a great gong note from Rafik's helmet. A gigantic buffet sent the man sprawling back. His comrades recoiled. They gathered themselves. Without thought, I flung myself forward to stand back to back with Rafik Avandil, A noose clung about my leg and I tripped headlong.

A figure bent over me. Hands gripped my throat. A harsh, husky voice said, "Not another word, dom!"

I could not speak. I levered up and other hands bore down on me. I was lifted like a log of lumber. A crazy vision of Rafik running fleetly along past blasphemous statues—he vanished with a wink of bright armor quenched by the shadows—the sound of men breathing hoarsely by me, a sudden exclamation.

The keen edge of a knife hovered under my chin. I could just see it. It was a thick, heavy long-knife, and it would slice through my windpipe as a butcher cuts up chops.

"Hold!" The men carrying me upended me and slammed me on my feet so my neck snapped my head forward and stars flew. I dragged the right-hand man around and smashed him into the left-hand one and a very hard, very sharp point came from nowhere and rested against my throat.

"Stand still, Prince! By Vox! You'll have us all killed!"

I stared owlishly.

In the erratic illumination I saw Naghan Vanki standing before me looking charged with rage, emotion almost making his features unrecognizable. Always before he had been smooth and bland and unremarkable.

"The cramph got away, jen," said one of his men, coming up. They all wore the black and silver, hard and supple leather, with steel bands and bracers. Vanki kept the point of his rapier at my throat. His men hung onto my arms.

"Keep silence, Prince. May I tell you something? You are a dead man unless—"

"I thought you served the racters, Vanki. Don't you know they are leagued with me now?" It was a ploy.

He started and then his face assumed that blank, indifferent look. This was the man I suspected had drugged me and thrown me into a thorny-ivy bush to perish miserably in the hostile territories. I had the desire to know, if I was to die now.

I asked him.

"You may be a prince now, the Prince Majister; then you were a savage clansman with ideas beyond his station. No one wanted you to marry the Princess Majestrix."

"In that you lie, Vanki. The Princess Majestrix wished it with all her heart."

"Aye! That is why when the other wanted to slit your throat there and then I counseled moderation. You owe your life to me, Prince."

"Alone, in the hostile territories, on foot, with the Klackadrin to cross?"

"You are here, alive, now."

"And for how much longer? How much is the cramph Makfaril paying you." I stopped suddenly. Then I gasped more than I liked as I spoke: "You, Naghan Vanki, are Makfaril!"

Without any change of expression, he said, "You are a prince, yet you are a clansman still, aye, and an onker!"

"Someone comes!" said one of his men, hissing from the shadows. In a bunch we melted into the darkness beyond the pillared chapel. Black and silver clothes, black and white for the racters, black feathers for the Chyyanists. I felt then that if Naghan Vanki, who on his own admission had connived at my death, was not Makfaril, then he was very high in the hierarchy and in all probability knew who the leader of the Chyyanists was.

It was pointless for me to call out. The masichieri would be less merciful than Naghan Vanki. They'd have slit my throat and gleed in the doing of it, back there in the hostile territories.

Without binding me in iron chains or stout lesten-hide ropes a man can only hold me for so long. There will come a time when he may be taken. I gave no thought to the silent ferocity of these hired men of Vanki's. They kept a perfect stillness. Perhaps Rafik Avandil had brought men with him down the rope ladder. So, taking my chance, I slipped the rapier point and dealt each of the wights holding my arms a most qruesome mischief with my knees, then ran fleetly into the darkness of the Cavern of Abominations.

In the maze of tumbled stonework and fallen rock, the pillared chapels and the half-ruined warren of rooms beyond, there was little chance Naghan Vanki and his men or the masichieri would find me. But, equally and frustratingly, I had as little chance of finding Himet the Mak or one of the other priests of the Black Feathers.

A sensible idea would be to get out of the place and rouse a strong body of loyal soldiers, from Natyzha, from the emperor, from my own Valkans, and return here with fire and sword. That would be the sensible course.

In matters of this nature I am woefully lacking in sense. I no longer had the faithful old bamboo sword-stick. The rasts had not taken my sailor knife, and I drew this now and held it ready as I padded through the semidarkness. The shafting light from above probably came from a higher cavern whose floor was fitted with fireglass crystal.

How far above that lay the surface I did not know, for we had descended that slimy spiral stairway to a considerable depth. However far into the bowels of Kregen we were, I had no mind to return to the surface without a priest of the Great Chyyan to prod along before me.

The grotesquely carved pillar around which I edged screened off what lay beyond. Tumbled walls and toppled arcades, all built within the cavern, surrounded me. I rounded the corner. . . .

The masichieri were surprised and sprang out under the flaring torches. There was only one thing I could do: I charged headlong for them. I bellowed "Hai!" and raced in with the knife held point up and thrusting for them.

I saw the slinger. I saw him unwind. I skidded on a fallen rock and tried to duck and then . . . The stone must have struck me fair and square between the eyes. I dropped headfirst into the deep dark cloak of Notor Zan.

Chapter Twenty

Makfaril's sacrifice

Someone was saying from a great distance: "The yetch is the Prince Majister of Vallia? It is difficult to believe." The words boomed and went up and down as though echoing in a gigantic sea shell. "What did he want creeping about down here?"

And the coarse answer: "By the Black Feathers! Whatever it was he will never find it now. Makfaril has ordained his death."

I opened my eyes. Well, cells are cells. This one cut from the rock boasted a barred window through which torchlight streamed, so I crawled across with all Beng Kishi's tinkers hammering out their bells in my skull, and listened as best I could.

"Come the Black Day and all the princes and Princesses will dangle-o!"

"Aye, dom. And then you'n me'll be princes."

They sounded apim. Masichieri. Hired killers. My head resonated and nausea clutched me. But escape must be attempted at once. Strike while the iron is hot. I tried to stand up and my legs buckled and I slumped back again. The guards talked on outside.

"Course, most of us will grab what loot we can and hightail it back home. Vallia is rich. By Havil! The plunder!"

So the cramph was from Havilfar somewhere, Hamal probably.

"Yes. You're right. But I'm going to sit in the throne for once, aye, and if any princes or kovs is about I'll use 'em for a footstool before we cut 'em up."

A hawk and a spit and: "Once they get this meeting over the priests can go and spread the word. I'm tired of waiting. The quicker they learn the day and go home and tell their people the better. Then, dom, then our swords will drink blood and our pockets will be filled!"

"Aye, may Armipand rot 'em all!"

My legs wavered. I leaned against the wall and shoved upright. I panted. I did not touch my forehead. The blow from the stone must have left a ghastly mess up there and if the blood had dried I did not wish to disturb it. Only my thick old vosk-skull of a head and the dip in the Pool of Baptism in far Aphrasöe had saved me. I stilled the trembling in my limbs. Talk about David and Goliath. That flung stone had nearly done for me. But I felt my strength coming back. I dragged deep lungfuls of air. I forced myself to stand free of the wall and pace about, grunting, working my muscles back to life.

". . . Beautiful piece. A waste to sacrifice her first."

I stopped and listened again.

"One of 'em got away. But the man's safely mewed up."

"Bitch women. Why can't they attend to women's affairs and leave men's to men?"

Thank God, I said to myself, Delia and Dayra and Lela were safe dwaburs away from here. Although nothing had ever been said about where they were going or where they were adventuring, I had somehow assumed it was in the north midlands of Vallia.

Well, this was getting me nowhere. While there was no way of telling just how professional these two masichieri were, they were mercanaries, and therefore I must give them the benefit of hard professional competence. If I made a single mistake they'd not wait for Makfaril to implement his ordinance on my death, whatever gruesome affair that was to be.

A trampling of iron-shod sandals in the corridor was followed by jocular remarks from the two guards to others of their ilk who passed giving me a little time.

"What a beauty! Treat her gently!"

"Ah! Makfaril's girls will see to her!"

"What I wouldn't give . . ."

I waited until the guards passed. Apart from the old scarlet breechclout I was naked. Simplicity, that was the only way. Simpleness in plans can defeat the most cunning of experienced professionals.

I leaned against the door and spoke through the iron bars. "Tell Makfaril I have vital information for him. *Bratch!*"

When Makfaril came I'd fling everything into one wild lunge and so finish the cramph.

But these two were incompetent professionals. One looked through the bars, saying, "How do we know you speak sooth?"

"Fetch Makfaril and you will soon see."

So, poor fools, they swung the door open to make sure of me. They were armed. I was naked. It made little difference.

I stood up and slid the thraxter from its scabbard. I took the other one's short compound reflex bow and his quiver of arrows and slung them over my shoulder. A knife, too, would be useful. . . . The two masichieri slumbered on the floor. I shut the door on them and shot the bars and bolts.

A short corridor lit by a single torch led onto a wider cellblock. Probably the sacrifices had been kept here in the old days. At the corner I halted as a screech of metal sounded. Cautiously, ready to fight or run—I was annoyed and did not wish to waste my strength on masichieri when Makfaril was here—I peered around the corner.

The scene was arresting in its action and before I could sort it all out in the tricky light it was all over.

A guard screamed and spun away from a door. I saw a girl drive a long think poniard into his neck, saw her as a fleeting black-clad sprite, her long limbs splendid as she sprang to the door. The sheening black leather stood out against her white skin. Her mass of brown hair obscured her face, but she was not Delia. She was not Delia. The door opened to her quick fingers and a man staggered out, looking ghastly, with blood dried upon his face and his dark hair draggling with caked blood and his left arm all broken and dangling awry. Quickly the girl dragged him along, taking no notice of his broken arm. She moved with feline grace, like a hunting cat—all the old images sprang into my mind. Like a tiger-girl she dragged the shambling man along and together they vanished around the corner.

I loped along the corridor and looked after them. The next set of cells lay dusty and deserted and of the panther-girl and the man she had rescued remained only a double line of footprints in the dust.

I wished her well. But I had my own zhantil to saddle.

Up. I must go up. Without doubt these cells for the sacrifices would be low down in this pestiferous place. So I hunted stairs and upward-sloping corridors, and only four guards died on the borrowed thraxter. The straight cut-and-thrust sword of Havilfar is keenly adapted to this work.

At the end of a long corridor which by its width and height indicated I must be leaving the deeper warrens, the figure of a girl moved across from one side passage to another. For a single instant I thought she was the girl who had rescued the bloodied, broken man. But this girl's black clothes riffled with black feathers, and she carried a wide silver bowl steaming with fragrant water. She vanished and I padded on. That splendid girl who had used her poniard so ruthlessly, she reminded me of Sosie ti Drakanium, Delia's messenger. Her gleaming tanned white skin and her long lissom legs—yes, well, there had been a sight more skin than black leather on view. All the same, I had not disposed of the two guards at my cell door, of whom she could have had no knowledge, her rescue would have gone awry.

Still, she could not know that.

As I prowled on, very much like a leem among ponsho pens, the absence of people made me realize that time was much later than I had thought. The palaces of Kregen—and there is an evocative phrase for you!—of which I had knowledge all contained runnels of secret passages and concealed doors. This ancient temple of abominations followed that pattern. I was perfectly confident I could find my way out to the surface and probably emerge through some hidden opening an ulm away from the ruined tower of Hjemur-Gebir, but I wanted to leave dragging a rascally priest of the Great Chyyan with me.

The deserted stone corridors, the decayed barrenness of it all as I wound my way back to the giant cavern of the idol of the toad-thing, convinced me the first meeting was already being held. The other meetings for later on, one of which I had arranged to visit, now meant nothing. This meeting, here, was the vital one. For Makfaril would tell his assembled priests the date of the Day of the Black Feathers. The priests would return to their congregations all over Vallia. They would scatter like a loathsome pestilence all over Vallia and prepare their followers and, come the Black Day, they would strike!

In the end the long ululations of a moaning, whining chant, a succession of weird cadences echoing through the dusty and deserted chambers, led me to the scene. I cautiously came out upon a high ledge of rock, drowned in shadow, and so could look out and down into the torchlit bowl of the cavern with the grotesquely evil idol crouching at the center on its ominous plinth. The black obsidian altar from which the long rusted streaks of dried blood cut corrosive swathes was covered by a wide-spread cloak of black feathers. The cloak was formed into the likeness of the four wings of a chyyan, covering the altar and what lay upon it.

When I had looked down from the balcony that had collapsed in Autonne upon a gathering of the Black Feathers I had had an inkling of what might follow. And here was the reality! This gathering was far removed from that first one. Here the long ranks of the black-feathered priests droned out their chant in perfect rhythms. Tall candle flames flickered among the torchlights, casting gleams that winked back from weapons and armor. The black arms lifted in ritual observances. A knot of high priests upon a fallen block of stone to one side led the chanting. I gazed at the scene, ignoring everything save the gigantic form of a chyyan, chained with silver chains, fluttering its four wings above the toad idol.

A real chyyan. Its rusty black feathers showed the true horror of the situation, as it clashed its wings and hissed viciously, its scarlet beak open and its scarlet claws striking wildly at the air.

The horror lay in this: how could any sane man regard this feral killer of the skies as a god? What difference lay between the living and breathing chyyan and the decayed stone idol of the toad-thing?

Half-naked girls partially clad in scraps of black feathers gyrated wildly. They swirled black-feathered fans. The stink of incense rose dizzyingly. The priests chanted, a long rigmarole of praises to the Great Chyyan and how he was immortally twinned in spirit with Makfaril. Staring down from the shadows of the ledge into the wild torchlights with the naked sprites dancing and the wafting coils of smoke and the chanting lines of priests, I felt the nausea well in me.

The chyyan clashed his wings and tried to drag his head away from the chain around his neck. The chain ran down to a small windlass plugged to the stone floor. The chyyan was captive—aye!—captive to the odious desires of Makfaril.

Captive the killer bird might be, but all the virulence of his nature showed itself in the venomous hissings and the violence of his movements. His scarlet beak gaped ready to rip and rend, his scarlet eyes gleamed like freshly spilled blood. The thunder of his wings and the hissings from the devilish beak clashed and blended with the sonorous chanting from the black-feathered ranks.

The masichieri stood around the walls, standing well clear of the blasphemous rotting statues in their niches, watchful, on guard. What they guarded against, deep here in the vile depths below Vondium, I did not know. The place must have borne some resemblance to the dire evil of Cottmer's Caverns. I saw the guards, their black leather, their metal, the black feathers adorning them. I saw their thraxters and the oval shields they bore, their bows.

When the chanting ceased a high priest stepped up onto the pedestal below the statue. He raised his arms. Above his head the chyyan hissed and spat and struck fiercely downward, his scarlet beak flashing above the priest's head.

Himet the Mak and the knot of other high priests stood in a solid block of blackness at the side. The high priest began a shrill chanting harangue, promising everything, promising all Vallia would be turned over to pillage and plunder, promising that Makfaril would make of them all new men and women.

"Behold, the Black Day dawns! Behold, Makfaril the beloved of the Great Chyyan will reveal to us the day chosen! On your knees, prostrate yourselves, perform the full incline for our leader, twinned spirit with the Great Chyyan! Makfaril! *Makfaril!*"

In a sighing rustling of feathers the whole congregation prostrated itself. Each man performed the full incline. I stared, fascinated. Power was being exercised here, power I understood, power I had fought against time and again.

The gargoyle head of the toad-thing moved. It lifted. The stone jaws gaped, wide and wider. The head lifted and the jaws gaped and a shaft of golden illumination sprang from the opening. A figure stood framed against that radiance, a tall strong figure silhouetted against the glow.

"Rise up, my people, and give thanks to the Great Chyyan!"

The voice boomed and rolled about the cavernous chamber in eerie echoes.

The figure stepped down from the blasphemous mouth of the toad. Clad all in black feathers, imitating a chyyan, the figure of Makfaril stood limned in the golden light.

"Sink me!" I whispered, and slid the bow into my hands. "By Zim-Zair! I'll feather you, you rast, aye, and with a shaft fletched with your own damned black feathers!"

The short compound reflex bow, a construction of laminates of wood and horn with a sinew backing, did not contain the supremely long powerful strike of a longbow, but it would serve. It took up an arrow and nocked it. I'd shoot the rast clean through his black heart. If it was Naghan Vanki then the treachery of the hostile territories would be avenged, although that was now the least of my concerns.

I lifted the bow.

Then I paused. There might be something to learn when the rast addressed these black priests of his.

He spoke, gesturing widely, almost laughing, so commanding a figure and so completely in his power were these poor duped fools.

"The Black Day dawns!" he bellowed in a roar. "Behold, the Day of the Black Feathers is at hand!"

The congregation, prostrate, let fly a long wailing cry of delight.

"Long and long have we waited. And to seal our compact, to prove to the Great Chyyan our love and devotion, we offer a sacrifice. We give a life into the Great Chyyan's keeping, earnest of our intention! We shall strike! Red will flow the blood! And all, my people, will be ours!"

At a signal priests stepped forward, prominent among them Himet the Mak. They ripped away the black feathered cloak in the guise of four chyyan wings. They tore it away from the sacrifice spread-eagled upon that blasphemous obsidian slab.

I stared.

White and voluptuous and naked, thonged by wrists and

ankles and yet still glaring up with blazing defiance, my Delia lay spread for the scarifice.

Redness, roaring, madness, blackness! They were winching down the chain, drawing the violently thrashing chyyan down by the neck. Its scarlet beak slashed the air above the altar, above the slab of sacrifice. Its scarlet eyes saw that superb white sacrifice spread out for it, and now it no longer fought the chain. Hungrily it darted its beaked head down to rip and tear and gorge upon that lovely flesh.

The bow spat.

The arrow winged true. The shaft gouged deeply into one scarlet eye and the chyyan screeched and thrashed and clashed its wings. Makfaril darted sideways with a ferocious leap and the second arrow splintered against the toad-thing where he had stood.

As he leaped, the black chyyan cloak spun away from him. The black feathers floated free. And Makfaril stood revealed clad all in glittering armor, with thraxter and rapier and parrying-stick, a glorious golden numim, powerful, ferocious, bellowing savage commands.

"By Vox, Rafik!" I said, and leaped.

Headlong I leaped from the high ledge and crashed down onto the heads of the priests. They scattered and I felt bones crunch and break. There was no time for me to be winded. I was up and running and the sword in my hand cut left and cut right and there were dead men in a blood-soaked swath behind me and I scarcely heeded them. Only one thing I saw. Like a maniac I raged through the press and reached the slab of black obsidian.

The screams and shouts roared in the cavern. Arrows splintered about me. I cut down two priests, saw Himet running away, shrieking, scrambled onto the plinth.

Four slashes, four sure quick cuts, and Delia was free.

The blood must be paining her cruelly, but she forced herself to stand beside me. Masichieri were running. If we were to die here then we would die. How we died would matter only to us. I did not forget my daughter Velia in those mad manic moments of blood. Death could touch me. I knew that.

"My heart!"

"They said you were safe!"

"So I was, until Melow was wounded."

I cut down the first of the masichieri. If I was exalted,

if I was drunk on the red rage and the red blood of battle, then I admit it. I fought. My scarlet breechclout felt wet and sticky with blood and my body gleamed a single crimson flame of blood. But so far none of the blood was mine. Delia had a dagger, snatched from the severed hand of a mercenary. Then she had a thraxter. We fought off the dais and back past the toad-thing. An arrow nicked my left shoulder. I stumbled back and hacked a priest across the face, drove the point past the guard of a masichieri, past his oval shield, deeply into his neck.

Delia slashed a fellow off my back and I withdrew and whirled back again and chopped the man trying to chop Delia.

Like two blood-splashed phantasms, we hacked and hewed our way toward the back of the statue.

The could not go on. There were just too many of them.

The blood stood out in livid patches across Delia's skin.

Black feathers swirled about me. Black chyyans painted on shields closed up and bore in.

A golden gleam glinted at the back of the masichieri. A great numim voice bellowed: "Do not kill him!"

As soon call off hunting dogs from the carcass of a kill when the hot madness is on them.

I slashed and beat away the lunging points, slid the slashing blows. Delia was a brilliant form of red and white, of tanned skin and spilled blood. I snarled deeply and charged headlong at the clustering shields. No coherent thought was left to me now. Only the desire to slay Makfaril and thus avenge our deaths. . . .

Somewhere through the madness beating in my skull I heard Delia yell. "Dray! Keep your fool head down!"

Through all the red roaring madness on me, through the thunder of blood in my head, the beat of blood about my body, the roar of warring multitudes in my brain, I heard my Delia. I dropped flat and squirmed about, and Delia was at my side, gasping and laughing, and a masichieri tumbled down on top of us with a long shaft feathered through him.

Screams burst out from horror-stricken throats.

From the walls, from the niches where the rotting idols slumbered, the Crimson Bowmen of Loh methodically swept the whole cavern with the arrow storm. That sleeting hail punctured skull and leather armor, struck through mail vest and oval shield alike. Among the Crimson Bowmen were the lithe and lissome forms of girls, all clad in trim rose-red tunics, slender and quick, shooting with a deftness to equal the men's.

"The Sisters did not forget me, then, after all!"

I looked for Seg as we shielded beneath a barrier of dead bodies, but I did not see him. This was the emperor's work. The Crimson Bowmen of Loh, and the Sisters of the Rose.

The shrieks died down to moaning whimpers and soon a dread silence hung over that cavern of death. Slowly Delia and I stood up. I swirled a black feathered cape about her glowing blood-spattered loveliness, and so we waited as Naghan Vanki walked slowly through the heaps of slain. The Bowmen had killed with that sleeting storm of clothyard shafts and not a priest or masichieri remained alive.

"So you were not Makfaril, Vanki," I said.

His expressionless features, white and contained, did not reveal a single iota of himself as he said, "Had I been, you would surely be dead, Prince."

Then, with cool insolence, he turned and bowed deeply to Delia. "Princess Majestrix," he said in that flat and chilling voice. "The emperor my master will be overjoyed that you live."

Delia is, after all, a princess, and knows how to conduct herself. She held out her hand. I saw the bloodstains.

"Thank you, Naghan. You have proved yourself a loyal servant to my father today. And to me."

"Always, my Princess, to you."

So that solved that problem.

Even then I still could not make up my mind how I regarded all those gallant men of Vallia who adored their princess and would gladly die for her—aye!—as so many did die and joy in the giving of their lives for that of my Delia.

"And Makfaril?" I said in my surely, oafish clansman's way.

"He ran back through the idol of Hjemur," said Vanki. Then, waspishly, he added, "I had thought you would stop him, Prince."

The cool effrontery of the man had no power to enrage me now. I felt amused. He served the emperor. He was the emperor's spy and, as I more then half-suspected then, the emperor's spy-master. Now girls crowded up and quickly more seemly clothes were found for the Princess Delia.

We walked toward the exit, past the droves of dead bodies. I saw the jiktar in command. He looked a little at a loss, for once Naghan Vanki's use for him was finished, Vanki lost all interest in him. I said, "Jiktar! Gather up all the arrows! Send search parties to comb out all the runnels. Have the dead disposed of and if you find any living, question them. Check all the cells." Then, because I was the Prince Majister and these things are expected of simpletons in that position, I added: "And, jiktar, you and your men are to be congratulated. You shot as I expect Bowmen of Loh to shoot. There are barrels to be broached tonight."

I did not mention the great word 'Jikai.' This had not been a jikai. Rather, mention of barrels brought vividly to mind what the shooting had been truly like. Fish . . .

Naghan Vanki and an advance party of his men had climbed down the rope ladder. Makfaril—Rafik Avandil—had discovered the ladder, but I had prevented his immediate arrest. Vanki was cutting about that. "And this villain Rafik has been close to you, Prince. He led us to you. Why he wished to have you under so close an observation we do not yet know. But, when he is found, we shall question him."

Naghan Vanki, the emperor's spy-master, might not know. But I knew. When my wizard Khe-Hi set up his sorcerous interference, preventing the monstrously egomaniacal wizard Phu-Si-Yantong from spying on me, that villain had sent his tool to seek me out and report my whereabouts and continue the spying on my movements. Vantong wished to rule all Vallian through me. Well, his plans to bring about the destruction of Vallian life and open the land to his greedy authority had fallen into ruins this day.

"And you suspected Avandil all along?"

"Since he came here from Hamal pretending to be a loyal cheerful Vallian koter. The emperor's agents never sleep. We dogged his footsteps, except when interfered with. That he was Makfaril was a surprise."

"And the emperor knew of this?"

A look of such cold hardness passed over Vanki's corpse-white face as to make his resemblance to the imagined devils of Cottmer's Caverns vivid and repulsive. "The emperor, may he live forever, knows we serve him as best we may. He has other problems weighing on his mind." Then Vanki looked at me with all the chilling presence of a dedicated, clever man who understands not only his own power but also his own limitations. "The racters . . . you must realize, Prince, how much more powerful they are now? Had you been seen visiting them you would have been taken up."

"But, Naghan," said Delia, smiling, holding my arm. "Not now, I think?"

"There is a night to be lived through yet, my princess."

I pointed to four Bowmen who marched in step. They carried a burden between them by arms and legs and the golden wink of glittering armor scintillated among the heaps of slain.

"You will not question Makfaril now, Vanki."

We looked down on the body of the numim Rafik Avandil, Makfaril, tool of Phu-Si-Yantong. From his throat above the golden rim of the corselet protruded the hilt of a long slender dagger. I pulled it out and the blood welled. The jewels clustered on the hilt were red, and they formed the outline of a rose.

"It is mine," said Delia. "But how—"

"What is more to the point, my love, is how you came here?"

We walked a little away from Vanki and his black-and-silver-clad men. The chamber of death bustled as the Bowmen did as I had commanded. Delia looked at me, her head on one side.

"Again, my heart? I will tell you all that I may in honor reveal. Melow was wounded and I saw her safely to our Delphondian villa here in Vondium. I went about the business that took me away—just for now let me keep that close, for I will tell you, I promise, when I am able—and I remember nothing from the moment I was drugged in some damned inn until they whipped that black covering off me and I saw—" She shivered and I put my arm about her. "It was wicked and scarlet! Hissing! I thought then that—"

"Yes, well," I said, an onker to the end. "You know what thought did."

When I asked about Dayra and Lela as we made our way through the maze of chambers and past the barracks and so up the circular slimy stair and out into the fresh air of Vondium, she told me they were well and as far as she knew dwaburs away and busy about business for the Sisters. She had left them with instructions to come and see their father as soon as they were able. Her smile was sweet, yet I saw the weariness in her. Her experiences had been horrific. Mine had been compounded of her horror, lumped together with my own and hurled full in my face, as a leem springs, near-shattering me when I saw the black-feathered cloak whipped away to reveal the naked body of my Delia spread for sacrifice.

The devilish hand of Yantong was in this, surely. The sacrifice of the Princess Majestrix would have been used in ways I could not comprehend. Chyyanism was finished. All the priests who would have carried the word for the day of uprising were dead. Makfaril was dead. The Day of the Black Feathers would never dawn in Vallia.

The simple people who had been hoodwinked would wait and they would grow restless. If they rose the insurrection would be in uncoordinated attacks, sporadic, local, able to be dealt with. Then the people would tire and lose faith and in the end they would curse the Great Chyyan and his twinned spirit, Makfaril.

"It is sad that people like the Racter party have triumphed," I said later, as we went through into our private apartments in our Valkan villa on its hill in Vondium. "But better, I think, than had the Great Chyyan triumphed."

"The racters are blind in their evil, as we know. Most are corrupted by their own wealth and power. But Makfaril he was not Phu-Si-Yantong then, after all. And my heart, Naghan Vanki, who is a monstrously clever man, said this numim kept close watch on you."

"Aye! Too close, I think." The callousness of Rafik Avandil seemed to me symptomatic of much that is evil about Kregen. Phu-Si-Yantong had spied on me in Delia's temple, knowing my own wizard could foil his lupal projections. So he had sent those poor doomed Rapa masichieri and Avandil, his tool, had slain them and appeared to save me, just to gain my confidence. I recalled what one of the Rapas had cried out in horror. And Rumil the Point—had he too been an instrument of Yantong's? I thought the Fristles heaven-sent to aid Avandil's schemes. So, smiling at Delia, I walked into our private room. "But the numim is dead, and with him for a time the schemes of Yantong."

"The racters have grown stronger, I think. But my father? They will seek to use him even more ruthlessly now."

"They believe they have a compact with me. That can be used to your father's advantage."

"But he has banished you from Vondium."

I looked up out of the window. She of the Veils cast down her golden light, tinged with a pink fuzziness. The Maiden with the Many Smiles stole gently over the fantastic silhouette of Vondium, bathing rooftops and spires with a second roseate wash of fire. All the stars of Kregen glowed in their brilliant constellations. I turned back to the sumptuously furnished room. Truly, life on Kregen is a hurly-burly of ups and downs. But who would have it any other way?

"Your father has been emperor for a long time. Now he has this Queen Lush of Lome to worry him, along with the new factions seeking to destroy him. I shall have to make him see sense."

"And if he will not? You called him an onker. He will not forget. He is my father, and he is a terrible man in his wrath, a true emperor."

"Perhaps onker was too harsh, for your father. Not for an emperor." I yawned. "I care not for tonight. . . . Now I am for the Baths of the Nine. Then I shall eat a stupendous meal. And then I shall sleep the rest of the night away."

"That, my love," said Delia, Delia of Delphond, Delia of the Blue Mountains, "is what you think."